Skelter's Final Duty

Stuart Pereira

To Marlyn

Stuart Pereira

2018

ISBN:1537196499
ISBN-13:9781537196497

DEDICATION

For all those in harm's way lying in ditches, in the heat and dust, rain, hail and snow, snatching at sleep half a world away from their loved ones.

CONTENTS

ACKNOWLEDGMENTS

UK
Special thanks to Mick Brennan and John Kerbotson for
allowing me to tap into their memories.

Robin Pereira for his professional design skills and
advice.

ROI
Ron Healy and Kiara Healy for their proof reading and
editing skills.

USA
Simon Melley for providing inspiration and
for his hospitality with Gilly Melley.

Everyone at the 'Key West Bed and Breakfast' for
looking after me during my research trips to the island,
particularly Liz and Tricia and Bailey for their warm
welcome and sense of humour and to Jody for
providing a relaxing, inspiring place to write.

By the same author

Novels:

South Atlantic Soldier
Helter Skelter
Skelter's Vengeance

Short Story collection:

Snapshots

Born in Cardiff in 1945 Stuart Pereira trained in Graphic Design, and Illustration and followed a career in museum exhibition design from 1965 to 2002. His short stories have won first prizes in two international competitions.

His first novel, published in 2012, follows two members of the 23rd Special Air Service Regiment (TAVR) in the Falklands war of 1982. The author served for 12 years in 23 SAS in the 1970s and 1980s.

Skelter's Final Duty

1
Sad News

Herefordshire
Sunday, October 3ʳᵈ 2004

Skelter blinked at the digital display on the alarm clock. Four a.m. This was no social call. He reached for the phone, surprised by the stab of chilly air on his naked arm. He pulled the handset under the duvet and thumbed the green button.

'Hello, who is this? Tommo? What's up? Mitch? Mitch is where?'

'Mark?' Lucy stretched and fumbled for the bedside lamp switch. 'What time is it?'

'I'm on the phone, Cariad.'

'I can see…'

'Shhh, love, please, it's important.' Skelter pulled back the duvet and swung his legs out of the bed. 'Need a piss, back in a mo, no, not you mate, talking to Lucy.' The insides of Skelter's mouth tasted like the bottom of a ferret's cage. Feet braving the cold bare floorboards, Skelter walked naked to the bathroom. Jamming the handset between his shoulder and ear, he squeezed toothpaste onto his brush and gave his teeth a vigorous peppermint scrub. 'Oh shit.' He spat the toothpaste into the basin, 'sure about this?'

Back in the bedroom Skelter slipped under the covers again. 'Which hospital? Hold on, mate, need a something to write on.' He rooted around in the bedside cabinet for a pen and found an old envelope. 'Fire away, mate.' The pen scrabbled across the paper. Dunstan Hospice, Coral Gables, Miami. 'Where the hell is my passport?

'Coffee?' said Lucy with a yawn, one hand on her husband's shoulder, the other reaching for a dressing gown. Skelter squeezed Lucy's hand.

He found Lucy in the kitchen surrounded by cardboard boxes and tea chests.

'Coffee,' she said, offering him a steaming mug. 'So what's wrong?'

'Mitch Mitchell, we went to thanksgiving dinner at his house in Florida.'

'Millennium trip – I remember. Lovely man, bad news?'

'He's sick,' said Skelter, 'very sick.'

'Oh, I am sorry, Mark.'

'Without Mitch I'd never have amounted to anything. He looked after me from the day I joined the Marines. It was Mitch that put me through the Navy education system. Been more of a father than my old man ever was.'

'How bad?'

'Terminal. Lung cancer. Not got long Tommo

reckons, few months maybe.'

'Is he still in Key West?'

Skelter shook his head, jaw clenched, a tight grip on the coffee mug. 'Got a house on the gulf now; Sanibel Island.'

'Millionaires row. When will you leave?'

'Soon as possible.'

'I'll call Daddy first thing, be a shame not to take advantage of such good connections. Nothing you can do now so come back to bed and get some sleep.'

Skelter swallowed hard but could not shift the lump in his throat. 'I'm going to ring around, try to get a flight. I can sleep on the plane.' He touched Lucy's cheek.

She kissed his hand. 'Can I do anything?'

'Go back to bed. I'll bring you a coffee when it's time to get up.'

Skelter searched the contacts on his mobile for the numbers but used the landline to call the airlines. After an hour of calls and hanging on hold, the earliest available flight he could find was Thursday.

He packed a large case and put essential items into a small rucksack. The most significant of these, a green soapstone Buddha, had been his constant companion ever since Jane had presented him with it high in the Himalayas; their last holiday before a terrorist bomb took her away. Buddha had been a sounding board for ideas, grievances and as the only tangible link to his late wife, a comfort in times of stress.

With bags packed and time on his hands, Skelter donned tracksuit and trainers and went for a run, his normal response to stress. Exercise is the finest medication for stress in the world, Judith had said, the day of his first session. He recalled his flippant response. Granny, eggs, teach, suck. He also remembered not being embarrassed by his rudeness. He had come a long way.

Skelter pounded the well-trodden circuit around winding country lanes, reel after reel of archived memories running through his head as he ran. *'Hope we're not too late,'* he said aloud to the fat green Buddha in his clenched fist. 'It doesn't sound good, buddy, not good at all.'

A closet novelist, Mitch Mitchell was the black sheep of the aristocratic family who – despite his background – joined 45 Commando as a ranker and twice refused a commission. Skelter had taken to this maverick from the start and he treated Skelter as a son. Later, seeing action together had welded an unbreakable bond, joining them at the hip.

Through half-closed eyes Skelter watched a tall ramrod-straight sergeant major Mitchell take his first parade and then put him through hell on his commando course, alternately berating and encouraging him. The man stood for no nonsense but he had a huge heart. Skelter watched the past unfold like a TV documentary and prayed for a miracle.

Steam rising from his hair and sweat top, Skelter stood in the still unfamiliar kitchen trying to recover his breath. After a few minutes of stretching he dived in to christen the new downstairs shower with a bar of soap from the kitchen sink. There was still much unpacking to do. At least he had remembered to dig out a towel before he set off. He dressed and headed upstairs with coffee for Lucy.

'Any luck with a flight?' she asked.

'Best I could find was a flight via Amsterdam and Atlanta. Twenty-seven hours.'

Lucy sat up and reached for the phone. 'What time is it?'

'Half seven.'

She tapped at the numbers.

'Think I'll walk into the village for a paper. Do you want anything, Cariad?'

'A Guardian. Oh and a couple of pints of milk.'

'Anything else?' 'Don't think so.' A voice at the other end of the line terminated her conversation with Skelter. 'Wilkins, it's Lucy is Daddy there? No, nothing's wrong, I need a favour.'

'Won't be long,' Skelter said. She blew him a kiss, as he turned and headed downstairs. He grabbed his body warmer from the top of a tea chest full of crockery and went out through the side door.

'Two pints of milk and one newspaper,' said Skelter, as he took a seat beside her at the breakfast bar.

Later, while sipping coffee from a steaming mug and munching a slice of butter basted wholemeal toast, he opened his Daily Express. Half way down page two the telephone rang. Lucy took the call. 'Good news. Overnight flight from Heathrow, Tuesday. Daddy says to wish you bon voyage. I explained the circumstances, and he asked me to pass on his best wishes to Mitch.' She peered into one of the tea chests, 'One thing, you won't have to worry about work.'

Skelter looked across the stacked boxes. 'Sorry, Cariad.'

'No problem, easier unpacking without you under my feet. Anyway all the heavy lifting's done and I'm sure Daddy will let me borrow Wilkins if necessary.'

'I'll try to get back for next week to help. You're right about work, could have been difficult.'

'Just get back for your birthday, old man.'

A look of mock hurt creased Skelter's weathered face 'Fifty is the new forty my girl, I'm not old.'

'Not until the seventeenth of next month.'

'That's five weeks away.'

'What about your next session with Judith?'

'Tomorrow.'

'That means you can keep your appointment.'

'Reckons I'm as good as sorted. Might sign me off this time. That woman knows her stuff.'

'Told you so,' said Lucy with a twinkle in her eye. 'No more nasty nightmares, and the wine bill has gone down.'

'You put your fair share of sauvignon away,' said Skelter with a grin.

'Touché.'

'Sorry for all I put you through the last six years.'

'It's fine, I'm just relieved you're well again.'

2

Therapy

Leominster
Monday, October 4th 2004

Skelter turned into the driveway and parked next to Judith's black BMW, got out and made his way through the side gate into the garden. Tired from lack of sleep and apprehensive about the impending counselling session, he followed the inlaid paving slabs across the lawn to the house and rang the bell. Dressed in black tailored trousers and grey cashmere sweater, Judith opened the door.

'Greetings, H, thanks for bringing the weather with you.'

'Not bad, is it?' he replied, trying to sound upbeat.

'Come in and make yourself comfortable.'

The former smithy had been transformed into a mint green haven of calm. Warm and cosy, thanks to the fire in the old blacksmith's forge, it enjoyed views across a large lily pond, complete with bulrushes and weeping willow. Skelter lowered himself into the recliner and took a deep breath.

'Relax,' said Judith. 'The meter isn't running yet. No rush, take it easy, settle in.'

Skelter closed his eyes, sank into the upholstery and

breathed steadily as he tried to focus on the place that to him personified relaxation; the Jacuzzi in the garden of the B&B in Key West. These days – thanks to Judith – he was more laid back. Coming off the Valium had been a challenge but he had been clean now for eight months. He imagined the water warm and bubbling, pounding his back as he looked up at the huge glaucous fan-shaped leaves of the Bismarck Palm towering overhead. His breathing settled and he could feel his heart rate slowing down. He opened his eyes and looked through the French windows towards the pond.

'I'm ready when you are,' he said.

'Excellent. How have you been since I saw you last? No major issues I trust?'

'Okay, thanks and no, not a single problem. So, what have you planned for me this week?'

Judith smiled. She looked briefly at her notes and then at Skelter.

'We have made significant progress in five years. So much that I am happy for you to leave my comfy couch and stand on your own two feet again. This will be our last session.'

Skelter had been expecting it but his heart beat doubled just the same.

'I will always be here if you need me, but I believe you are ready. We have one last thing do. I want you to relax. Consider where you are on your journey. The flash backs, nightmares, panic attacks. Remember them?' Judith consulted her notes. 'You have had no episodes in the last six months. Is that still the case?'

Skelter steadied his breathing. 'Yes, yes it is.'

'Good,' said Judith. She ran her fingers through her silver hair and tucked the loose ends behind a diamond studded ear. 'In order for you to appreciate how much progress we have made I shall play you the transcript of our first session. Just close your eyes, relax, let the tape take you back, okay?'

'Sure, whatever you say doc. You've done a tidy job up to now.' He dropped his eyelids and settled in to the soft upholstery as the music began. He would miss the soothing strings that made his mind more receptive. He had fought hard against it in the beginning but gradually he learned to accept it as Judith built the bridge of trust that now linked them.

The tape began with a low hiss *'Okay so what have you planned for me?'*

'Before I address that, I have a question. I want you to see a colleague of mine, who has considerable experience in working with ex service personnel.'

'This colleague, she another psychologist?'

'He, is a psychiatrist. If he concurs then I would like you to consider a form of hypnotherapy, possibly combined with medication.'

'Like I told you doc, I'm open to anything.'

'Excellent.' The sound of dainty feet on parquet followed by *'Coffee?'*

'White no sugar please.'

'Describe your symptoms, how do they impact on your life day to day,' her voice sounded far away.

'Coffee, white, no sugar.'

'Thank you, Doc.'

'Well?'

The tape returned to a low hiss for several seconds.

'I get nightmares, well one nightmare mainly, although it has

15

eased off lately.'

'Why do you think the nightmare has eased?'

'I know why, it's because I remembered the cause, after twenty-five years of trying.'

'What exactly did you remember?'

'I was eighteen, working as a steward on a beat up steamer out of Cardiff. We were ashore in Marseilles, crawling the dockside dives. I got legless. Somebody jumped me in an alley and beat the shit out of me, left me for dead. I would have died too if Otto hadn't found me, him and Duke.'

'Tell me about Otto and Duke.'

'Otto was a bear of a man, most powerful man I ever met, worked as a circus strongman before he joined the Legion. He served on the Russian front with the Waffen SS in the war. Duke was not much older than me, twenty-two I think. He got drafted to Vietnam in sixty-eight, did two tours. You'd like him, doc, he was completely out of his tree.'

'When you say Legion, I assume that you are referring to the French Foreign Legion?'

'That's the one, I can't see either of those two rattling poppy tins for the British legion. I thought you wanted to record this?'

'I am, the tape's running.'

The cassette returned to hiss mode *'When you went for the coffee? You started it then?'*

'So, what else besides nightmares?'

'Distraction, loss of concentration...' hissing again

'What are you distracted from, not your work, is it?'

'Any chance of another coffee?'

'You've not finished the one you have. Is it because I am a woman?'

'Excuse me?'

'Nothing you say will shock me. Your work cannot be the problem or you would have been discharged long ago if not killed.

That leaves domestic. You are in a relationship…'

'Don't take any prisoners do you Doc? Ok, ok, it affects me in the friendly weapon department.' The sound of lungs being emptied battled with the hiss of the cassette. *'Not always, a bit hit and miss, if you know what I mean.'*

'Far more common than you might believe. I think we should stop the clock there for ten minutes.'

The hard plastic click of the pause button fast-forwarded Skelter from 1999 back to the present. He opened his eyes.

'Remember that stuttering beginning? How far away is that now, H?'

Tears welled up in his eyes. He patted himself down.

'Forgotten something?' asked Judith.

'It's okay. Left him in my rucksack.'

'Buddha?'

'Yeah.'

A huge smile broke across Judith's face and her eyes sparkled. 'Imagine if that had happened back then? You would have been beside yourself. Now look at you.'

Skelter smiled back. 'It's been one hell of a long journey.'

'We'll break there for five minutes. Why don't you take a walk around the garden? I'll make a fresh brew.'

Skelter got up and walked outside into the late summer sunshine. The leaves would begin to turn in a few weeks. He walked down the garden and gazed into the depths of the pond. A large tadpole with fully developed back legs was eating a worm that had fallen into the water. Skelter watched fascinated as a dragonfly nymph crept up from behind the tadpole, struck with its hinged claw and thrust the unfortunate tadpole into its jaws. So which are we, H, boy, tadpole or dragonfly nymph?

'So, H?' Judith asked as he walked back in. 'Are you ready for part two?'

'Bring it on Doc.'

He settled in and soaked up the music, the ever present, reliable comfort blanket that preceded every session. The clack of the machine, coupled with the short hiss transported Skelter back to 1999.

'Describe your earliest memory of violence?'

'I thought you were going to hypnotise me?'

'One step at a time, Mr Skelter. We need to establish a starting point.'

'H.'

'I'm sorry?'

'If I'm going to share intimate details of my private life with you it's H.'

'As you wish. So, H, what is your earliest memory of violence?'

The hissing again – it went on for several seconds.

'It was a Friday. Dad got paid on Fridays. It was thirsty work in the steelworks he told me. I never saw my Dad on Fridays. I never saw him, but I heard him. Around midnight. He woke me up, shouting and swearing, banging and bawling. Mam hated Fridays. I hated my Dad. One day I'd be grown up tall and strong. He'd be older and slower and weaker. Then he'd learn fear, be scared like Mam turning in his gut till he was sick like us. Friday fever we called it. Waiting and sweating, little Annie wetting herself as she heard the door go. He'd learn, cos I'd teach him. No mercy. He'd be begging but it wouldn't do no good. I'd throw him out. Put new locks on the doors. But first I'd smash his hands with the ballpein hammer I hid under my pillow. Smash them so they could never make fists again, his toes too. No more kicking.'

'Was it only at the weekends?'

'Friday night after chucking out time. Pay day. Pub day. He got a skinful, came in angry and took it out on Mam. Repeat performance on Saturday if he had any of his wages left.'

'How old were you?'

'A kid, a little kid, four, five?'

'How did you feel about it at the time?'

'Delighted. How do think I felt?' More hiss 'This isn't going to work. You might be ok for Lucy, but not for me. No offence, Judith.'

'None taken, H. You are here of your own free will. I would point out you have forty-seven minutes left. You might take advantage of the services the Brigadier has paid good money for. They are expensive.'

'I don't doubt it.'

'Do you know why?' More hissing as the tape rolled over a background of silence. 'My services command a high fee because I'm good, H, I am very good. I have been practicing in this field for thirty years. I may be unconventional but I get results. Your scepticism is healthy and perfectly normal. If you work with me I am confident we can resolve many of your issues. What have you got to lose? Forty-five minutes, well?'

'Forty-five minutes, you say.'

'Forty-two now, tell me how you felt about your father's violence towards your mother.'

'It was so deliberate, calculated. I wanted to smash his face in. I thought of nothing else. I planned to do it as soon as I was big enough.'

'Planned?'

'I hated him. I lived for the day I would be big enough and strong enough.'

'Your plan, did you ever…?'

'The night before my tenth birthday I learned two new words.

19

Coronary thrombosis. I had no idea what they meant, only that it was something bad. Mam and Auntie Vi were talking in the kitchen. I was hanging my coat in the hall. I wasn't looking forward to my birthday, I never looked forward to birthdays, it was just another day to me. It couldn't have fallen on a worse day. I remember thinking why did it have to be on a Friday? Mam made a sponge with icing and candles on the top. There was no money for presents. I could smell the Victoria sponge, warm from the oven, taste the sharp sugary tang of raspberry jam. Mam called from the kitchen: "That you Cariad?" she said, she always called me Cariad, except when Dad was around.'

'Why is that?'

'He would have got angry. Soft, sissy name. Wouldn't have his boy called darling. "Come by yer" she said, I remember so clear. "Your Auntie Vi's brought you toffees" she said, that's when I knew something was wrong. It was Friday see? Auntie Vi always came on Mondays. Mam was smiling. She looked really happy. Mam never looked happy on Fridays. I remember Auntie Vi holding out her arms. I went over and let her kiss me. I loved toffees see. I asked what was wrong, Mam said Lawrie Bennett from the steelworks had been round. There'd been an accident. It was Dad. Had to get an ambulance, but it was too late, he was dead'

'How did your father's death make you feel?'

'Cheated, the bastard cheated me. I wanted to use the hammer on him. I wanted to beat that man so bad, to smash his bones to dust. I longed to hear him scream for mercy.'

'Do you still fantasise about taking a hammer to your father?'
'Sometimes.'

'How often?'

The tape hissed forward a few revolutions. *'Couldn't really say, random, not often, depends.'*

'Upon what?'
'I need water, mouth's dry.'

'*On the table beside you.*'

The sound of pouring water and swallowing emanated from the machine. '*Not sure really, I think maybe it depends what I am doing.*'

'*Such as?*'

'*After a contact. when the shooting's stopped when it's all gone quiet.*'

'*When the adrenaline's slowing down?*'

'*Yes.*'

'*When you imagine hitting him with the hammer, how does that make you feel now?*'

'*Good, but bad at the same time. I can't explain it.*'

'*I think we should leave it there for now. Is there anything you want to ask me?*'

'*I know what is wrong with me, Doc, I have PTSD. I know exactly what caused it and when. What I want to know is can it be cured?*'

'*Who diagnosed your PTSD?*' The tape went back to silent hissing mode once more. '*Suppose your rifle stopped working, and I was to offer an explanation as to the cause. How seriously would you value my input?*'

'*Point taken, Doc.*'

'*Post-Traumatic Stress Disorder is not uncommon in your profession and you might be right but leave the diagnosis to the professionals. As to whether it can be cured, there is no simple answer. It can be treated. Patients can be taught ways of dealing with their symptoms. I have had significant success with several veterans who have had their lives transformed by treatment. No magic bullet, I'm afraid H, but we can make a big difference. You are in a fortunate position. You have no financial responsibility for the treatment. I would urge you to take advantage of it.*'

'*Ok, Doc, you're the boss. So what happens next?*'

'*I will see you in a week. In the meanwhile, try to keep an open mind about the cause of your problem. The obvious is not always the right answer. The cause can be multifaceted and complex.'*

The tape stopped with a clack.

'Are you ready to take the stabilisers off and balance by yourself?'

'I think I am, Judith, I really think I am now. Thank you for persevering with me. I apologise for being such a stroppy sod in the beginning.'

'You have an excellent chance to put most of this behind you and the skills and tools to manage your condition into the future. The key thing is you have a completely changed lifestyle. All that violence is behind you. Gone forever, and that makes you able to handle it.'

Skelter stood up and held out his hand. 'You have given me back a life I thought lost forever. Thank you.'

'Pleased to have been of service. Off you pop then and be sure to give my love to Lucy.'

'Will do and thanks again, Judith.'

Skelter drove back in a state of euphoria. Judith had succeeded beyond all expectation. He pulled in at a garage for fuel and called Lucy.

'I should be with you in twenty minutes, Cariad.'

'I'll put the coffee on. How did it go?'

'Tell you when I get there, got to go I'm blocking someone in.'

The smell of coffee and sizzling bacon greeted Skelter as he crossed the threshold into the kitchen

'Well?'

'I've been officially discharged.'

'Oh, well done. She is good, isn't she? Any other news?'

'No, that's it. Oh, she sends her love. What's with the bacon?'

'Got fresh rolls from the bakers. Thought I'd treat you,' she said flipping the rashers.

'Cheers. What you been up to then?'

'Work. What else? Coming on well, I'm almost ready to send the next batch of illustrations to the publishers.' Lucy sliced a batch roll and slid in two thick rashers of crispy best back. 'There you go. Coffee's on the table.'

Skelter leaned across and planted a kiss on her cheek. 'Thanks.'

'It's only a bacon roll, Mark.'

'For everything else too,' he said. 'I dont understand what I've done to deserve you, Cariad. You are a real glutton for punishment.'

'We don't choose who we fall for, it just happens,' said Lucy.

'Shit happens,' said Skelter.

'Thanks a bunch.'

Skelter paused mid bite, recovered. 'Cracking bacon banjo, girl.'

3

Mitch

Florida
Wednesday/Thursday/Friday
October 6/7/8th 2004

In sharp contrast to the oppressive heat outside, the air conditioning in the private clinic raised goose bumps on Skelter's arms. A pleasant young receptionist typed the patient's name into her computer and directed him to a room on the second floor. Mitch Mitchell was a big man, 'was' − as in past tense. Skelter had prepared himself for a shock but the sight of his old friend rocked his foundations. The powerful athletic figure he knew, now reduced to a parchment covered skeleton, with look of resignation in his eyes.

'Thanks for coming, son, I wouldn't bother you but...'

'No sweat. I owe you more than I can ever repay.'

'Not much time left.' Mitch was struggling to speak.

'Envelope in the locker.' He waved a frail hand to the bedside. Inside was a large brown envelope, stuffed full with 20-dollar bills.

Mitch tapped the envelope, 'Inside, a letter.'

Skelter took out the smaller, white envelope, removed the folded sheet of paper and read:

Maria Solina
Schooner Wharf Bar
Key West, Florida.

Dear Maria,

I have been fortunate to call you my friend ever since you took me in and gave me a place to stay all those years ago. I was in a bad way then and you straightened me out. I know you have since looked up to me as a father. This made my feelings towards you difficult to handle sometimes. You are never far from my thoughts and now it seems the time approaches for me to leave this Earth. I have no regrets, life has been good. I have no family so I wish you to have what I leave behind. I am sending a trusted friend with an envelope for you. It contains money, a letter from my lawyer, (I know we never discussed your immigration status but do not worry, he is very discreet). He will arrange the sale of my house on Sanibel Island. A copy of my Will is also enclosed. The house and my other assets in the US will realise enough for you to give up any or all of your three jobs and put Juan, Pedro and Eva through college.

I fear I have drunk my last Margarita in the Schooner Wharf. May God watch over you and your family.

Much love,
Mitch.

Also in the envelope was a bunch of keys, with an address label attached.

'House keys, car and the Chelsea tractor.' He winked. 'See you at the house when you get back, take the car or four by four, whichever.' He began coughing, his breathing, laboured.

Skelter buzzed for a nurse. Mitch looked worn out. 'I'll set off first thing Mitch. Don't worry, I'll sort it.'

A weary half smile stole across Mitch's face as a young nurse in a crisp starched uniform entered the room. 'One thing, H, I am going home tomorrow, to Sanibel.'

Skelter raised an eyebrow. 'You sure that's wise?'

A knowing smile spread across Mitch's haggard face. 'Private air ambulance. Two nurses round the clock at home. Got way more than I can spend now, son.'

Skelter nodded slowly, 'I better go, you need to rest.' Their eyes met in understanding.

'You should leave now,' said the nurse.

Skelter nodded, but failed to keep the surprise from his face. Mitch managed a weak wink as his visitor picked up the envelopes, letter and keys and walked out.

An hour after sunrise the following day Skelter was looking down at the clear blue waters of the Gulf of Mexico gliding beneath the aircraft, eating up the miles to Key West.

'Where are we going, sir?' asked the taxi driver.

'William Street, four fifteen, please.'

Without a word the man released the brake and the

cab moved forward heading for the main gate.

'First trip to Key West, sir?'

'No.' Skelter looked out of the window.

The driver took the hint. He cut down Eaton hung a left south onto William and stopped next to a new tourist rental convertible. Skelter thanked the driver, paid him and lifted his sports bag out of the back. He opened the white picket gate and walked up the steps and into the grand entrance. It was like coming home. Diz was at the desk busy checking the screen while talking on the phone. She put the phone down. 'Assholes, what part of fully booked did they not understand?' She shook her head and rolled her eyes up in to the top of her head.

'Someone pulling on your chain Dizzy?'

'Mark Skelter, what a lovely surprise, I wasn't expecting you until next April. You are incredibly lucky. Last minute cancellation, sudden bereavement.' Dizzy frowned, her fingers combing through her long raven locks.

'Did I say something wrong, H?' she said, noting the sadness in his face.

'No, no, great to see you Dizzy.'

'Likewise. Lucy and you will be here in April as planned?'

'Absolutely. This was a last minute thing. I spoke to someone called Lula, I think. Lucky you had room.'

'You certainly were. Business is brisk these days.' Dizzy took a set of keys from the drawer and handed them to Skelter. 'You are in the Bella's room on the first floor, with shared bathroom for seven days. You have stayed before so I can spare you the introduction speech if you wish. Breakfast is between eight thirty and ten.'

'I'm okay,' thanks. 'I can remember my way around.'

Dizzy flashed a faultless set of pearly whites. 'That's fine,' she said, 'I'll leave you to it.'

'New picture?' Skelter asked, observing a small watercolour on the wall opposite the desk. It depicted the back porch from the garden, complete with orchids, hibiscus and royal purple painted steps to the side door.

'One of our guests painted it.'

'Lucy will love that.' He picked up his bag and headed upstairs. The single room was compact but had everything he needed. There were two windows, letting in loads of light, more drawers than he could use and a choice of two bathrooms along the hall, shared with three other rooms. Somebody had thoughtfully switched on the air conditioning and the atmosphere was cool and pleasant. He unzipped his case, took out a toilet bag and picked the large, soft white towel from the bed and walked along the landing.

Skelter breakfasted alone in the garden in the shade of a large sour-orange tree. It was hot and the mercury was still rising. He ate a toasted buttered cinnamon and raisin bagel followed by figs and coffee. At 10.30 he walked out the front gate, turned right and walked the two blocks towards Front Street.

A warm breeze wafted across the gravel patio, stirring the palm fronds around The Schooner Wharf Bar. Six customers occupied three of the small glass-topped tables. The tourists sat in pairs on the white plastic garden chairs, nursing Margaritas and Mojitos, browning their pasty white knees, faces shielded from the hot sun by the cotton canvas parasols. Skelter took a seat at the bar, one of three areas with a roof. The other two were the kitchen on the far side of the gravel and the wooden stage to Skelter's right, at the front of the patio.

'Hi, what can I get you?'

He was big and moved slow and easy, fresh faced and smiling.

'Rolling Rock, please,' Skelter replied. 'Davey still play here?' he asked, inclining his head towards the stage.

The man plunged his hand into the ice filled trough behind the bar and pulled out a beer, took the cap off the bottle and handed it to him with a small round paper coaster.

'Not today. Today we have Magpie from noon through five pm.'

'Excellent. It'll be good listening to live music here again,' said Skelter, recalling with a wisp of sadness, the occasion when he first stumbled across the bar many years ago.

'You were here before? I'm good with faces but...'

'About four years ago.'

'I remember now,' he said. 'You were with a guy that smoked a pipe, right? Called himself Brick. You're H.'

'That's right,' said Skelter, 'well remembered.'

'Part of the job. Welcome back.'

Skelter lifted the bottle towards his lips. 'Thank you er...'

'Duncan and you're welcome.'

He raised the bottle in salute. 'Pleased to renew the acquaintance, Duncan.' He necked half the contents and looked around the bar. A pair of forty-something tourists in white socks and sandals, bellies bursting out of brand new XXL T-shirts, sat at a table near the kitchen. Three stools along the bar, nursing a margarita apiece, two blue rinse cruise-ship gals clucked away in a nest of designer bags from Duval Street's tourist traps. Beyond them at the end of the bar sat a local the colour of seasoned cedar wood dressed in cut-offs and flip flops looking like part of the furniture.

Skelter had well settled in at the bar by the time Magpie arrived and plugged in for a sound check. They were a duo – her black him white. 'I'll have another Rolling Rock please, Duncan, and can I get an order of fish tacos?'

'Sure,' the man said, passing Skelter the bottle. 'You want blue cheese dip with that, right?'

'Damn but you're good,' said Skelter.

'I'll take that,' said Duncan.

Skelter passed a relaxing couple of hours listening to Magpie's island-blend of folk rock music. They were good, with beautiful polished harmonies. Solid music, professional and relaxing to listen to. Skelter approached the stage, put a couple of dollar bills in the jar and requested Jimmy Buffet's "A Pirate Looks at Forty". The tacos arrived. He dived in with relish.

'Please pass my thanks to the chef,' said Skelter licking the last traces of sauce from his fingers, 'terrific.'

'Why thank you, I will.'

Skelter stayed until the end of Magpie's first set and then drained his last bottle. 'I'd like to clear my tab if that's okay?'

'Absolutely.'

Skelter unzipped his cargo pocket and paid cash, a novelty in that part of the world. He tipped the bartender a five-dollar bill. He wanted him to remember when he started asking questions about Maria, but that would keep for now. It was a small island and visitors asking questions were likely to be regarded with suspicion.

Duncan thanked him, screwed up the coaster and replaced it with a fresh one. Skelter slid from the barstool and wandered out into the sun and onto the boardwalk. The water was alive with fish, including several tarpon, some almost a metre long. Skelter walked along the jetty to Harpoon Harry's for coffee and doughnuts.

Fortified with three cups and a brace of sugar rings, he made his way back for another Schooner Wharf session. Magpie was half way through the last set when Skelter took the last free barstool. Duncan was still on shift and two Rolling Rocks in he slipped Maria's name into the conversation.

'I have a friend, Mitch Mitchell, comes here twice a year. He says to say hi for him. Did you know him?'

'Doesn't ring any bells,' said Duncan shaking his head.

'He used to be friendly with one of your waitresses, Maria. Maria Solina.'

'Sorry, Maria works weekends,' Duncan said, his eyes narrowing. 'Got to go,' he said, 'customer.' He walked the length of the bar and spoke to a pair of heavies around his age with sharp crew cuts and big necks. They both clocked him. Skelter took a notebook and pen from his pocket and scribbled a note on a page which he tore from the book. It was twenty minutes before they approached him all friendly and smiling.

'Word is you're looking for Maria,' said the taller of the two. 'Name's Elmore, this is Jimmy. We're friends of Maria.'

'Nice to meet you.' Skelter replied studying the men's body language.

'We'd be happy to take you to see her. How is Mitch by the way?'

'Not so good. He gave me some stuff he wanted her to have.'

'Sorry to hear that. We could take it for you if you like?' said the shorter wider one.

'No offence,' said Skelter, 'but I promised I'd deliver it personally. If you don't mind showing me where she lives I would be grateful.'

'Sure thing,' said the tall guy, 'follow us.'

4

Confrontation

Key West
Friday, October 8th 2004

Skelter called Duncan over and paid the tab. He took a ten-dollar bill from his wallet, wrapped it around the scribbled note and passed it to him. The two men led the way. Maria lived in a small shotgun shack somewhere south of Eaton, but that was all he knew. As he followed the two guys along the waterfront towards the naval base, his suspicions were confirmed. They were chatty, real friendly, but they were not Oscar material. *They'll make their move where the pier meets the security fence, let us get level, step back and cut off escape. Boy are they in for a surprise Buddha buddy.*

The fence loomed ahead, water on both sides, the two apes behind. He patted the Buddha in his pocket *we're not going for a swim, boy.* The pitch of the tall guy's voice went up an octave as they reached a point some fifty yards from where Skelter guessed the guys would strike. *Any second now.* Skelter stopped suddenly, skipped back three paces and stood with his back against one of the massive wooden piles that supported the dock. Thicker than a telegraph pole they rose three feet above the walkway.

The men turned about.

'Cut the crap boys and get it off your chest,' said Skelter.

The short one spoke. 'We don't like people hassling our friends, amigo.'

'Maria's lucky to have you guys looking out for her but I really do have stuff for her. Important stuff.'

The tall guy stepped forward a pace. Skelter put up his hand. He stopped.

'Hear me out. You don't want to hurt Maria, do you?'

The wide one crabbed left, right on the edge of the eight-foot-wide boardwalk.

'Last chance,' Skelter said.

Puzzlement claimed the would-be muggers' faces. Body mass and biceps, but short on brains.

'Listen boy...'

'Silence!' Skelter barked.

Open mouthed, shocked and confused, initiative surrendered, the apes looked at one another. 'Think I'm new to this, I take it you both swim?'

The two apes exchanged looks. The tall one moved first followed a second later by the other. Tall boy steamed in, a vicious kick, straight at Skelter's groin. Fast and accurate. Skelter side-stepped faster. The man's soft-toed deck shoe struck the wooden pile where Skelter had stood a second before, with a sickening, bone breaking crunch. The man's scream merged with the sound of his buddy splashing into the sea as Skelter yielded to the muscle mass hurled at him by falling backwards onto the dock while firmly planting the sole of his foot into his attacker's stomach, using the man's own momentum to send him arcing through the air over his head and into the water. It was over in seconds. The tall guy was screaming in agony holding his foot. Skelter looked down at him while his buddy splashed spluttered and cursed from his early bath beside them.

'Had to do this the hard way, didn't we?' said Skelter, 'I'm a friend. I can help Maria. Help her a lot.'

'We thought you were from immigration,' the man blubbed, moaning and wailing.

'I guessed as much, but you're wrong. I need to see her. You could help but either way, I will find her.'

At that moment Jimmy climbed onto the boardwalk, soaked and shaken. He had gone in hard. When he saw the state Elmore was in. what fight he had left drained away with the water that poured from his ugly frame.

'You okay Elmore?' Jimmy asked in a high-pitched voice.

'Bust my foot, broke my freakin' toes goddamnit. Jesus, man.'

Skelter looked at the dripping dude. As if reading his mind, the man said, 'No trouble buddy. We don't want no trouble.'

'Not now you don't. Pity you didn't listen.' It was then that Skelter noticed the group of people coming along the jetty towards him, five or six of them. Adrenaline rising he turned to face them. Right at the front was a woman: small, dark, early fifties.

'You,' she said, 'what is wrong with Mitch? Why is he in hospital? Tell me.'

'Maria?' Skelter queried.

'Si, Maria.'

'Aren't you worried about your friends?' said Skelter, indicating the two now being helped by four youths and the Biker from the Schooner Wharf.

'They are big enough to look after themselves,' she replied.

Skelter raised his eyebrows

'Mitch, tell me about Mitch, please,' Maria said.

'This is for you,' he said, taking the package from his cargo pocket, 'from Mitch. There's more back at the place I'm staying. He has no family. Everything is yours, house, car, boat – everything. It's all legal and above board. Proper Will, drawn up by lawyers.'

'You mean he is...'

'He's dying. I'm so sorry. He is like a father to me, Maria.'

She was crying now, her tears silent but sincere.

Someone helped Elmore back along the pier while Jimmy squelched in his wake.

'Come,' said Maria, 'come to my house, I must thank you.' Skelter fell in alongside her and walked in silence the whole way to her home.

The house was small but cosy. Maria made coffee and offered Skelter home baked banana cake, which he gratefully accepted.

'I want to see him,' Maria said. 'There are things to say, things never said. He is a good man. He is the finest man I have ever known. I cannot lose him. Not now.'

'Maria...' Skelter began.

'I know, but you do not understand.'

'He loves you, Maria.'

'I know.' Her tears began to flow again.

'Not like a daughter...'

'I know, I know.' She beat her fists on the table. 'Why are men so stupid in affairs of the heart?' She struggled to compose herself and looked directly into Skelter's eyes. 'Mitch is good and kind. I have a husband who is a no good drunk but I am good Catholic. I stay with him, but my heart is with Mitch, always with Mitch. I love him...' she paused. 'I love him as a woman loves a man. The aching is not just in my heart but my body, too. A woman knows when a man looks at her that way. He would not speak of it because of our ages, but eighteen years means nothing to love.'

5

Visitation

Sanibel Island
Saturday, October 9th 2004

Maria insisted that Skelter stay the night after he refused point blank, to set off to see Mitch at such a late hour. They set off early, with Maria at the wheel of her brown over cream seventy-nine Ford pickup. 'Chico maybe old but he is still my baby,' she said, patting the peeling plastic dash.

'Chico?' said Skelter.

'You men give your trucks girls' names.'

'Point taken,' said Skelter as she floored the pedal on the highway towards the bridge.

'You might want to ease off the gas, Maria, before the cops get on your tail. We'll get there sooner if we don't get pulled over.'

She lifted her foot a touch. 'You are right of course,

but I need so bad to see him.'

Skelter placed a hand lightly on her arm. 'I know,' he said. 'So, what about you and Mitch?'

Maria relaxed her grip on the wheel a little, sighed and spoke. 'It was a very hot day, no wind, he came in and sat at the bar. He ordered beer and smiled this great, big smile. His teeth were so white, so perfect. His voice soft with an accent like Sir Laurence Olivier. I remember my stomach had little tingling pains. I did not know what it was. It hurt, but it felt so good.'

'When was this?'

'It was just before Christmas 1992. He was charming and smiling then, but it did not last.' There was a tremor in her voice.

'Oh?' said Skelter.

'He came often to the bar, always he sat at the same place on the corner facing the stage, he liked the music. But he became more sad, and he drank too much and that just made him more sad. He was in much pain.'

'The cancer?'

'No, this was a different pain, a pain of the heart. For such a pain, there is only one cure, but I am a married woman.'

Skelter watched the tears slowly slide down Maria's cheeks. 'I'm sorry I didn't mean to...'

'Do not worry, H, it is good to talk. This I have kept inside for much too long.'

'You knew?'

'Of course. We became friends, and I fell in love with him as he was in love with me, but I have a husband. The church...'

'I understand,' said Skelter. 'It must have been very painful for you.'

Maria wiped her cheeks with the back of her hand. 'We need gas,' she said.

'Maybe we can get a cup of coffee?' said Skelter. 'We've been going over two hours.'

She flashed her tear-filled eyes at him and, tight lipped, she shook her head.

'A couple to go?'

She nodded. 'I cried myself to sleep many nights,' she said. 'I longed to put my arms around him and take away his pain, but that would have been a sin. I went to confession. I knew that what I wanted I could not have.'

Maria pulled into a gas station on Key Largo. Tears were flowing freely now. 'I...restroom.'

'Go,' said Skelter. 'I'll fill her up.' He paid for the fuel, picked up coffee and a bag of donuts.

Mitch's home was not too easy to find even with the directions Skelter had been given, written in a shaky hand on the back of a map of Sanibel. It was, however, breathtaking. The narrow lane to the property had expensive looking luxury properties on the left as they approached, while the right appeared to be virgin forest and coastal swamp.

'We're on the right road,' said Skelter, 'here's the parking for the wildlife reserve.' There were just two vehicles in the small lot but a large information board confirmed they were on track. 'Should be half a mile down the road.'

Maria shifted in her seat in a state of agitated excitement, hands gripping the steering wheel, her eyes straining ahead.

'This looks like it,' said Skelter. 'Last one on the

street.'

Maria pulled up in the driveway in front of the triple garage. The twin turreted, white painted, clapboard residence was substantial. Just visible through the palm trees at the side of the house the blue/green waters of one of the inlets from the gulf. Skelter pressed the bell while Maria hopped from one impatient foot to the other. The door was opened by a nurse.

'Where is he?' Maria demanded. 'I must see him. Now.'

Skelter followed the two women through to the back of the house. Mitch lay semi-recumbent in a day bed on the terrace catching the cooling breeze from the waterway.

Maria hurried over and knelt beside him. She took his face in her hands, threw the church out of the window and kissed him.

The nurse made a sound as if to protest but Skelter caught her arm and steered her back the way they came. 'They should be alone,' he said.

'But.'

'He's dying. She is the best medicine he will ever get. Trust me. Now why don't you show me to the kitchen and I'll put the coffee on. I'm sorry, I didn't catch your name.'

'Lena, it's Lena.'

'Well, Lena, you can call me H. Coffee?'

She glanced in the direction of the terrace. There were sounds of gentle sobbing. She looked at Skelter. 'Okay, you win.'

'Not giving you too much of a hard time is he, Lena?'

Skelter asked as he poured his second cup of coffee. 'He can be a bit of a pain. It's the soldier in him, he can't help it.'

'Don't worry, it slides right over me. I was born in Fort Bragg, right on the base. My Daddy was in the military, both my brothers too. He's a sweet man, really. I nursed him here for a while before he went to the hospital.'

Skelter suggested a tour of the house. Lena smiled.

'Mitch told me to expect you and gave strict instructions you were to be treated as close family. I guess he is in safe hands,' she said, looking at Maria.

'None safer,' said Skelter, 'err, no offence.'

'None taken,' she said with a broad smile. 'This way, H.'

Later, Maria and Skelter sat watching the sunset from the terrace, while next to them Mitch lay sleeping soundly. Lena was elsewhere in the house.

'Mitch tells me you are like a son to him.'

'Kind of, I guess, but there is only ten years between us. He took me under his wing when I joined the Marines.'

'He helped you to be a soldier?'

Skelter smiled recalling his first day at Lympstone. 'Not exactly,' he said. 'I was a soldier before I joined. He helped me with my schooling. I went to sea when I was very young so missed out on my education. Mitch enrolled me in the Royal Navy education system. He's been very good to me.' Skelter's eyes started misting up.

'Yes,' said Maria, 'he is a very good man with a big heart, and my heart is his. Do you think I am a bad woman for being so sinful, H?'

Skelter smiled and placed a hand over hers. 'You are not at all bad. God will understand. Any comfort you can bring to each other in the short time you have can only be good. Mitch needs you and you need him. Love can never be bad, Maria.'

'You think that is so, H?'

'I am certain of it. Absolutely.'

She let out a long sigh and sank back into the cushions of the recliner. 'Thank you.'

The two sat in silence watching the rising moon reflect its silver light on the water. At the bottom of the gently sloping, manicured lawn, a substantial wooden jetty jutted out into the inlet. Skelter stood up and went to explore. At the end of the jetty, sitting upon a tackle box. an old man sat with his back to him with a fishing rod in his hand. Moored alongside, a classic 1947 Chris Craft cabin cruiser gave the scene the air of a Hollywood film set. The backdrop of lights from the houses and moored cruisers on the far bank of the channel reinforced the illusion. Skelter approached the jetty slowly and quietly, so as not to frighten the fish. It was not until he took his first steps onto the wooden planking that he realised that the old fisherman was not going to catch anything. Not only did his rod have no line, but he was a work of art. A life-like, life-size, fibreglass sculpture. He patted the fisherman on the shoulder, with a chuckle.

'You are beautiful,' said Skelter, admiring the classic lines of the mahogany superstructure.

'Who is?' said a voice from somewhere close behind.

'Ah, Lena, I was just admiring the boat.'

'It is his baby,' the nurse replied. 'So sad he will not

get the chance to take her out again.'

'I guess there's no point asking....'

Lena shook her head, her eyes showing sympathy for him. 'Impossible to tell, I'm afraid. He is a fighter, and it is not the most aggressive condition I have seen, but it has spread too far. We can eliminate the pain and keep him comfortable, but that is all. He may carry on for months, we just don't know.'

6

Windfall

Sanibel Island
Sunday, October 10th 2004

The smell of fresh-brewed coffee enticed Skelter from his room. He found Maria at Mitch's side, fast asleep on the recliner. Someone had covered her with a light blanket and closed the terrace doors.

'Morning, Mitch, been here all night has she?' Skelter asked, knowing full well that she had.

Mitch nodded. 'Open up will you, laddie?'

Skelter unlatched the smoked glass concertina folders and slid them silently into the wall cavities on each side of the opening. The sudden increase in light level had no effect upon the sleeping Maria. It was at this point that Skelter noticed a nurse sat at a small desk in the corner. 'Morning,' he said.

'Good morning, sir, I am Katya.' The accent was

unmistakably East European.

'Katya is from Hungary. Pretty, isn't she?' Katya blushed and turned away to her paperwork. Mitch seemed perkier than the night before.

'How are you feeling?'

'A little better, not so tired. Good to see you, laddie. Sorry it has to be like this.'

Skelter shook his head slowly, stuck for words. Mitch beckoned him to the other side of the bed from Maria. Skelter complied and knelt close to the pillow.

Mitch clutched at Skelter's sleeve, pulling him close. His grip was surprising, given his condition. 'Do ye still have contacts with the private sector?'

Skelter nodded, surprised at the question. 'What's up?'

'Not sure yet, I might need a job doing. I must talk to Maria. She may be in a spot of bother with some bad people. Drug dealers. Can you stick around a day or two?'

'You just try to stop me,' said Skelter.

Mitch smiled. 'Thanks, I owe you.'

'Au contraire, mon ami, au contraire.'

'Time for your medication, Mr Mitchell.'

Maria stirred but did not wake.

'Mitch, Katya, please.'

'That would not be appropriate sir.' Mitch looked at Skelter.

'Don't look at me, you're on your own with this one. I'm going for some coffee.' Skelter followed his nose to the kitchen, where he found a line of mugs next to the percolator. He filled one and took a walk outside. The sun was warm, a light cooling breeze wafted in across the water under a cloudless cobalt sky. He wandered across the grass and down to the mooring and stood on the jetty, drinking his coffee while he admired the classic lines of the Chris Craft. He took the Buddha statue from his pocket and placed it on the top of one of the supporting posts. *'Don't make 'em like this anymore, do they, Buddha, buddy?'* he said aloud to the little figurine. *'Wonder what kind of job he's got in mind? Better be something I can pass on to some of the youngsters to handle, Lucy will kill me if I get involved. Shit, Lucy. Better go give her a call. It'll be after lunch at home.'* He turned and headed up the shallow slope towards the house in search of a telephone.

'How is everything, Cariad? All well I hope.'

Lucy's response was muted. 'Never mind here, Mark, how is Mitch?'

'He's a bit brighter today. He was out of it for most of yesterday, morphine. He appreciates the situation, and he's handling it well but I don't think he'll be around too far into the new year. Before the primroses bloom in the lanes at home, I reckon.'

'Oh Mark. Not in any pain is he?'

'Not too much, the nurses have that under control. Did I say he was at home; two nurses around the clock? He's well looked after and Maria is with him.'

'Maria?'

'She's an old friend, close friend of his. His house is amazing,' said Skelter, changing the subject. 'Right on the water – got a dock, a beautiful 1940s cabin cruiser, views to die for...' *Shit why did I say that?* 'Look I have to go. Call you later, okay?'

'All right, give Mitch my love, take care. Love you.'

'You, too, Cariad.'

Maria sat beside Mitch stroking his face, their eyes locked and ranged into each other's. The air crackled with unresolvable sexual tension fuelled by a love beyond Skelter's experience. He felt uncomfortable and backed up towards the door, just as nurse Katya came through it. Several packs of pills skidded across the marble floor as the two collided.

'Sorry, wasn't looking,' said Skelter as he dropped to his knees to retrieve the medication.

'No harm done,' said Katya.

The incident had broken the spell. Maria stood up, muttered something, which included the word bathroom and excused herself.

'You always were a clumsy bastard,' croaked Mitch. 'Come and sit with me a while.'

'You're looking better,' said Skelter. 'I guess that's the Maria effect.'

Mitch nodded without raising his head from the pillow. 'I can't thank you enough for bringing her.'

'Get out of here, I owe you shed loads.'

Mitch's face clouded over to serious mode. 'Don't have too much time left. Here's the thing. Maria's son Luis works in communications for the Coast Guard. He is feeding intel to a drug gang to help them avoid detection. They are a nasty bunch. He doesn't want to but these guys are holding his sister as a hostage. Not sure where yet. I'll know in a couple of days.' Mitch paused and reached out for drink.

'Here, let me.' Skelter handed him the covered vessel.

The patient took it and closed his trembling lips

around the straw.

'No rush,' said Skelter, 'take your time.'

'Time is something I don't have, laddie.' Mitch put the drink on the bedside table. 'If we get Eva back, Maria can start a new life away from here.'

'Okay, let's see if I've got this right. I guess the police are out because Maria is an illegal and immigration would send her back to Cuba?'

Mitch nodded.

'Any intel on the size and capability of the gang?'

'Four-man team should do it easy. They are well armed, will kill in a heartbeat, but poor discipline.' Mitch picked up his drink and sucked on the straw.

'You seem remarkably well-informed,' said Skelter, 'considering you only just found this out. Maria tell you all this, did she?'

'I may be dying laddie but I'm still playing with a full deck. To answer that question and the other you daren't ask, I spent a few years when I first moved here smuggling weed from Mexico and Belize. I know this gang. They run coke, something I wouldn't touch. Point is, I made a packet. I also inherited the family estate on Speyside, including the distillery. Funding the operation is not an issue. I have made my will and you are sole executor. My attorney will be by this afternoon to talk to you about it.'

Skelter placed his hand on the man's forearm. 'You should rest now, mate. Take a nap. Don't worry, just come up with the intel I'll sort the rest.'

Mitch closed his eyes and relaxed into the pillow with a thin smile.

Skelter rose from his seat and turned towards the door. 'How long…' he asked.

'Time enough,' Maria replied from the doorway. 'I did not mean to...'

'It's what we do,' he said, 'and we're very good at it.'

'I am so scared for Eva. She is so young.'

Skelter lifted his chin and raised his eyebrows.

'Seventeen. It will be her eighteenth birthday at Christmas.'

'Don't worry it will be okay, she will be home to celebrate it with you, trust me.' *Why did I do that? I have no intel, no idea about the job yet.*

'Thank you, H, you are a good man but my heart says to me it will not be so easy.'

Before Skelter could find an appropriate response the nurse intervened. 'Medication time,' she said.

At that moment the doorbell rang. 'That will be Shawna,' said the nurse.

'I'll get it,' Skelter said, seizing the opportunity to escape. He opened the door to a fifty-something black woman in a rainbow-coloured kaftan. She thrust a large, double-bagged, brown paper grocery bag into his arms and breezed past him before he had time to react. He turned and followed her into the kitchen. 'And you are?' she asked.

Skelter put the bag on the work surface. 'H, I'm H,' he said.

'Shawna. How many for lunch, today, H?'

'Not sure,' said Skelter, wrong-footed.

'Then go find out.'

'Yes, Ma'am.' He went through to the terrace. 'Where did Mitch find her?' He asked Katya with a grin.

'She's looked after him for years. She sure can cook.'

'She wants to know how many for lunch.'

'Four,' said Katya. 'Mitch is on liquid supplements.'

Skelter returned to the kitchen with the information.

Lunch was Cuban pork with rice and re-fried beans. It looked, smelled and tasted delicious. After he had eaten, Skelter used the house phone to call the UK. He left messages on Brick Lennon and Turbo Thompson's mobile voicemail and home answerphone asking them to call him on Mitch's landline. Not much else he could do but wait for Mitch's attorney to arrive. He walked through to the terrace but seeing Maria with her head on his friend's chest and holding his hand, he did a quick about-face and headed outside through the French doors in the kitchen. He sat on the edge of the stone fountain – a comic piece in the shape of a dolphin wearing an eye patch and a bandana. *Fingers crossed Brick or Turbo can recommend some good operatives for the job. Not so close to the action these days.* Skelter felt a pang of envy. Part of him longed for the old days. *Old days, that's a laugh you've been out of it less than five years.*

'Mr Skelter?'

The man wore a suit. It was thirty degrees. 'You must be the lawyer.'

'Guilty as charged, sir,' said the man mopping his forehead with a neatly folded light blue handkerchief, exactly matching the colour of his suit. 'Alex Morgan, Morgan and Barrett.'

'Perhaps we should go inside,' said Skelter leading the way.

They went into Mitch's den – a real man-cave – the walls a photographic record of Mitch's life interspersed with memorabilia. Skelter planted his backside in the leather swivel chair and leaned forward across the desk. Alex Morgan perched on the edge of a nut-brown, leather Chesterfield. Morgan opened his briefcase and took out a slim file.

'I am authorised to disclose the contents of Mr Mitchell's Will. This is, in my experience, quite unusual with you being one of the main beneficiaries.'

Skelter sat upright.

'You didn't know?'

'Not a clue. I just thought maybe a memento.'

Skelter went down to the boat to try digest the news, his head and heart in turmoil. A life-changing windfall, but his close friend had to die for him to realise it. 'I don't talk to you very often these days Lord, but couldn't you fix the cancer instead? I don't want his money. He doesn't deserve to die, not like this.' Skelter had a sick feeling in the pit of his stomach. He looked at the magnificent view across the waterway to the manicured lawns and swimming pools on the far bank. It was a privileged landscape but one which his friend would not enjoy for very much longer. Maria, if she chose to, could enjoy it without worry into her old age. What he was going to do with a Speyside estate and an award winning distillery, he had absolutely no idea. The responsibility for maintaining so much land – not to mention tenants and employees – scared the living shit out of him.

7
Intel Windfall

Sanibel Island
Sunday/Monday, October 10/11th 2004

Skelter sat with Mitch and Maria after an evening meal of Chilli, trying to come to terms with the impending windfall, humbled that Mitch had thought so highly of him.

'Spit it out, laddie. Get it off your chest.'

'I don't know what to say mate, I'm...'

'Don't get too excited. There will be death duties. My ill-gotten gains are safe; bank safety deposit boxes,' he said. 'Keys in the safe. Remember the date you got your Green Beret?'

'Of course, why?'

'Combination. Stop looking like a startled deer, for Christ's sake. Who else could I leave it to? You're like a son to me.'

'I know, but…'

'But nothing. Go into the lounge a get yourself a large malt,' said Mitch with a wink, 'and a glass of water.'

Maria gave Mitch a disapproving look.

'What? They can't make things any worse, can they?'

Maria rolled her eyes up into her head.

'I'll get the Scotch,' said Skelter.

When he returned Katya was taking Mitch's blood pressure, while Lena stood by ready for the handover. She spotted the large whisky in Skelter's hand, fixed him with an accusing stare. 'Don't waste my time with the whisky is for you routine. He's not allowed, not with the drugs….'

'Hello. I'm right here, Lena,' said Mitch in a tired voice.

'She is right, Mitch,' said Maria. 'Please. We have little time. Do not make it any less, I beg you.'

Mitch slumped back onto the pillow in recognition of losing the argument.

'Cheers,' said Skelter taking a sip of the golden peaty liquid.

'Bastard,' whispered Mitch.

The telephone rang at ten forty-five. Lena answered it. 'He is resting, can I take a message? Yes, I will make sure he gets it. Who? Yes, he is here. Hold on.' She covered the mouthpiece with her hand. 'A man called Stan, he wants to speak to you.'

Skelter took the phone. 'What can I do for you?'

'Mitch asked me to gather some intel for him. I've got pretty much what he wanted. Who, where, when. I'll call round in the morning to brief you. Tell Shawna to lay an extra place for breakfast, see ya.'

The line went dead.

Skelter rose early and took a walk around the garden. When he returned to the house, Shawna was already in the kitchen scrambling eggs and slicing ham. The smell of baking cornbread filled the air.

'Shawna, there will be one more for breakfast,' said Skelter.

'That would be me,' announced a voice from the doorway.

'What are you doing here, Stan?'

'I was lured by the irresistible aroma of your fabulous cooking, Shawna.'

'Cut the bullshit Stan Kelly,' she replied with a laugh. 'I ain't buying.'

Skelter held out a hand. Stan grasped it. They shook. Stan's grip was firm and strong, his grin wide and mischievous.

'Heard a lot about you, H. Some of it good.' He winked.

'You have me at a disadvantage,' said Skelter.

'I'll fill you in after brekky.'

After breakfast, Skelter and Stan retreated to the boat where they would not be disturbed. Mitch was still sleeping, with both Maria and the nurse in attendance. The two men sat in the stern enjoying the warming rays of the early morning sun. Stan passed Skelter a folder. He flicked through the notes and photographs. 'I am impressed. So much detail in such a short time. How…?'

Stan winked and tapped the side of his nose, twice.

'Best not ask. You know the drill. Let's just say that Mitch and I go back a long way and we worked together in the import business when he first moved over here.'

'So how did you meet?'

'Falklands, Mitch was attached to us, Naval Gunfire Liaison. Did a great job getting us artillery support. He's a good bloke, for a cabbage head. A brave man.'

'Cabbage head? That makes you a Para, then?'

Stan nodded. 'Aye.'

'I was a Marine,' said Skelter. 'Not like you lot to have anything good to say about the Royals.'

Stan's smile was disarming. 'Up to your necks in the same flying shit storm the colour of your beret doesn't seem to matter that much, especially when you're the best.'

'True,' said Skelter with conviction.

'You were there?'

Skelter nodded.

'So, let me run through the intel with you, H,' said Stan. 'The key player is Lope Valdez, the Wolf, as he likes to be called. He runs his operation from...' Stan flipped a page in the file. 'Here we are.'

Skelter looked at the three aerial photographs. They were clear and sharp and had probably been taken from around fifteen hundred feet.

'Knuckle Cay, not much of an island, but the Wolf owns it. Administratively, it falls under the Bahamas, but they don't bother him. Palm greasing. I guess he paid them a lot of money for it. He claims it as a wildlife sanctuary – bullshit, of course. The main feature is the airstrip. Twelve-hundred feet plus. Only practical way on or off the island. See the cluster of buildings at the northern end: this is the main house, this long outbuilding – accommodation for staff and bodyguards; around eight at any one time we think.'

'Eight bodyguards?' said Skelter.

'This man has made a lot of enemies. Also, unusually he samples his own merchandise, been a user for years. Makes him paranoid.'

Skelter tapped the photograph with his finger, 'This building here?'

'Not certain, but my gut says it's a desalination plant. No fresh water on the island. No food sources either, beyond fish and coconuts.'

'This area here, any idea what that is?' said Skelter pointing at the far end of the airstrip, squinting as he rotated the picture.

'That'll be the fuel dump for the aircraft. It's fifty-five nautical miles to Marathon Key. Almost a hundred to the Everglades, where they fly the drugs in. They use three aircraft, including a Twin Otter. It can haul three thousand pounds four hundred miles on full tanks.'

'How come you know so much about this?'

'Hobby of mine, flying, I take guys up skydiving most weekends. You'd be welcome to come along to the club.'

'Cheers, I might take you up on that when this is put to bed.' Skelter studied the file in detail with Stan for over an hour. The ex-Para was a goldmine of information. 'How reliable is this intel, Stan?'

'Pretty much on the money that the girl will be on the island. Wolf only leaves occasionally to check operations in the Everglades. Not likely he would take her with him. Most of this has been cross-checked from at least two sources. Money has changed hands, which is a risk factor but the recipients have scores to settle with Wolf. They would benefit commercially if he was out of the picture.'

'Fair enough. Well, thanks a lot mate, that is very comprehensive. All I need now is to raise a team and figure out how to get on this bare arsed blot on the ocean.'

'Good luck with that, mate. Any coffee?' said Stan.

'Great idea, I could do with a stimulant.'

The pair walked back to the house in the glorious sunshine. 'Such a bastard,' said Stan. 'Why is it the good ones go early and arseholes live on?'

'Always the same. Just look at this place? Beautiful. By rights, he should enjoy it into old age.'

'You ever thought of moving to warmer climes, H? Lots of great properties in this neck of the woods.'

Skelter smiled. 'Not at the moment but I have to admit the idea is not without appeal. Don't worry, Stan, if I ever do, you will be the first to know.'

'Here, take one,' said Stan offering an embossed business card, 'in case you need me for anything.'

Mitch was awake. Maria was not in attendance, the nurse was at the desk, head in a book.

'I've given your friend here a full update, Mitch,' said Stan. 'How are you feeling mate?'

'Not too bad, considering. Thank you for coming up with the goods, Stan. It means a lot.'

'Anytime. Look, gotta go, I left the wife minding the office on her own.'

Mitch nodded.

'Stan's in real estate, he found me this place.' said Mitch after he had left.

Skelter smiled. 'Yes, he's given me one of his business cards. And very nice it is, too, this place of yours. So where is Maria?'

'I sent her off for a shower and told her to get to bed, poor lassie's worn out. You get what you need from Stan?'

'Pretty much, just need to come up with a plan and get a team together. This one will take a lot of resources…'

'You tell me what you need. I'll make sure you get it. Money is no object on this, okay?'

'Understood.' Skelter looked at his old comrade, saddened by the shadow of a once tall aristocratic athlete, but gratified to see the fire of his spirit still burning within. He reached into his pocket and stroked the smooth bald head of the little soapstone god. *If ever I have to face anything like this, Buddha, I only hope I can do it with as much dignity.*

8

Touching Base

Sanibel Island
Monday, October 11th 2004

Skelter sat in the kitchen drinking coffee, trying to figure out a way of approaching the island. Stan had thoughtfully provided a map of the area but it was not much help. He was on the point of giving his brain a rest and getting a shower when the phone rang. He left it for the nurse to pick up but he needn't have bothered. Katya came in and offered him the handset.

'It is for you Mr Skelter, someone called Herbie or Herbo, I think, I am not sure.'

Skelter took the phone, 'Thank you, Katya. Turbo? How are you mate, long time no see. How's tricks?' Skelter glanced at his watch. Almost noon, seven a.m. at home. 'You're up early.'

'Aye. I'm off to work in twenty minutes, minding a spoilt brat rich kid. It's doing my head in. Only three more days fank fuck.'

'I'll cut to the chase, I need to put a team together for a one-off job over here. Two to three weeks max. Wondered if you could recommend anyone? I'm a bit out of touch with the new talent.'

'What's the job?'

'It's for a friend, not a love job, well paid. Seventeen-year-old girl, unwilling guest of a group of lowlife drug dealers. I want to get her back to her mother.'

'I could do with a holiday in the sun and, as I say, three days and I'm out of work... again.'

'Whoa I wasn't expecting you... I mean I'm only the organiser, I won't be at the sharp end.'

'To be honest, H, I need the money.'

'When can I get you to have long chat?'

'Call me Wednesday, around the same time, if it will keep?'

'No desperate rush, she's okay for now as far as we can tell. I'll do that. And thanks for calling back, mate. Cheers.'

It was almost midnight when the call came through from Brick Lennon, which surprised Skelter. Skelter was glad of the distraction. He had toyed with a number of possible approaches to the island including kayak, zodiac inflatable and even swimming in. He was not happy with any of them.

'Now then, Mucker, what's it all about?'

'Bloody good to hear you, Brick, didn't expect a call this late, must be five in the morning over there. All well with you I hope?'

'It is, but you didn't ask me to call to talk shite, now did you?'

Skelter chuckled to himself, same old Brick. 'Bang on mate. I'm looking for a team to do a job – hostage rescue. Can you recommend any guys who might be interested?'

'How many?'

'Four.'

'How many you got?'

'One.'

'Location, duration?'

Skelter spent ten minutes laying it out and answering Brick's questions, after which the big man posed one final one.

'A couple of good guys I could recommend. I'm not as young as I used to be but I'm still on the circuit, pretty much up to speed. I'd like a shot at it myself, though. Work is a bit thin on the ground right now, to be honest. Your call, of course, H.'

It was getting more complicated than Skelter expected. *He was teetering on the brink. Lucy would kill me. I daren't.* Brick's voice brought him back to earth.

'You still there, H?'

'Sorry, just having a thought process crisis. I wasn't thinking of including myself. I planned on organising from behind the scenes, but you and my old mate Turbo, well, it is kind of tempting. It would be cracking to do one last one with you blokes, and I'd only need one more bloke. It would almost certainly prove fatal, mind.'

'What?'

'Lucy, mate, she will kill me for sure.' The sound of laughter crackled down the line. That did it. Skelter tipped over the edge. 'Okay you're in. I'll get back to you with the details on Thursday, if that's okay?'

'Fine, Mucker. Call me on this number, better write it down.'

Skelter scribbled on the palm of his hand with a biro. 'Speak to you then. Cheers.' Skelter ended the call. He sat in silence for a long time and then dug deep into the cargo pocket of his shorts. He pulled out the little green Buddha. *'Well, my fine, fat friend, what have I done? You must think I'm off my chump.'*

The lack of response did nothing for Skelter's enthusiasm for the discussion. *'She is going to go ballistic, really, she will do me serious damage, you know she will.'*

Skelter buttonholed Maria while Mitch was asleep. He persuaded her to take a walk down to the dock.

'Let's sit,' he said, offering her his hand. She took it and stepped onto the boat. 'Okay, Maria, when and how did your daughter get into this situation?'

'Eva did not come home from her dance class. It was two months ago. Two men came to my house and told me she was staying with a friend. They called her on their phone. She said she was well and I should not worry but I must not tell the police. She said she would call me every week on my cell phone and that she was being well cared for. I didn't know what to do. Eva is a good girl, H. She has never been in trouble.'

Skelter leaned towards Maria, closely scrutinising her expression. 'Think carefully now. How did she seem to you, did she sound scared, nervous?'

Maria wiped the start of a tear from the corner of her eye. 'It is strange. She was very calm, like she really was just staying over with a friend. She made me promise not to tell the police, I had no choice, immigration would send me back to Cuba.'

'That's good, she isn't in danger at the moment from the sound of it.' He placed a hand on her shoulder. 'Chin up. We'll bring her back to you.'

'You really can do this?'

'We can. It will take a while to prepare, I must get the team and practice the plan before we execute it.'

'You have a plan? What is this plan?'

Skelter looked out over the water at a couple of pelicans squabbling over a fish. 'The plan must remain secret,' said Skelter, knowing full well that so far he had not managed to come up with anything.

Maria looked embarrassed. 'Of course, I am sorry.'

'That's okay. Now, what about your son? Was he... were they close?'

'Oh yes, very close. Very, very close.'

Skelter scoured her face with narrowed eyes

'Of course, sometimes, they fight, as all brothers and sisters do, but she loved Luis very much and he loved her too.' Maria's voice started to tremble. 'If anything'

'Nothing is going to happen to her. Don't get upset, she will be with you in no time and thanks to Mitch, we can help you both to find a new place away from trouble. Luis too. A fresh start, Maria.'

Maria nodded but did not look convinced.

9

Reaching Out

Sanibel Island
Wednesday, October 13th 2004

Tuesday came and went in a blur. Wednesday dawned with Skelter nursing a headache, not a hangover, for other than the single glass of malt, he had not touched alcohol since he arrived at Mitch's. He needed a clear head if he was to devise a viable plan, not that the strategy had worked so far. He borrowed the keys to Maria's truck and went for a drive to try to clear the logjam. The weather was fine and hot but it did nothing to lift Skelter's mood. He drove north along the beach road for a little while and then pulled over to the side to watch a pair of Ospreys whirling and wheeling as one dropped a large fish which the other one caught flying upside down as it swooped majestically below. It was an impressive display of aerobatics. He sat upon the sand

and stared out to sea at pelicans riding on the sun-sparkled water around three hundred metres away. Further out, a couple of jet skiers tore across the sea. The clear visibility, which made this possible, was normal for the time of year in that part of the world. Skelter could not see how they could approach the target in daylight. Even at night the moon would be likely to give them away. The Wolf had chosen his lair well. The only possibility seemed to be underwater, launched from a boat. Skelter returned to the truck, subdued. He took his little, green mentor from his pocket and placed him on the dashboard. *'I need to bring Turbo and Brick out here, asap. Three heads are better than one. Sorry, Buddy, I mean four heads.'*

He did not want to draw Mitch in to the problem. The man had enough to contend with. Running it past Turbo and Brick might come up with a workable answer.

After lunch, Skelter rang Turbo. 'Can you get here tomorrow?' he asked.

'You do realise it's seven o'clock at night here? That is real short notice. I'll never get a flight.'

'Already sorted. I have it on hold, just need to call the airline and confirm. I'll have it waiting in your name at the American Airlines' desk, Terminal three, Heathrow. Be at Leeds Bradford by five am. Take off at six forty-five, connecting flight at Heathrow eleven-twenty, flying first class. Bring enough gear for three weeks.'

'Did you say first class? Fuck me this must be some job.'

'It's important to me, mate. I'll call you back to confirm your flight number. Got to go.'

Skelter made a similar call to Brick, but he insisted on paying his own fare. The number was a mobile one.

'Keep the receipt and I'll reimburse you the fare,' said Skelter. He knew better than to ask Brick where in the world he was or what he was up to. Finally, he called both men back to confirm flight numbers and arrange to meet them at Miami Airport. Brick was evasive about his flight but said he could be there at the time Turbo's was due, so no problem. Skelter felt better for making something happen. It was progress of a sort. He left the den and went out to the terrace. Mitch was awake with the ever faithful Maria glued to his side.

'How's the patient?' asked Skelter.

'I am doing fine, thank you,' Mitch answered. 'How did you get on?'

'Two good guys coming in tomorrow. They'll need beds,' he said. He was not worried − he had counted six bedrooms on his guided tour with Lena. 'Made a big dent in this,' said Skelter, holding out an American Express charge card.

'Keep it, laddie, you'll need it. It is no use to me anymore.'

'Okay, I suppose you're right.'

'How's the plan coming?'

'Fine, just working on the details,' Skelter lied, glancing at Maria, who was too into Mitch to notice.

Mitch looked at Skelter with a tired wry smile and managed a wink.

'Okay if I call Lucy?' Skelter asked.

Mitch nodded.

'Time for your medication, Mitch,' said Lena from her desk in the corner, as Skelter turned to leave the room.

'Lucy, how's the move going?'

'Mark, lovely to hear you. It's going well, Wilkins has been brilliant, and Daddy says I can have him to help for as long as I need. Isn't that wonderful? Nothing broken so far, but we still have half the boxes to unpack yet. Fingers crossed.'

'Sounds like you have it all under control. I had a meeting with Mitch's lawyer and it is going to take a week or two to tie up the legal side of things. I need to be here to catch up on stuff we missed when we drifted apart. It seems to be doing him good. Only thing we can do now is to make what time he has left the best we can for him.'

'I am sure you will do just that. Give him my love will you?'

'I will.' He deliberately neglected to mention anything about being a beneficiary of Mitch's will. It seemed inappropriate while his friend lay upon his sick bed still breathing the same air. Besides, it made sense to keep it in the bank for when Lucy discovered, as she surely would, what he was about to get involved in. It might just take the edge off her fury.

They chatted for a while, trading small talk, weather, usual stuff. Lucy wound it up as she had dinner in the oven.

'Better get your chicken out before it gets burnt, then,' said Skelter, feeling faintly ridiculous talking domestic trivia while his mind wrestled with the problem of invading the stronghold of a drugs baron surrounded by armed bodyguards.

'Yes, better had. Love you,'

'You too, Cariad.'

Skelter ended the call and stared out through the kitchen doors to the garden. He walked outside and sat upon the edge of the fountain. He spent hours out there kicking ideas around for the assault on Wolf's lair without success and felt like he was about to disappear up his own exhaust. Something caught his eye, high in the sky. A red-shouldered hawk carving a lazy figure of eight in the blue. It was then Skelter saw the feather – russet edged white – drifting across his vision, side slipping towards the lawn only to rise at the last minute born up by warm air reflected from the flagstones of the barbecue area. He watched, fascinated, and made bets with himself as to whether it would make landfall or settle in the sea of grass. He urged it on, his mood rising and falling with the fortunes of the feather. Miraculously it landed on a small, curved bench supported on two cast concrete dolphins.

Skelter leapt to his feet and marched into the kitchen.

'Phone, Shawna, have you seen the phone?'

'Right next to the door.'

Skelter picked up the handset and dug his wallet out of the cargo pocket of his shorts. He took out the card and dialled the number. 'Stan? Me, H. Can we meet for a coffee? I'd like to run some stuff by you.'

'Sure, how about tomorrow? I'm here until six. Mitch can give you directions or Shawna if she's there.'

'Cheers. I'll drive over after lunch. I have to go to Miami later to pick someone up from the airport.'

'Chicken,' said Shawna as Skelter put the phone down.

'Sorry?'

'Dinner, we have fried chicken, with Spanish rice.'

'Sounds great,' said Skelter from a faraway place, only vaguely aware of the delicious aroma of southern fried spices filling the air, 'thanks, Shawna.'

'You are very welcome.'

Mitch sipped on his straw while Maria sat quietly at his side, thumbing through a National Geographic magazine.

'I need to go out tomorrow afternoon, to see Stan the man and I have to collect the guys from the airport after,' said Skelter.

Maria looked up. 'Of course. You still have the keys to the truck?'

Skelter nodded.

'Take my car,' said Mitch. 'In the garage, keys on my desk in the den. Full tank of gas. More comfortable, no offence, Maria, besides lassie, it will be yours soon.'

'Do not speak of this,' she said, choking back tears.

'There now, don't upset yourself, it is just how it is,' said Mitch, squeezing her hand in his.

10

Team Players

Sanibel Island/Miami
Thursday, October 14th 2004

Skelter wasn't sure what he was expecting when he entered the garage, but it wasn't a Maserati Quattroporte. He was not much of a petrol head, but there was no mistaking the trident badge and Italian styling. He almost had second thoughts about taking it but as Mitch had said, he wasn't going to need it. The foot-well was a bit cramped and there were only two seats in the back, one of which would almost certainly be needed for a suitcase, but what the hell. The experience was too much to turn down. As soon as he got on the highway, he realised keeping under the speed limit would be a problem. He was halfway to Stan's before the question of insurance occurred to him.

Stan's office was smart and stylish, the man came out from behind his desk and greeted Skelter with a grin. 'How do you take your coffee?'

'Cream no sugar, thanks.'

Stan leaned around the door and spoke to someone out of Skelter's sightline. He turned back to his visitor. 'Have a seat, mate, what's on your mind?'

'This Wolf character, he knows how to pick a spot. I've been racking my brain to find a way of getting to it. Only way I can see is by air. I've got a contact at home who may be able to get me a pilot, but...'

'Are you asking me...?'

'Good God no, I just want to pick your brains on the logistics. What sort of aircraft, that kind of thing, tell me I'm crazy, or say if you think there's a chance.'

Stan gave Skelter a quizzical look. 'You're certainly crazy, no doubt at all about that. Ah coffee, thank you, Anna.' The young woman placed a tray on the desk and left, closing the door behind her. 'You think you can persuade someone to land an aircraft on the airstrip of a drug lord's island, sixty miles from land and then what? Charge out guns blazing like the Israelis at Entebbe?'

'Not quite.' Skelter leaned forward. 'Would it be possible to navigate an aircraft, at night to the island from Florida, one capable of carrying four passengers with full assault kit, plus parachutes.'

Stan picked up his cup and sipped the coffee slowly. He said nothing for some time. 'You are certifiable, you do know that.' It was a statement rather than a question. 'Suppose it was possible, and you managed to pull it off. Four men safely on the ground on an un-recce'd DZ, a small one at that, then what? Take out the bad guys, rescue the damsel?'

'Well, is it possible?'

Stan sipped at his coffee once more. 'In theory, but it is risky to say the least. It would need a good pilot. You realise you are proposing a full military operation, with civilians? If you get caught, you are looking at serious jail time.'

Skelter looked Stan in the eye. 'Ex armed forces, if you don't mind. Don't recognise the term civilian.'

Stan shook his head slowly from side to side. 'That's not how the cops here will see it.'

'Look,' Skelter said, 'this Wolf character, no one will mourn his passing if he goes out of business and if all goes well we may be able to take these guys without casualties on either side.'

Stan couldn't hold it in any longer, he laughed long and loud. 'I say one thing for you, H, you're long on optimism. How are your team on freefall? Up to date are they?'

'I was going to speak to you about that. I wondered if we could get refreshers at this club of yours.'

The humour left Stan's face. 'You are serious aren't you?'

Skelter nodded. 'I owe Mitch a lot. Without him, I would never have amounted to anything.'

Stan drained his cup. 'More coffee?'

'I'm okay, thanks. I've taken up too much of your time already.'

'You need to give serious consideration to your chances of getting away without getting arrested. That said, give me a chance to sleep on it. I might be able to help with the para training, sourcing an aircraft possibly. No promises.'

'Understood. Any help at all would be much appreciated, but don't stick your neck out, I don't want to get you in trouble with the local sheriff.'

'Don't you worry. I can get into trouble all by myself.'

Skelter stood up, shook Stan's hand and bid him farewell.

The long, arrow-straight highway to Miami was bounded on both sides by flat swampland and forest. The Maserati made all the difference, the smooth engine purred along at a modest sixty miles an hour as the radio lulled Skelter in to air-conditioned relax mode with smooth easy listening.

The flight was on time. First to appear, Turbo Thompson strode out into the sunlight hauling a suitcase almost as tall as he was.

'Good to see you,' said Skelter, 'flight okay?'

'Champion, ta. I could get used to this first class malarkey. It's like a fucking bed, your own video, drinks on tap, owt you want. Tasty stewardess, too.'

'Flight attendant,' corrected Skelter, 'they call them flight attendants these days.'

'Stuff that P.C. bollocks she was tasty, pal, I'm telling you.'

Skelter spotted Brick heading his way. 'Here he is.'

'Now then Mucker, how's tricks?'

'Pretty good thanks. Brick meet Turbo, Turbo, Brick.' The two men shook hands, Brick openly surprised at Turbo's diminutive stature.

'Five three,' said Turbo, 'save you over taxing your brain, but I'm from Yorkshire.'

'Okay,' said a bemused Brick.

'You two are going to get on fine, I can tell. This way gents.' Skelter led them to the car park. As soon as they set off, Brick pulled an already full pipe from his tobacco pouch and lit up.

'You didn't say you'd won the lottery,' said Turbo as Skelter unlocked the Maserati.

'Take five and finish your smoke, Brick,' said Skelter, 'no rush. One of your suitcases will have to go on the back seat, not built for carrying kit, these. Borrowed, by the way, not mine.'

'Nice motor just the same,' said Brick, through a blue/grey cloud.

'You boys hungry, we can stop for grub on the way, if you like?'

'How far?' Brick asked.

'Under three hours.'

Brick looked at Turbo.

He shrugged. 'I'm easy.'

'Might as well go then, H.'

Skelter engaged drive and set off. Turbo sat in the back as the head room there was less than generous, his suitcase on the seat beside him strapped in like a passenger. 'How the other half lives, eh?' he said, stroking the premium leather. 'You wouldn't be softening us up by any chance, H? Sticky job?'

'Let's say challenging,' he replied. 'I'll brief you later.'

Turbo was openly impressed by Mitch's home, while Brick took the place in his stride. Both settled in their rooms and then met up with Skelter, who introduced them to their host and to Maria.

'Thanks for coming, lads, I appreciate it. Sorry I can't

get up. Why don't you get yourselves a beer out of the refrigerator? Or something stronger?'

'Beer's fine thanks,' said Turbo looking at Brick.

'Suits me.'

Mitch settled back in the pillows. He looked tired. 'Laddie.'

'I'll sort it, Mitch. Ok if we use your den to go over the details?' Mitch blinked acknowledgement, the morphine suppressing any stronger response. 'Come on let's get you two reprobates a drink.'

'I should warn you before we start,' said Skelter, 'the plan needs work. It is a little thin in places.'

'I said he was softening us up,' said Turbo.

'Let's see what you've got,' said Brick. 'Any chance of another beer before we start? First one never touches the sides.'

'I'll go,' said Turbo. 'H?'

'Aye, I'll have one.'

'Makes a fair impression for a little un,' said Brick.

'What he lacks in altitude, he makes up for in attitude. Don't be fooled, he's one of the most experienced men I've worked with; fourteen years in The Regiment, five years in 2 Para before that. Remember the Somalia job I told you about? That's where he lost his ear lobe. Close encounter with a bullet. He picked up some shrapnel at Goose Green, too.'

Turbo returned with three cans of Heineken. Skelter took them through the file and outlined the plan, such as it was. The two listened intently, without comment, and appeared to absorb everything Skelter put before them. At the end of the presentation, for – in truth – that is what it was, rather than a briefing, both men remained silent.

'Well?' said Skelter.

'Let me see if I have got this right,' said Brick. 'You want three, possibly four men, to parachute – at night – from six thousand feet, in civilian sports chutes, with weapons and equipment, from a civvy aircraft flown by a stranger – probably also a civilian – land on a tiny island with no DZ lights to neutralise a gang of armed villains, with non-lethal force. This is after a hundred-mile flight, at low level over the sea. You then plan to rescue the hostage, take over the airstrip so the pilot can land and fly us all back to the mainland, avoiding detection by the Navy, Air Force and Coast Guard of the most powerful and sophisticated military nation in the world.'

'That pretty much sums it up, yes,' said Skelter.

Brick took a large intake of breath and shook his head very slowly. 'The last time I fitted a parachute was 1976. I jumped into the African bush from a thirty-year-old Dakota.'

'Like riding a bike,' said Turbo.

'So when did you last jump, smart arse?'

'Military, four years ago, civvy, last month.'

'Turbo was an APJI,' Skelter explained. 'He skydives for fun now.'

Brick scratched his head in silence and took a swig from the can.

'You won't have jumped in a while either, H,' said Turbo, 'and as I recall you were never what you might call enthusiastic. Not saying you can't or won't, but to hit a DZ that small takes a bit of practice, especially at night.'

'I have a contact at a local skydiving club, a Brit. He's a friend of Mitch's, pretty sound and he's ex 3 Para.'

'Think he'll fill the vacancy?' Turbo asked.

'Haven't asked, but I doubt it. Too much to lose, mate. Successful business, wife, family, et cetera. He would have to be crazy.'

'So would we,' said Brick, now thoughtfully sucking on his unlit curved briar.

'Does that mean I can count you out? Not that I would blame you,' said Skelter, disheartened.

'Not at this stage, but let's just say I have a few reservations.'

'The money will reflect the risks involved, top bat and more. You can name your price.'

'You know that's not the issue, H.'

'He's speaking for his self,' interjected Turbo.

Skelter rubbed the back of his neck and straightened up. 'Look, it's getting on, let's call it a night, take a fresh look in the morning. What do you say?' The nods confirmed it. Cans were drained, and the meeting broke up.

Skelter looked in on Mitch, but he was asleep. Lena had managed to persuade Maria to go to bed. 'Night, Lena.'

'Night, H.'

11

Plan? What Plan?

Sanibel Island
Friday, October 15th 2004

Skelter had been awake for what seemed like hours, his brain overloaded with a deluge of permutations of his wafer thin plan. He battled hard to stay positive, but the negative 'what ifs' were piling up faster than he could shift them. By the time he reached the kitchen for breakfast, he was feeling beat up and flat.

'What's up wi' you this morning?' said Turbo, 'you got a face like a smacked arse.'

It was just the lift he needed. 'Need coffee, that's all, I'll be all right when I get some caffeine in me. Brick sleeping in?' Skelter asked.

'Outside polluting the atmosphere wi' his smoke discharger. He was up before me.'

Skelter sliced a bagel and popped it into the toaster.

'I'm going to check on Mitch,' he said.

Katya smiled from her seat at the desk and Maria stirred slightly, dozing on a sun lounger alongside Mitch's bed, with her arm across his chest. The man was sleeping. Skelter cursed the injustices of religion and social convention that had kept two people so obviously in love, apart. *Negativity again, focus on the positive. They are together now, aren't they? They might never have had the chance but for the cancer.* 'How is he?' Skelter asked Katya.

'He is doing quite well, really. No pain and we have not needed to increase the medication.'

'That's good.' It occurred to him that Mitch probably lied about how bad the pain was. He would not want to be dosed up with morphine, sleeping all day. Mitch's drug of choice was Maria.

Brick was in the kitchen when Skelter returned. 'Sleep okay?'

'Fine, you?'

'Same,' Skelter lied.

'Oh yeah?'

Skelter shrugged.

'Don't worry mate, somefing'll turn up,' Turbo said, slapping him on the shoulder, 'in fact I've got an idea on method of entry.'

'I'm all ears mate.'

'Tandem,' said Turbo.

'Stupid twat,' said Skelter. 'Stop taking the piss.'

'You're not listening…'

'Invade an island by bicycle,' said Brick, 'there's a novelty'.

Skelter and Brick both regarded the diminutive

mercenary with quizzical doubt.

'Tandem parachutes. If we get another experienced skydiver, we can pair up.'

It went quiet.

'Well?' Turbo asked.

The men looked at one another in silence for several seconds. Brick spoke first.

'He's got a point.'

'Turbo you are a bloody genius,' said Skelter, now beaming from ear to ear.

Brick leaned against the worktop, coffee in hand stroking his luxuriant Zapata moustache. 'We'll need to look at equipment load,' he said. 'Has anyone tried tandem jumping with assault kit?'

'I doubt it,' said Skelter, with a smile. *That's it my friend, climb aboard. Get with the program,* said the voice of the Buddha in his head.

'What about a practice run with dummy loads? We can jettison if necessary. How much kit are we going to need? Only weapons and ammo. Talking of which?'

'Don't worry. I'm sure I can get anything we want, this is the land of the NRA, remember. Anyway Mitch is very well connected, and nothing talks louder than a dollar bill.'

'What we need now is a practice jump, H.'

'Ok, I'll give Stan a call, meanwhile can you and Brick give some thought to weapons and assault kit. Draw up a list. Keep it light as possible.'

Skelter finished his breakfast and then called Stan at his office. Following a fruitful conversation, he wandered down to the boat dock for some solitude. He pulled a notebook from the pocket of his shorts and began to compile lists of contingencies. Turbo's enthusiasm had pumped fresh fire into his veins and now that it looked like Brick was coming on board his mood lifted.

The aromatic whiff of St Bruno wafted up Skelter's nostrils. He looked up from his note-making.

'Not disturbing you, am I?' said Brick. 'The old grey matter works better with a full head of steam.'

'Not at all. By the way I've arranged to meet Stan at the club in the morning to take us up for a tandem.'

'Excellent. Still reservations mind, but we're on the right road Mucker. Keep at it. I'll leave you in peace.' He wandered away towards the house, a cloud of brown smoke billowing around his broad shoulders. Fifty-four but still solid. Skelter was delighted to have him aboard.

After lunch Skelter sat in the boat with his two companions and thrashed out the details of the equipment that they might need and tried to gauge just how much they could safely carry. As well as pistols and automatic weapons, the list included non-lethal CS gas, Tasers, and flash-bangs,

Skelter shook his head. 'Why is ammo so heavy?'

'A container drop could work,' Brick suggested, 'a Bergen, with ammo?'

'Worth a try, but chances of it hitting the island won't be high.'

'It might land in the wrong place and alert the bad guys, too. No, I think we best rule that one out boys.'

'That doesn't leave us with much. We must give priority to non-lethal – which means one pistol and three mags each plus an MP5 or similar – between two. The key weapon has to be surprise. They won't be expecting. When we relieve them of their body-guarding responsibilities we can use their weapons.'

Turbo grinned like a lunatic. 'Who Dares Wins, eh, H? Now you're thinking, super soldier.'

'Cheers, you mad bastard, that's just what I wanted to hear. More coffee anyone?'

There were no takers.

'One thing we should talk about is who we can get to fill our vacancy, so any suggestions will be well received. The other is money. The offer is double the usual rate plus a twenty percent bonus on successful completion. It is generous, to reflect the level of risk. I know it's not all about the cash, but we all need to live.'

For once, Turbo did not produce an appropriate quip. Brick listened without expression. 'I think I'll just pop outside for a smoke,' he said.

'I would not like to play poker with that man.'

Turbo nodded. 'Me, neither.'

'So, mate, what do you say?'

'I will have that coffee,' he replied, taking a hip flask from his pocket. He poured a generous measure into his mug. 'H?'

'I'm fine mate, you fill your boots.'

'Purely medicinal, you know, for shock.'

Skelter nodded and smiled.

12

It Takes Two to Tandem

Silverlakes Flying Club
Saturday, October 16ᵗʰ 2004

'Beer'll not be cheap here,' said Turbo as they passed manicured shrubs at the imposing entrance to Silverlakes Flying Club The clubhouse confirmed this.

'Just as well we're here to work then,' said Skelter.

Stan appeared at the entrance. 'Come on in, lads, sign the visitors book, then I can show you around.'

The club was modern and well equipped and the professional set up convinced Skelter that free falling onto the island could work. The sticking point was weight They could only carry a bare minimum of kit.

'Here we have the main hangar,' said Stan, there's another smaller one. Both aircraft are flying just now, but here's my baby.' Stan pointed to the framed picture hanging on the wall. 'Cessna Cargomaster. She'll hold the team and all the kit with room to spare. Not British Airways comfort class, but after a Hercules...'

'She'll do fine, I'm sure, Stan,' Skelter said.

'Anyone asks, you're here on a jolly, okay? So if you follow me, we'll run you through the drills then we can get you kitted out to jump later today.'

The men filed out and walked across the airfield to the pre-flight building.

As soon as they had completed ground-training Stan led the boys across to the hangar to be fitted with chutes. While two instructors briefed Skelter and Brick on the tandem rigs, Stan took Turbo to one side. The two men became engrossed in conversation, but Skelter was too busy and too far away to listen in.

Once he had fitted his chute, Skelter ran through his well-remembered checklist. Moments later his jump instructor gave him a thorough check twice over. Skelter climbed aboard the Cessna with his tandem partner, followed by Brick and his instructor. Last in Turbo and Stan – also wearing a chute.

'Thought I'd join you,' said Stan, 'don't worry, Julie's a better pilot than me. She's got twice as many hours in.'

Once settled inside the aircraft, Skelter stood while the instructor attached himself to Skelter's harness. It was a strange experience and one he was not entirely comfortable with as an experienced freefall parachutist, albeit one whose skills were somewhat rusty. He considered it necessary to undergo the same training as Brick, to offer support to his friend and appreciate the problems he might face. Brick took it in his stride and appeared relaxed. Skelter reckoned he would have lit his pipe and had a smoke during the descent if it had been feasible.

After eight minutes climbing, the Cessna levelled off and made a slow lazy turn towards the exit point above the drop zone. All jumpers had remained standing throughout the flight. The blast of air and noise that filled the cabin as the dispatcher pulled the door open heightened Skelter's senses. He psyched himself up for the jump. *Ready Buddha? Time to hit the silk as the yanks say.*

Stan and Turbo first, Brick next then him. He wondered how good the thirty-year-old strapped to his back would prove to be. He hated relinquishing control to a complete stranger. The next few seconds were a blur. The wind slapped Skelter's cheeks as he caught the slipstream ten thousand feet above the patchwork of regular housing developments that punctuated the flat lake-laced greenery.

Skelter's head tilted back as he arched his body and put his arms out and up, a nano-second ahead of the tap on his arm that would remind him to. *Position stable, clear vision, no problems.* The sound of speed thundered in his ears as the pair accelerated towards terminal velocity at one hundred and twenty-five miles per hour.

At five thousand feet the instructor tapped Skelter's helmet to indicate he was about to deploy the parachute. The sudden deceleration to thirty miles an hour stirred memories of his HALO course, as the insane rushing, gushing, wind dissolved into the calm quiet of a moderate breeze. The harness jerked his shoulders upwards and his legs swung down from behind to settle below him where they belonged. Skelter snapped his head up to check the canopy for malfunctions, thumping the man on his back in the chin. Fortunately, his padded helmet absorbed most of the impact.

'Sorry, force of habit,' he said.

'No problem. You okay?' asked the tandem stranger.

'Fine,' Skelter answered looking first around him for signs of life. Two chutes blossomed below and to the right, a third caught his eye somewhat lower. He took a brief moment to admire the view.

'Want to take control?' said the young skydiver.

'Yeah,' Skelter gave him a thumbs up and gripped the toggles. He went into a right hand turn swiftly following it with another faster one in the opposite direction, cracking a wide smile as the old experiences flooded back. He handed over control at around eight hundred feet and prepared for landing.

'Remember to lift your feet,' said a voice in Skelter's ear. 'Resist the temptation to go with your training. Let me take care of the landing.'

'Roger that,' Skelter replied, glancing down as the ground rushed up to meet them. At the last second with perfect timing the instructor turned into wind and planted his boots on the ground, trotting forward a few steps as Skelter's trainers touched the grass.

'Thanks, fella, that was good.'

'You're welcome, sir,' said the man.

13
TAFF

Silverlakes Flying Club
Saturday, October 16th 2004.

Lunch in the clubhouse presented the perfect opportunity to discuss the plan's feasibility, now that they had looked at tandem jumping.

Turbo kicked off. 'Stan and me put our heads together, H, and he's another idea which should solve the weight limit problem. You tell 'im Stan.'

'I'm all ears,' said Skelter.

'TAFF. That's the way to go. Tandem Accelerated Free Fall. We run a course over two days. Two tandem and eight solo jumps. Start with two instructors to each jumper. One holding each side through free fall. Radio comms through the helmet, hand signals. You'll piss it. Get accredited too. Turbo doesn't need it, already ticketed, you just need a refresher. By the end Brick will have enough skill to do the job and with a chute a piece you can carry more weight. We won't be able to jump with kit at the club, but I can arrange something, I'm sure.'

'What about accuracy?' Skelter asked.

'Turbo?' said Stan.

'You'll be fine, H,' said the diminutive ex-SAS soldier. 'I'll exit with Puffing Billy here, hold on and steer him right until time to deploy chutes. We should be close enough not to miss by then.'

Brick looked sceptically at Turbo, while thoughtfully stroking his moustache. 'Thanks for that vote of confidence, short arse.'

'You're welcome,' said Turbo, biting a huge chunk from a slice of pizza with a wide grin.

Skelter grinned too. This TAFF idea sounds like a possible plan. 'How soon could we get on a course?'

'I can take you through induction and ground training first phase this afternoon. Start jumping tomorrow.'

'You're kidding?'

'Not at all, mate, and don't worry about payment. Mitch will sort that.'

'That's terrific,' said Skelter.

Stan smiled, not a full blown happy smile. More a slow, sentimental, reflective one. 'Cabbage head he might have been, but he was a good cabbage head.'

'Was?'

'He's retired, H, but we all know the score. I'm going to miss him.'

'Yeah, me too.'

'Any progress on finding a fourth man?' said Stan.

'Not yet', Skelter replied, 'tried a couple but they are

already on jobs. Don't suppose you...'

'Crossed my mind but no, mate. I envy you the rush, but not enough to risk my marriage. She would crucify me.'

'Shame.'

Stan's face creased into a frown. 'Found your pilot yet?'

Skelter looked into the man's eyes.

'Not as risky,' Stan said. The frown relented a little. 'Still some adrenaline to be had....'

Skelter's eyes widened,

'No promises, but ...'

'Sure,' Skelter smiled broadly and noted from the facial reactions of Brick and Turbo, that they were comfortable with the possibility.

'Have to be a rented aircraft,' said Stan.

'Naturally, I have a contact who can get us one through unofficial channels.'

After lunch, Brick and Skelter made another tandem descent following which all four men went into the training centre to begin the next phase. Stan stood by to guide them through while Turbo observed. After completing the paperwork, they went through the drills, practising the positions while balanced by their midriffs face down on a wheeled stool.

By the time it was too dark to fly, Skelter and Brick had completed two jumps, each with a pair of instructors gripping their harness and passing instructions.

'So far so good,' said Skelter.

'Aye, cheers for that, Stan,' said Brick.

'Yeah, fanks' added Turbo. 'Been a big 'elp, pal.'

'Come and have a drink in the bar, lads,' said Stan.

'Sorry boys, I don't want to break up the party before it gets started, but I need to see Mitch about kit and such and call my contact in UK. Besides, we have an early start in the morning.'

Neither Turbo, nor Brick, were impressed but common sense prevailed. In less than an hour, they were rolling down the road to Sanibel.

Mitch had rallied somewhat, relaxed and semi-recumbent against a mountain of pillows, his head on Maria's shoulder. The woman certainly seemed to have a positive effect upon the patient. She acknowledged Skelter with the warmest of smiles. Skelter smiled back and gave Mitch a look. He got the message immediately.

'Maria, could you excuse us please.'

She nodded, rose to her feet and leaned down to kiss Mitch's forehead. 'Of course. Would you like some coffee?'

'I'm fine thanks,' said Skelter.

'We'll have a brew, won't we,' said Brick taking the lead.

'Aye, or a beer maybe?' answered Turbo, following Maria towards the kitchen.

'Lena, would you excuse us?'

The nurse rose from her chair and followed the others with 'try not to tire my patient,' as a parting shot.

'Well, laddie?' Mitch asked when they were alone.

'Getting there, Mitch, expect a bill from Stan's skydiving club, a hefty one I'm afraid.'

'No skin off my nose.' Mitch started to laugh.

'What's so damn funny?'

'You, apologising. You risk your neck for me and I

am funding the enterprise, including your fee, out of your inheritance. It's your money.' Mitch collapsed in a fit of laughter, which quickly changed to coughing.

Lena marched in barging Skelter out of the way. She settled Mitch down and gave him medication for the cough. She turned on Skelter. 'I told you not...'

'Lena, leave it,' said Mitch. 'Not his fault, I'm fine now... Leave us please.'

The nurse gave both men an icy look. 'Behave, or I will be back.'

'Promise,' said Mitch.

Skelter nodded in agreement.

'Make sure you do.'

'That is one scary woman,' Skelter said when she left. He leaned in close and lowered his voice. 'We need the kit from the list I drew up.'

'It is being sourced. I expect to have everything you asked for by Thursday.'

'That is impressive,' said Skelter. 'How'd you do it?'

'Uncle Sam,' said Mitch. 'Only in the USA.'

'That's great. Don't you worry, we'll get her back safe.'

'I know,' said Mitch. 'You understand I don't have much time left?'

Skelter nodded, gently squeezed the man's bony shoulder and got up to leave. 'I should call home.'

'Use the den, laddie, and thank you.'

Skelter winked and made for the door. He stuck his head in the kitchen. 'He's ready for visitors now.'

Maria's face lit up and she went out past him immediately. Lena rinsed her coffee cup under the tap and followed.

'Everything okay, H?' Turbo asked.

'Fine, I'm having an early night soon as I've made a few phone calls.'

Brick grinned and turned to Turbo. 'Think he's trying to tell us something?'

'Could be, miserable bastard.'

'See you bright and early for breakfast, then.' Skelter turned and left, before the sarcasm hit full flow.

He called Rollo, in Ross on Wye but had no luck. After leaving a cryptic message on the answerphone, he rang Lucy, but with the same result. He checked his watch. *Idiot, remember to engage brain first. They'll both be in bed.* He would rise extra early and try then.

When he finally settled on the pillow, he felt confident that the operation would succeed. He could feel it in his gut. Things had progressed well. He just needed a pilot, a plane and one more man for the team. Piece of cake, really.

14
TAFF 2

Silverlakes Flying Club
Sunday, October 17th 2004

'Cariad, how's it going?'

'Mark, lovely to hear you. It's going very well. Half way through the illustrations for the book on pond plants. Weather's pretty decent at the moment so I'm really enjoying my morning run. Daddy's here. He's taking me to lunch at The Bells later, isn't that good?'

'Lucky girl, I'm drooling at the thought of their homemade steak and ale pie. Rollo's with you, you say? I wouldn't mind a quick word with him before you ring off.'

'What are you up to?'

'Nothing, Cariad, I just want his opinion on something is all. Shame on you for being so suspicious.'

'I know you of old, Mark Skelter. You and he just

can't lie down and let it go. You love all that "Boys Own" comic book nonsense.'

Skelter took a deep breath. *If you only knew.* 'You've got too vivid an imagination. We are both retired, remember?'

'Of course you are,' said the voice at the other end, 'anyway he's here now, so I suppose you had better have a word. We don't want you going into a sulk, do we?'

'Cheeky... No, not you, Rollo, I was wondering if you had got anywhere with finding us an aircraft.'

'There is a chap I have in mind. I gave him your friend's number. He's reliable and he is good. Uses the name Smoke on the Water; native American, service background. He should be in touch in the next couple of days. He is strictly cash. Half up front rest on completion.'

'That shouldn't be a problem. Thanks, Rollo.'

'Anytime, I'll hand you back to my daughter, when I can locate her.'

His free hand went instinctively to his pocket and the Buddha. *Christ, I hope she's not earwigging on the extension.* Skelter listened for the tell-tale click. Sure enough, there it was. *Fuck!*

Lucy gave no indication that she had any idea what was going on, but she was eager to end the conversation, saying she was famished and wanted her lunch.

It won't just be the fish that's grilled, thought Skelter. *Poor Rollo, still, he can handle it.* Right now, Skelter wanted to get on with organising the kit and run through the logistics. He was beginning to enjoy himself back in the groove. First up, breakfast, then freefall training.

Training at Silverlakes began well. The weather was perfect – six-knot breeze, scattered light white clouds under a vivid cerulean sky. By lunchtime they were on the home strait and Brick was absorbing everything they threw at him. They had come a long way in three days, Skelter reflected. He was well pleased.

When the time came for Brick's final guided jump, Skelter went up to lend moral support, not that he needed to. The aircraft levelled off at six thousand feet above the drop zone, Brick and Stan stood in the door with Turbo breathing down their necks. The red light came on and they braced for exit. Red changed to green, and the two jumpers leapt out with Turbo glued to their backs. Skelter threw himself after them into the prop-washed wind with a gasp. He got himself into a stable position as, below and to his right, Turbo tracked across and linked up with Stan and Brick. He watched the two instructors guide their student with cool precision onto the correct course.

At two thousand feet, Turbo and Stan let go of Brick's harness and tracked away a short distance. Brick's chute streamed out to deploy and he flew up towards Skelter. In a heartbeat the big man slowed right down and flashed past to hang above him. Skelter pulled his own cord and felt the rush of deceleration as his canopy breathed and deployed.

Look up, check canopy, no defects, all sound; down, check below, all round, three sixty. His heart was hammering. *How does anyone get to like this shit? I don't get it. Gets the job done but I can't call it fun. Look for the target marker? There, white cross, bang on.*

The ground was coming up fast now, *steady, steady, turn into wind, toggles...*

Below him, Stan and Turbo's chutes already trailed over the grass, both men hauling in on their rigging lines.

*Two hundred, one-fifty, ease in and...*Skelter trotted forward across the grass within twenty feet of the others who had straddled the target cross. He looked up just in time to see Brick's boots a microsecond before they grazed his forearm.

'Sorry about that, Mucker, but you stole my parking spot,' Brick said when he had recovered from the landing.

'No worries. That landing was spot on. Well done mate.'

'Cheers, you did okay yourself.'

15

Quartermaster's Stores

Everglades
Tuesday, October 19th 2004

Skelter rose early on Tuesday and went for a run around the neighbourhood. He jogged past houses larger and grander than Mitch's and not a few less so. The whole area smelled of money. He wondered just how much the houses sold for, but more than that – what kind of people lived in them. Bankers, wankers, saints and sinners? He must have sweated five pounds, at least, and he wound down with a walk around Mitch's garden, drying himself with a towel. He would shower later, but first, as had become his habit, he went to the dock. As he sat on the planking, dangling his legs in the cool water he admired the graceful lines of the Chris Craft. Before long, his nose twitched at the unmistakable aroma of Brick's tobacco.

'Mitch wants you, H,' said the big man.

'On my way,' said Skelter, getting up and stretching. 'Morning to you.'

'And to you, Mucker.'

Mitch was sitting up with Katya as she took his blood pressure. 'Morning, laddie, I have news. Call this number,' he said, passing Skelter a scrap of paper.

'Please, you must keep still...'

Mitch ignored the nurse's plea. 'The guy's name is Judd. Cellphone. Arrange to meet him. He's our QM.'

'Sir, please, keep still. I cannot take...'

'Yes, yes, okay. Katya. He's waiting for the call, H. Use the den.'

'Okay, cheers.'

The phone had hardly rung when a Southern voice on the other end said: 'State your business.'

'Name's H. Mitch Mitchell said you can supply me with some equipment.'

'Drive down to Naples, take the interstate, follow I75 East to 29 then turn South on 29 through Everglades City and keep going until you run out of road. I'll be waiting. It's a two-hour drive. I'll see you at one o'clock. Come dressed like a local going fishing.'

The line went dead.

Long, straight, flat and sun-baked, the highway gave little visual relief. The median separating east and westbound carriageways, a green ribbon stretching to the horizon, land at either side alternating between tangled forestation and open swamp.

'How much stuff has this guy got for us, H?' Turbo asked. 'Sure there's enough room in this old pickup?'

'Cut the sarcasm, I want to blend in. Where we're

going, a Maserati would stick out like a turd on a snooker table, besides, it's short on luggage space. Maria's truck is perfect.'

'That mazzawhat'sit would stick out anywhere.'

'So, what's this place again?' asked Brick.

'Not sure of the name, Chockalocolate or something. It's just beyond Everglades City, which according to Mitch is more of an overgrown village than a city. Anyway, we can't miss it - the road ends there.'

'Know anything about this bloke, do we?'

'Sod all other than Mitch vouches for him, which is good enough for me.'

After an hour and a half, Skelter slowed to make the turn south on 29. The landscape opened up as the forest thinned out into scrubland and the road downgraded to a single carriageway. The sparse traffic on I75 turned to almost no traffic. Along the right of the highway twin grey galvanised steel posts carried heavy power cables. Beyond these, occasional flashes of sunlight bounced off bodies of water.

A short while later, a square green sign proclaimed Everglades City: Florida's Outstanding Rural Community of the year, 1998. Soon after that the town was behind them and the houses had given way to large stretches of open water

'Not so big in the city stakes, is it?' said Brick.

'We're an hour early,' said Skelter. 'What about a coffee?'

'Suits me, I could do with a pipe. How far are we?'

'Less than a mile, in fact this looks like we could be there.'

Just after the sign welcoming them to Chokoloskee Island, Skelter turned off the road, onto a parking lot, in front of a waterside restaurant called the Stone Crab. They de-bussed and in less time than it takes to tell, Brick billowed smoke like a Cardiff-bound collier butting through a Bristol Channel headwind.

Refreshed after coffee and bagels, Skelter drove around slow enough for the three men to take in their surroundings but not slow enough to draw attention. The island was a half mile long and slightly less across.

He drove past an eclectic scattering of houses, huts and mobile homes until he reached the end of the road and stopped as arranged. He parked next to an empty circular structure resembling a cross between a wall-less Iron Age hut and a bandstand. Nailed to a small solitary adjacent tree, a sign in large red capital letters read TROPICAL LOUNGE. Beneath it, standing in silence upon one leg – a life-size, bright pink, plastic flamingo. Beyond the pointed thatched roof, a bright, blue sky reflected in the wide, shallow waters of the gulf, sheltered by a distant line of mangrove trees.

'Bit remote, but pleasant enough,' Skelter remarked, as he strolled over to check out the half dozen or so small boats sitting on trailers on the gravel lot. There were two small, wooden dwellings and a couple of mobile homes, but no sign of life.

He checked his watch. Five-to-one. Brick jumped out and moved away towards the water, behind the thatched building, while Turbo instinctively walked into a stand of pine trees and stood in the shadows. Skelter stayed in the cab but left the door open. It was hot. Too hot to remain there for long. It didn't matter, for within a couple of minutes a man in shorts and T-shirt stepped out of a trailer home nestling in the trees at the far side of the clearing. He walked towards the pickup, carrying a bait box and a couple of fishing rods.

'Come for some fishing?' the man said.

Skelter nodded. He recognised the man's distinct twang.

'This way boys,' said the man.

He led them behind the trailer home and along a path through a mix of pine scrub and mangrove to a small boat moored alongside a jetty. The humidity was high, the sun mercilessly hot. Mosquitos zipped around their heads – except Brick's, of course. His smoke discharger did a great job discouraging them. The man with the fishing gear untied the bowline and held it while the men stepped aboard, then took his place at the stern. He pulled the starter cord twice. The outboard fired into life.

'Good day for it,' said Skelter.

There was no response. The boat scudded across the water for a quarter of a mile and then entered a creek which wound through the mangrove swamp. Turbo pointed to an alligator sunning itself on a mud bank. 'Hand bag, hand bag,' he said, taunting the unresponsive creature.

Brick shook his head lazily from side to side.

'That'll put the wind up the bastard,' said Turbo.

Twenty minutes after entering the creek, they turned into a passage so narrow they could reach out and touch the trees on either side. Eventually they reached a small islet with a shack. The man ran the bow against a couple of truck tyres tied to mangrove root and secured the stern line.

Well-concealed and hidden from above, under a

canopy of foliage, the shack was a ramshackle affair slightly bigger than a single-car garage.

'Okay, here's the deal. I don't normally bring strangers all the way out here but Mitch has vouched for you so I'm sure you guys are cool. I got a list. This is what I have, nearest match to the list.' He pointed to the small, crude wooden table that occupied the middle of the space. Two wooden chairs and three upturned crates. 'Take a seat.'

Brick ignored the gesture and moved to the one window where he stood scanning the outside. The door remained open to let light into the dark interior. Turbo looked at Skelter as the man fumbled with a bunch of keys, unlocking the first of three steel cabinets at the back of the shack. Skelter nodded, Turbo shrugged. Both men sat down.

The man placed a brand new Taser and a box of eight CS gas grenades in front of Skelter and Turbo. They examined the equipment as Judd went back to the cabinet. In no time, the table was groaning under the weight of non-lethal ordnance.

'Can you get any more Tasers?' asked Skelter.

'That's just a sample, got six more in the cupboard,' said Judd, 'Pepper spray, many as you can carry.'

'What about guns?' Turbo asked. 'This stuff's all very well…'

Judd returned to the table with a haversack. 'Try these to start.'

Turbo pulled out four ballistic nylon slip cases, fleece lined. Three contained well used Beretta 9mm pistols, one a gleaming stainless steel Smith and Wesson of the same calibre.

'Okay so far,' said Skelter, 'but...'

'Patience buddy, I also save the best for last. Before I show you the diamond, let's talk business. The Tasers and guns I can do for rent. Full charge as retainer, balance back if returned in perfect condition. CS, pepper and such, sale only. I'll give you fifty percent back on ammo.'

'Deal,' said Skelter. Under the circumstances the guy was being reasonable. After all, where else could he take his shopping list?

The piéce de resistance was well worth the wait. Judd produced two strange looking weapons that reminded Skelter of the weapons used by Gorillas in the original film "Planet Of The Apes" with Charlton Heston.

'Atchisson 12-gauge auto.' The man slid on a large, round drum magazine. 'Twenty rounds,' he said almost salivating. 'Three hundred and sixty rounds a minute. How cool is that? These babies are so new, they're not on sale yet. Pre-production prototypes, upgraded version of the old nineteen eighties model. Expensive, but wait till you try.' Judd handed one to Skelter and a heavy knapsack to Turbo, then walked to the door. 'This way.'

They followed him outside to the back of the shack. Twenty feet away, dozens of plastic bottles filled with water hung on twine at various heights from a tree branch.

'One thing, guys, forget all you learned about shotguns. Do not, I repeat do not, lean in. This baby has zero recoil.' Judd pulled back the bolt and pushed the safety before passing it to Turbo. 'Go ahead, get your rocks off.'

Both he and Skelter emptied the shotguns in seconds.

Bottles danced and disintegrated, exploding in an orgy of water and lead.

Turbo's eyes were wide with wonder. 'Awesome, that was awesome.'

'I want one for Christmas,' said Brick.

Skelter nodded, examining the weapon with admiration. 'How...?'

'Got a real long recoil system. Goes right to the end of the butt. Absorbs all the energy so you don't feel it. Keeps it smack on target. Cool yeah? But we're not done yet.' He turned to Turbo. 'Get another magazine outa the bag will ya?'

Turbo swapped the empty one on the gun for the fresh one.

'Let your buddy try. Not the bottles, what's left of them. Try those.' He pointed to two large heavy looking plastic Jerrycans, full of water, standing on a couple of tree stumps.

Brick fired. The first round knocked a can backwards, off the stump. The second round delivered the same blow to the other. Brick shot several more rounds at the cans, hitting them every time.

'Fucking useless,' said Turbo, won't even penetrate plastic.

Brick looked at Skelter. Skelter shrugged. Judd took a cartridge from his pocket and gave it to Skelter.

'Plastic mini baton round, won't kill ya, but packs a punch like Tyson.'

When they reached the jetty at the end of the road it was almost four thirty. Skelter shook Judd's hand and agreed the price for the package.

'I'll have the stuff delivered to Mitch's, including the ammo quantities you asked for day after tomorrow, after dark.'

'Cash will be waiting,' said Skelter, 'and thanks.' The men parted company.

'Can we stop for some grub?' said Turbo, 'my stomach finks me throat's been cut.'

'I second that,' said Brick, puffing away on his pipe as they walked to the truck.

'Unanimous,' Skelter said, 'didn't we pass a steakhouse on the way through Everglades City?'

16
New Recruit

Sanibel Island
Wednesday, October 20th 2004

Skelter was up early, drinking coffee in the kitchen when Maria walked in. 'What's wrong, is it Mitch?' he asked.

'No, yes, no, he is the same, but the pain. He refuses the morphine. Speak to him, please, H.'

'Wouldn't do any good, Maria. He knows what he's doing, we both do.'

'But...'

Maria stepped forward. Skelter felt awkward, out of his depth. She broke and buried her head in his chest. He held her until the sobbing subsided, at which point she broke away, embarrassed. 'So sorry. I should not...'

'Nonsense, of course you should, you need to. How you've kept it together until now is a mystery. I wish I could take his place. He won't take the morphine because he knows it shortens his time with you. Being with you is the most precious thing he has. He'll not give it up without a fight.'

She nodded, wiping her tears with a handkerchief. 'I know, I know, I just wanted… It hurts so much to see him in pain.'

'He is no stranger to pain, Maria, trust me Mitch can handle it. Now go back to him, you are the best medicine he has. Don't waste a minute.'

Maria smiled, squeezed Skelter's arm and went through the door to get back to Mitch. Skelter opened the French doors, went outside into the warm bright sunshine and expelled all the air from his lungs. He wondered if they could pull the job off with three men, rather than four.

Skelter stood by the fountain, mulling it over as the sound of a striking match close by announced Brick's arrival. 'What's up? Where's granddad's trench lighter?'

Brick paused between puffs. 'Needs a new flint.'

'Have a word with Mitch, never smoked, but carried a Zippo with him everywhere.'

'Cheers, I will. Looks like he's struggling a bit this morning.'

'Yes, we need to crack on. I want to get this job done before…' The sentence was left unfinished.

Brick nodded. 'Any sign of a fourth man? I know the pilot's in the pipeline.'

Skelter shook his head. 'Do you reckon we could pull it off with three?'

The big man looked over the water. He stroked his moustache and said nothing.

'I take it you don't think so?'

'Not for me to say, H. This is your gig. If we take casualties…'

'You're right. I'd better find someone. And quick too.'

Skelter took a telephone call, mid-morning, from Stan Kelly.

'Morning H, just checking to see how it's going. Still need a pilot?'

'Position's open, if you want it. Want another for the ground team too. What's the matter, skydiving not enough anymore, Stan? Need more adrenaline?'

'My wife will cut my balls off and hang them on the Christmas tree, if she finds out I'm flying you, so keep your gob shut.'

Skelter let out a huge sigh, beaming from ear to ear. 'Good man. Of course, Mum's the word. Welcome aboard. You won't get a bigger rush, not even from skydiving.' The phone went quiet. Seconds ticked by. 'Stan? You still there?'

'Got to go, mate, Call you back.'

Skelter allowed himself a hint of a smile.

Twenty minutes later, true to his word Stan called again. 'What's up?' said Skelter, stifling a burst of mirth, 'your good lady walk in on you?'

'Close call mate. All right if I drop round tonight? We can iron out details.'

'Sure Stan, any time to suit you. I'm not going anywhere.'

'See you around seven.'

The line went dead. Skelter chuckled.

'Good news, boys, Stan has agreed to fly us,' said Skelter. Turbo and Brick looked pleased and relieved.

'So what are we short of?' said Brick.

Skelter took a battered notebook from his pocket and started to make a list with a stub of pencil.

'Respirators, we'll need them,' said Turbo.

'Sorted mate, and cable ties and gaffer tape for handcuffs. Our main deficiency is the fourth man.'

'Not much time, H,' Turbo said.

'Thanks for pointing out the bleeding obvious,' Skelter said.

'Okay don't get out yer pram.'

Skelter exhaled loudly. 'Sorry mate.'

'No worries.'

Brick patted his friend on the shoulder. 'We share your pain, H.'

'Medic Kit,' said Turbo.

Skelter scribbled a note on the page, 'good man, T.'

They spent most of the day going over drills for the operation, including casualty evacuation procedures, prisoner containment and exfiltration to Florida. The lack of a fourth man still plagued Skelter's thoughts, causing much anxiety.

They broke up for dinner: Paella, Shawna's signature dish. Skelter felt guilty for not having spent more than a few minutes with Mitch and was about to put that right when Stan arrived. He was not alone.

'Evening gents, can I introduce a friend of mine. Laz, this is H, the low altitude guy is Turbo and the bloke who stole Pancho Villa's moustache is Brick.'

The men exchanged handshakes. Skelter looked hard at the young man; thirty at most, clean cut, lean and fit looking.

'Laz may be able to fill your vacancy, H. I would have mentioned him before but he has been away.'

'Let's go into the den,' said Skelter.

The men gathered around Mitch's big old desk.

'Been away?' Skelter said. 'Work or vacation?'

Laz looked at Stan.

'Laz has been a guest of the state of Wisconsin. Three years, aggravated assault.' Stan shrugged. 'The guy had it coming.'

'How long you known each other?'

'We met on an exchange visit to Fort Bragg '506th infantry,' said Laz anticipating the next question. 'Eighty-second airborne.'

'Laz got an honourable discharge,' said Stan. 'Silver star for Iraq.'

Skelter looked at the newcomer and then Stan, who nodded, 'Let's go to the kitchen Laz, get some coffee.'

'Just show me,' said the young man, 'I'll put the pot on, you can come back and talk about me. It's okay, guys.'

With Laz in the kitchen, organising the brew, the rest of the crew got together in the den.

Stan scanned the faces around the desk. 'I understand your concerns,' he said, 'but he's up to the job and you are running out of time. He knows to stay where he is until I call him.'

'I'm against,' said Brick. 'Late in the day to take on untried, untested, unknown.'

'Turbo?'

'I sympathise with Brick but I can't see how we can do the job with three of us. What about jumping, Stan?'

'Lazarus used to be an instructor at Silverlakes. Half

a day refresh, no more.'

Skelter chewed it over. 'What about the aggravated assault? Three years, for a first offence? Who did he beat up?'

'His brother in law.'

Skelter's eyes narrowed, beneath a furrowed brow.

'The man had been beating his wife, Laz's sister.'

'Still, three years?'

'He was a police officer. Completely out of character, I promise you. I've known Laz since he was a teenager.'

'Rank?' asked Skelter.

'Lieutenant.'

Eyes widened around the table.

'A fucking Rupert,' said Turbo, shaking his head.

'I'm still against,' said Brick, 'but...' He paused and stroked his moustache with a hard, calloused hand. 'Like Turbo says: if we are going to do this, we're not going to get a better offer.'

Skelter went into contemplative mode once again. He kicked the possibilities around and came to the inevitable conclusion. 'Okay, Stan, let's have him in.'

When Stan went out to fetch him, Skelter turned to the other two. 'Not ideal, I know, but he's the only game in town. It's not like we haven't faced this kind of situation before, having to work with strangers.'

Turbo shrugged, Brick remained tight-lipped and impassive. The door opened and Stan walked in with Laz, who had a tray of coffee in his hands.

'Just one rule,' said Skelter. 'When we go live, I give the orders. Your previous rank means nothing, clear?'

'Clear.' Lazarus seemed happy with the ruling.

'Right,' said Skelter, 'let's run through the plan, so far.'

Maria came out with the telephone in her hand. 'Sorry to disturb you. Someone says he is Smoke on the Water? A joke perhaps? The name I mean.'

Skelter took the hand set. 'Thanks. I was expecting this.' He turned away and Maria walked back towards the house. 'This is H. You have a package for me?'

'Correct,' said a gravelly voice so deep it seemed subterranean. 'Where and when?'

'Sunday, an hour before sunset, near as you can to Naples,' said Skelter, not wishing to mention Sanibel.

'Take this down,' said gravel voice.

Skelter noted the coordinates in his notebook.

'Bring the deposit. Don't be late.'

'I need a contact number.' Skelter wrote the number in his notebook. 'Done,' he said. The call clicked off.

Skelter exhaled again with a sound like a punctured life raft. *Another item ticked off the list, thank God. This work seems more stressful than I remember. Must be old age creeping in.*

17
Briefing

Sanibel Island
Wednesday, October 20th 2004

The men went into the garage, drove the Maserati and Mitch's Range Rover out and parked them next to Maria's pickup. Skelter found two trestles and a sheet of plywood and the men positioned themselves around the makeshift table. Stan produced two felt marker pens from his car and, with the aid of the photographs he had supplied previously, sketched an outline map of the island on the plywood. Using small tins of varnish to portray the men of the assault team Skelter initialled the tops B and T in black marker and S and L in red. He had to keep Laz close. The other two he trusted, even though they had never worked together. In an ideal world he would pair with Brick or Turbo – men he had worked on ops with, men he could read and who could read him, but, each pair needed a skilled skydiver.

They went over the plan once, twice, three times. Maria brought them more coffee and later they broke off for food. Shawna's southern fried chicken with Spanish rice and black beans. After they had eaten, Skelter took Stan out into the garden. The waning moon glistened upon the water as a breeze stirred the surface. The scent of jasmine hung heavy in the air and the night filled with the chorus of frogs from the water's edge.

'Here's the number of the guy who can supply the plane,' said Skelter, handing Stan a page torn from his notebook. 'I guess you'll need to talk to him. Smoke on the Water.'

'Are you serious?' said Stan.

'His nickname, that's what he calls himself.'

'Deep Purple fan?'

'Cherokee Indian. What's the chance of an intel update, Stan?'

'I spoke to a disgruntled employee last night. He expects Wolf to stay put until the next major shipment and that won't be for a month. I'll have another word though, just to be sure. All we need now is the plane.'

'Don't worry, the guy is reliable. I have it on the best authority. All you need to do is get us to the landing strip. I gave the GPS coordinates to the pilot.'

'Mitch give you the landing site?'

'Yeah.'

'I know it. We used it back in the day.'

'Quel surprise,' said Skelter. 'The pilot will fly in. We swap the keys for our truck. Pay the deposit and you fly us out. We return the plane to the same location after the job, pay the balance and he'll fly it out. All he wants from you is the all-up weight and flight time and distance to calculate fuel load.'

'What aircraft type, H, do you know?'

'I asked for a Cargomaster. Can't promise but my man says he'll get as close as he can.'

'No shit?' said Stan, clearly impressed. 'You really are well connected.'

Skelter allowed the remark to slide. 'All we have to do is work out when. The weapons and most of the other kit is scheduled for delivery tomorrow. Are the parachutes organised?'

'Yes, not new but perfectly serviceable ex SF rigs, so all set for attaching Bergens.'

'Excellent.'

'Thought I'd find you out here.' The deep voice cut through the cloud of smoke that preceded it.

'Not very tactical, that smoke generator,' said Stan, 'you can whiff it for a furlong. Not unpleasant, though.'

'I never load it on the job. Just suck it dry.' Brick cocked his head towards the light coming from the kitchen door. 'The troops are waiting for orders.'

Skelter nodded. 'Right then, see you in the briefing room when you've finished your smoke.'

The men reconvened around the makeshift table. Skelter ran through the logistics, equipment list and timescale for deliveries. He kept the details of the aircraft and the exact date to himself. 'It looks like we could be going pretty soon, gents. From now on, if you come here, assume we might be on that night. Not sure how you can square that with your missus, Stan.'

'Me neither, mate, but I'll think of something. If I don't, then no flowers, thanks, donations to Para Reg.

benevolent fund.'

There was a ripple of low-level laughter, the first to lighten the serious mood in the gathering.

'Well, boys, let's go through it one more time, okay? Stan?'

Stan Kelly picked up a four-inch paintbrush and held it at waist height, flat and parallel to the table top. 'I fly in on the deck to a mile from the target.' He raised the brush and canted it over. 'Turn and climb up to six thousand feet.' He now held brush above his head and swept it theatrically through the air to line up with the edge of the map. 'Line up for the run and... We will need to rig up jumping lights. Torches might do it.'

'Okay, next. Turbo?'

'Brick and me exit on green, go stable, track to heading for target DZ.'

'Location?'

'Small beach at southern end of island, beyond stand of trees, which should hide us from view.'

'Okay, Laz and I will be right behind you. What next? Brick?'

'We move up to the main house, two by two. Recon for hostiles and trip wires, then Turbo and me move away to the barracks hut.'

'If we meet any hostiles?' said Skelter.

'Avoid if possible, if not take them out quiet, without deadly force.'

'And if it goes noisy?'

'Priority one storm the barracks, gas and flash bangs, tag, bag and gag 'em then make for the house.'

'Good. And while this is going on? Laz?'

'You and I gain entry to the house, clear it room by room until we get the target. Immobilise the Wolf and any other. Make for the barracks to assist if needed.'

'Stan?'

I'm holding at low altitude, eastward, waiting for green flare on ground. Soon as I see it, I'll come in, land and pick you up and fly us all back, wave hopping to the mainland. We rendezvous with the phantom pilot, get in the trucks and head for home before daylight.

'Good, let's go through the kit list. Each of us will carry two Tasers, pepper spray, respirator and four grenades: two gas and two flash bang. One shotgun per team, pistol plus four magazines for each man. Fill your pockets with cable ties and a roll of gaffer tape each. Water bottles, watches and torch. Have I missed anything?'

'Shotguns. How many mags?' said Turbo.

'One on and two spare for each team. It's all we have. Non-lethal ammo only.'

Skelter turned to the recruit. 'You haven't asked about money.'

'I just got out of the Pen. Work is thin on the ground. I reckon this has to be worth a shot. Stan said it would be worth my while. Besides, what else am I qualified for?'

'Ten for the job, plus fifteen percent bonus if we deliver the girl unharmed. Any questions?'

Laz looked at Skelter with a huge grin. 'None at all, Chief.'

Skelter exhaled long and slow. 'In that case business for today is concluded.'

Mitch seemed to be holding his own and Lena had accepted his refusal of painkillers. Katya was less accommodating, however.

'Tell that bloody woman I will decide when I need morphine, not her,' he said.

'Mitch, please do not be angry,' said Maria, 'she only wishes to help.'

'She's right,' Skelter said, 'stop giving the women a hard time. You are lucky to have them in your corner. Take it easy, okay?'

Mitch relaxed back into the mountain of white pillows. He looked all in, the skin drawn over his skull, like a tight fitting latex mask in ash grey.

'Maria,' said Skelter.

'I know, you want me to leave, that is fine, I must change anyway. Do not to tire him, please.'

'I won't. Not much to discuss.'

Maria leaned over the frail figure, touched his cheek with her fingertips and kissed him upon the forehead. 'Try to relax,' she said.

Mitch responded with a weak grin and a wave of his bony hand. 'Well, laddie, how is it?' he said when Maria had left the room.

'All good. Everything's in place except the assault kit and that's coming today. I plan to go on Sunday. Back here Monday morning, done and dusted. Don't you worry now, it'll all be fine.'

Skelter felt Mitch's fingers scratching at his arm. 'I was never worried, laddie. Not with you in charge. You are the best there is, always were. I know, I taught you.'

'One thing, Mitch, got any binos?'

'Window ledge, in my bedroom.'

18
Kit Fest

Sanibel Island
Thursday, October 21st 2004

Mid-afternoon, an anonymous grey van with blacked out windows pulled into the drive and backed in to the garage. Brick and Turbo unloaded the kit. Skelter checked the items against the list in his notebook. Once satisfied, he handed a fat envelope to the driver, who stuffed it in his pocket.

'You not going to count it?' Skelter asked.

The man shook his head and said, with no trace of humour. 'I know where you live.'

Brick winked and gave the man a smile, which threw the guy until he cottoned on that it was a wind up.

The man climbed back into the cab and drove off. Turbo tapped the button on the remote and the roller door trundled to the floor.

'Bergens?' asked Skelter.

Brick held up a couple of the olive green rucksacks.

'Let's get sorted then,' said Skelter. The men lined up the Bergens against the wall and distributed the contents of the cardboard boxes, allocating items to the right individuals. They finished in less than forty-five minutes.

'That just leaves the overalls and chutes,' said Skelter; 'Stan's department.'

'Do you think his missus will let him live when she finds out?' said Turbo.

'No idea,' said Skelter 'to be honest, I'm more concerned about what Lucy might do to me. What about you Brick? Anyone waiting at home for you these days?'

The broad face slackened, his hand reached instinctively for his pipe. He slipped it into his mouth and began to chew the mouthpiece like a hungry rat with a piece of electrical cable.

'Brick?'

He looked uncomfortable. 'You are bound to find out sooner or later,' he said. 'We've been together for three and a half years.'

'Who?'

'She can't come home, of course, not since the last job.'

Skelter frowned so deep his forehead resembled the top of a shepherd's pie.

Brick's eyebrows arched. 'Penny not hit the slot yet?'

'What language are you two speaking?' said Turbo. 'I'm totally lost here.'

'Bugger me, Brick,' said Skelter as the coin dropped and tripped the light in his brain. 'Are you serious, you and Caroline Warren? Wow. How is she?'

'Still drinking you mean? Not anymore. Getting

therapy, working hard at it too. We're living on Dominica. Not Bell's house, renting a bungalow near the beach. You know he died, right?'

Skelter winced inwardly. 'Yeah, I did hear something.' Skelter searched Brick's face for any clue he might know that he was responsible for the death of Caroline's boss. *You think he knows, Buddha buddy? I wouldn't be surprised.*

'Left her a small fortune,' Brick continued, 'she won't touch it. Just takes the pension.'

Skelter was gobsmacked.

Turbo's face lit up. 'Not that lass that was secretary to what's is name, Bell? She's a stunner.'

Surprise registered on Brick's face

'Turbo, here, was with me in Somalia, remember?' Skelter said.

'Course, you mentioned it when we met.' He turned to Turbo. 'So, you helped rescue Richard Bell, did you?'

'Aye. Give Caroline my best, mate, I'm really happy for both of you, but what she sees in an ugly mug like yours, beats me.'

'Thanks, Mucker, appreciate that.'

Later, when Brick went for a stroll outside to satisfy his craving for the dark treacly St. Bruno, Skelter filled in the blanks for Turbo.

'Brick and I did a bodyguard job, here in Florida, looking after Bell. Rollo was involved, so you know what that means.'

'Smoke and mirrors.'

'Exactly, anyway, it got complicated. Bell had upset powerful people in the government at home and here, in the US, so we took him out of circulation. He wound up exiled in the Caribbean, along with Caroline. Bell met with an accident a few years ago.'

'What kind of accident?'

'The fatal kind,' said Skelter.

Turbo studied Skelter's face. 'Fair enough, H.' he said, with a slight smile.

Skelter went to his room to ring Lucy. He lay on the bed and picked up the phone, but just stared at the handset. Brick's news about Caroline reawakened a haunting memory. An episode he believed to be buried for good. Five years of expert therapy; five years coming to terms with a chequered past littered with trauma. He turned to Buddha, perched upon the bedside cabinet. *Well, fat boy, if Bell was still around, she wouldn't be with Brick, now would she? So, that's a positive, isn't it? The evil bastard deserved to die. He really did, you can see that, can't you?'* Skelter lay back, and let his head sink into the pillow, as the memory flooded in. He had neither the energy, nor will to resist it.

That day in 1999, when he hired the fishing boat in Isles de Saintes. Lucy sleeping as he crept from the holiday bungalow, the walk down the steep hill to the harbour in the dark, the slap of wind against canvas as the sails filled with nature's energy and drove the vessel out into the blue waters of the Caribbean. He managed a smile as the image of the lilac dawn that fateful day passed through his mind.

It wasn't even as if he had formed a proper plan. Surprise the bastard at home, give him a bloody good kicking, that was the extent of his planning. It went so well, the isolated anchorage, the short swim ashore, the climb up the rocks. He had not expected to find Bell's place so easily nor had he expected a total lack of security. It had been a piece of piss. Then, to discover Bell off his face on narcotics and strapped to that machine, talk about poetic justice. All he had to do was gag the shit bag to stop him releasing the Velcro or the cut-off switch with his teeth. Then it was a simple matter of overriding the timer. The man wasn't supposed to die. Who could have anticipated a heart attack? An eye for an eye: that was the intention. Let him know how it feels to be sodomised.

What confused Skelter was the fact that he cared at all. Getting soft perhaps? Maybe Judith was right: perhaps his humanity was rising above the chaos. *Come on, shake yourself out of it. Get a grip man, call her.*

The phone rang for ages. He was on the verge of hanging up when Lucy's breathless voice cut through the air. 'Is that you Mark? I was in the garage, dumping boxes, I only just heard the phone. It will make a great gym. It's massive. Workshop too.'

'Steady girl, slow down, you sound as if you're about to explode.'

'Can't help it. Such a super house, and all ours, our first home together. I'm excited. Wilkins has been a godsend. He is so organised.'

'Of course he's organised, he's a brigadier's batman for God's sake. Anyway I'm glad to know the move's going okay. Probably better without me under your feet.'

The sound of laughter filled Skelter's ear.

'You might be right, handsome. How's the patient?'

'Holding his own at the moment. Refusing morphine to spin out his time with Maria. She's stuck to him like glue twenty-four-seven since we arrived. Bloody heart breaking. All the years they might have had.'

'You'll be away a while then?'

'A week, at least.'

'Do you want me to call work and explain the situation in case...'

'Would you? That would be great, Cariad. I really appreciate the offer.'

'Consider it done and don't worry, I'll have a lovely new home for you to return to.'

'I owe you, big time.'

'Don't you fret, you're going to pay handsomely. I guarantee it. Look, I have to get on, Wilkins is working his little nuts off in the house. Love you, bye.'

'You too, bye.' *'That was short and sweet,'* said Skelter to the Buddha nestling in his fist. *'Not a whiff of trouble, Rollo's worked his magic again. Spun some bullshit story to take the heat off, no doubt. The move is proving to be a useful distraction.'*

'Off for an early night, boys,' Skelter announced after dinner. 'Meet after breakfast to run through contingencies but, after that, take a break. Go live on Sunday, subject to the aircraft being available, which I am assured will be the case, just need to make the call to check tomorrow. Weather forecast is perfect; near full moon, light winds, ten percent chance of rain. Looks like the Gods are on our side for once. See you in the morning.'

'Yeah, night, H,' said Turbo and Brick in unison.

Skelter looked in on Mitch, but the man lay sleeping, cradled in Maria's arms. The woman was also asleep. They looked at peace together. He crept out and away to his room and flopped on the bed to contemplate the coming operation. This was new territory and he had no mandate. They were going to commit a criminal act. What was more worrying was the prospect of facing real bullets, while armed with plastic ones. *You must be fucking crazy, H, my boy. Off your nut. Not too late to call it off, mate. What if one of the team gets injured? Broken leg on the drop, ok, but try explaining a gunshot wound to the local hospital – if you can get him out, that is. Not like you can call for a casevac chopper is it? We could all wind up in jail.*

The permutations rattled around in his head, like ball bearings in a pinball machine. After a couple of hours, his stomach forced him to the bathroom. Shawna's risotto vomited into the toilet bowl, as his guts retched until he emptied them. The shower sluiced his vomit-splashed body until the smell had vanished, replaced by the sharp scent of citrus shampoo. Wrapped in a huge white bath sheet, he went to bed exhausted, but sleep did not come for a long time, held at bay by the rattling pinball.

19
Time Out

Sanibel Island
Friday, October 22nd 2004

Skelter took his breakfast coffee and sat beside Mitch and Maria. She immediately got to her feet, but Skelter waved his hand, palm down. 'Please, not business this time, I just want a moment with my old friend.'

Maria smiled and resumed her seat. Mitch turned his head on the pillow and managed a weak smile in Skelter's direction.

He smiled back. 'How you holding up, my friend?'

'Okay, laddie, thanks to Maria. Glad you managed to persuade her to visit this grouchy old bugger.'

Maria leaned across and fiddled with the pillows, wiped a tear away and kissed the back of Mitch's hand, then held it to her cheek. 'It is not fair,' she said.

'Hush now, woman, don't upset yourself,' said Mitch.

127

His voice rose and fell in pitch, unsteady, making it difficult to follow what he said. 'Make the most of what we have. Be grateful for it.'

Skelter smiled. Mitch looked genuinely happy, despite the awful circumstances.

Lena appeared beside them, holding the blood pressure monitor and thermometer.

Skelter nodded to the nurse. 'Our cue for more coffee, Maria.'

Maria stood up and made way for Lena to perform her duties.

'How are you managing?' Skelter asked Maria when they reached the kitchen. She dropped onto a chair at the table and ran her slim fingers through her hair. 'I need to wash this,' she said. She sounded detached, as if looking down from on high.

'Take a break. Turbo and Brick have gone to the beach. You should do something...'

'I will not leave him. I cannot. Mitch is all I have until my Eva returns. She will return, H?'

Skelter swallowed hard. 'Of course. Preparations are almost complete. Not long now.'

Maria said nothing, but there was no mistaking the pleading in her eyes.

'A few days, that's all, I promise.' *Why did you say that? You've no idea if things will go according to plan. When do they ever follow the plan?* Skelter thought for a moment until the light flashed inside his head. 'Hold on. I've got an idea. Wait here.' He left her and went back out to the terrace. Lena was finishing up. 'I saw a wheelchair folded up in the garage,' he said.

'Lena laughed. We've tried, he won't use it.'

'Wanna bet?' said Skelter, heading for the garage.

When he returned, Maria was there, too. 'Okay Mitch, bin the non-cooperation shit and tell me where the keys to the boat are.'

Mitch's face changed from defiant to compliant as the significance of the request dawned upon him.

'Top drawer, right side, desk.' The voice was strained but joyful. Like a kid anticipating Santa's visit at Christmas.

'You are coming too, Lena.'

Getting Mitch into the chair was not difficult. He weighed next to nothing. Transferring him to the boat was a challenge, but accomplished without trauma. With Mitch in the stern, flanked by Maria and Lena Skelter cast off and checked the fuel. She had an almost full tank. He took the helm and fired up the engine. A glance behind caught the enormous grin on Mitch's haggard face as Maria snuggled into his emaciated frame. It felt good to be doing something positive for his old comrade. He set off at a steady four knots and gently followed the intra-coastal waterway past picture-postcard houses set in beautifully manicured gardens. Each had a dock, with large luxury vessels moored at most. So much money crammed onto one small island.

After half an hour of exploring the canals and basins, Skelter steered out into the Gulf. The passengers were treated to close up views of ospreys nesting on the tops of the channel markers as they threaded Westward through the narrows and under bridges. Mitch remarked to the women that the laddie had learnt well from the master.

'I heard that, Mitch. Self-praise is no recommendation, you know,' said Skelter, with a laugh on his lips.

They made it into the turquoise waters of the Gulf where they encountered a large loggerhead turtle, much to the delight of Maria and Lena. Mitch continued to grin like an idiot, which became infectious. They stayed out for two hours, before Skelter decided he'd better turn for home. The weather had been perfect, the sea calm and there were no noisy speedboats or jet skis to intrude and spoil the tranquillity.

When they finally made it to the dock, Brick and Turbo were waiting, sitting in the warm sun, nursing cold beers.

'Got your note, Mucker. Had a good trip?'

Skelter nodded, pleased to see them. Getting the patient ashore would be a breeze now.

By the time they settled Mitch in his day bed, it was past lunchtime.

Maria kissed Skelter on the cheek. 'That was a great idea, H, we had a lovely time. God bless you.'

'Me too,' said Lena. 'I really enjoyed that. More to the point, he did. Thank you, H, it was real good of you.'

'My pleasure,' said Skelter, looking over to a soundly sleeping Mitch. 'Well, if you don't mind, I'll get myself a beer and join the boys.'

'I think you deserve one, what you say Lena?' said Maria.

'Absolutely.'

Skelter took a beer from the refrigerator and sat at the table with the other two. 'How was the beach?' he asked.

'Lucky pint-size here hasn't got a dicky ticker, it might have proved fatal,' said Brick.

'You can talk, walrus-features. You were looking hard enough. You shoulda seen 'em, H. Tits like ripe melons, big enough to drown in, unbelievable.'

'Glad you enjoyed yourself, mate. A good day all round, just what's needed to settle the nerves before the show.'

'We're all set then?' said Brick.

'Everything's in place, ready to roll.' Skelter eyeballed the two men. 'You both still up for this? Any doubts, now is the time.'

'We're fine.'

'Speak for yourself,' said Turbo.

Skelter felt his heart slide down to his canvas espadrilles. 'What's the problem?'

'There is no problem, I just don't want walrus face speaking for me.'

'Are you trying to give me a heart attack?'

'If I wanted to do that, I'd drag you to the beach to look at all those melons,' said Turbo.

'You're nuts.'

'Maybe, but it's a great way to go.'

'Bloody perv,' said Brick, getting out of his chair. 'I've had enough of this barrack-room banter, I'm off for a smoke.'

Skelter and Turbo watched as Brick mashed the dark tobacco flakes in his palm with the heel of his other hand. The smell was captivating. He stuffed the bowl and walked towards the door. He paused, looked back at Skelter and held his grandfather's old brass trench lighter aloft. He flicked the wheel with his thumb. It lit first time. 'You were right about Mitch having flints,' he said.

When he had left, Skelter turned to Turbo. 'Well, what do you think of Laz?'

'Like you said, he's the only game in town. He's qualified, operational experience. Until we get on the ground, who knows. Could be a natural, could be a nightmare. He's on your team, it's up to you to keep him right. Too late to start worrying now.'

Skelter called Lucy. The conversation felt strained, she was subdued. 'Everything ok, Lucy? You seem a bit quiet.'

'Fine, Mark, everything is fine at this end,' she said, stressing the last two words.

'Sure?'

'Said so, didn't I? Look after yourself okay? Be careful, please.'

'Cariad?'

'I'm not a bloody fool, Mark, and Daddy isn't as smart as he thinks. Don't say anything, I don't want to know, just come back in one piece.'

Skelter was lost for words.

'You had better,' she said. 'Have to go now, I love you, Mark Skelter.'

The line went dead before he had a chance to reply.

20

Pre Match Nerves

Sanibel Island
Saturday, October 23rd 2004

The luminous dial on Skelter's watch showed 1.45 a.m. The last time he looked it was 1.35. Sleep eluded him. He swung his legs out of the bed and went to the bathroom, took a leak and cleaned his teeth. Slipping into a pair of shorts and pulling a T-shirt over his head, he went downstairs to the kitchen. He pushed a tall glass against the lever under the ice dispenser and watched the cubes rattle into the glass. After topping it up with cold water, he went outside and walked to the boat dock. More than anywhere else on the property, he felt at peace aboard her. It was a good place to think.

So, what you got yourself into this time, boy? No choice, of course, not really. Non-lethal ammo, what possessed you, you dozy twat? The home team won't be using non-lethal; won't be playing by your rules, either. He looked over the stern, at the lights across the water. The reflections in the coal-black canal a picture of calm and quiet beauty, at odds with his tumble-drier brain. He sipped at the iced water, while the frog chorus echoed across the shallows in the humid air. The little, green, fat figure came out of Skelter's pocket, rotated slowly around his master's fingers. *'We need something more deadly than rubber bullets and birdshot, Buddha man. We need assault rifles. Not really thought it through, have we? I'm a civilian. Ok, ex armed forces, but that means what it says: ex, formerly known as, no longer a part of, not subject to military rules. Subject to civil law; the law of the US – federal law. Get caught and we're toast. No back up plan, no get out of jail free card; nothing. Nothing but one shot at getting it one hundred percent right. One single shot at the title. One slip and we'll be lucky to make it to the State Penitentiary alive. More likely wind up in a shallow grave on that tiny, barren island.* He lifted the glass to take a drink. The ice cubes rattled and clinked. He tried to stop his hand from shaking. He failed.

'Sweet Lord, help me out here, please.' The words surprised him. He had not intended to speak out loud. It freaked him a little.

'I don't want to lose anyone, Fat Man,' he said, his hand stroking the smooth, hard figure. *'Not another Tash. So help me, I couldn't bear to lose another man, Buddha. I know these guys don't have kids, well, Sam does, at least I think he does. Shit, why don't I know more about them. Laz might have a kid, I suppose but...Oh fuck it. Fuck it, fuck it, fuck it.'* Skelter hurled the glass far out into the darkness and dropped his head into his hands, as the sound of the splash punctuated the amphibian chorus.

Forty-five minutes later, the men were up to speed and half an hour after that, Skelter was confident they had mastered the awesome Atchisson shotgun, which was simplicity itself.

'This stuff is all very well, Mucker, but our lives are on the line here. We need something more serious in the firepower department for backup. I know we can't go around killing civilians but they'll be using live rounds. Pistol's no much use against assault rifles.'

'Got it covered, Brick. Coffee break first, then I shall reveal all.'

Brick's frown eased but did not entirely disappear. He was going to take some convincing. No matter, it would happen.

'Turbo, with me, coffee can wait a few minutes.'

Skelter led the way to the house and into the den, the closet and beyond. The gun store might, more accurately, be described as an armoury. Barely three feet wide by around seven feet long, it had steel shelves across the full width of the end wall, floor to the two-metre ceiling. It was a 30 centimetres deep, which left two metres by two of wall, racked with guns. For once, Turbo was lost for words. He let out a long, low whistle.

'Take your pick, any except the Steyr, That's mine. Put it to one side and go and get a coffee. Not a word mind, Laz is still an unknown quantity. I'll pick for him if necessary,' said Skelter.

Turbo, like a kid in sweet shop, tried the lot. He settled on a Ruger Mini 14, for which he found ammunition and three magazines. 'I always fancied one of these. Just like the A Team, eh, H?'

'Go get your coffee.'

Skelter stood looking at a wall lined with lethal weapons. He shook his head in bemused wonder that a private citizen would be allowed such an arsenal. Grateful under the circumstances, he felt uncomfortable at the same time. A lifetime of service in the military had forged an affinity with firearms; they were the tools of his trade, but he grew up in a country where the police were, for the most part, unarmed.

Skelter returned to the garage. 'Right boys, to address concerns raised by Brick, I have secured extra weapons. Understand me on this, they are defensive, last resort. Clear?'

'What kind of…?'

'Are we clear?' said Skelter, cutting off Laz before he could finish his question.

'Yes, Chief.'

'Automatic rifles, for you, an AR15. Now, everyone sure what we need to do?' Nods all round. 'Okay stand down until after lunch. Meet here at two. I'll issue weapons tomorrow. Three magazines each, last resort, remember. If we are forced to use them, I shall consider the mission a failure. Do not let me down, okay? That's it.' Skelter inclined his head towards the door as he eyeballed Brick. When Laz and Turbo had left the garage, he spoke to him. 'Come with me, I've something to show you.'

As the two men squeezed into the hot, stuffy space, Brick failed to conceal his surprise at the treasure trove.

'Must be a few grand's worth in here,' he said, stroking his moustache as he eyed the wall of weapons. 'Uzi, Winchester, H&K. It's an impressive collection.'

'Aye, what do you fancy?' Skelter asked.

Brick picked several from the rack, weighed them, checked each for balance and finally settled on a compact Colt commando.

Skelter nodded approval.

'Defensive only. Small island, two buildings, confined space. Not likely to be engaging at distance. Three mags you said?'

'That's it, ninety rounds, remember, you have to jump with all this.'

'Suits me, Mucker, so what's yours?'

'The Steyr, used them before on attachment with the Australian SAS. They swear by them. Your team partner's earmarked this one,' said Skelter, tapping the Ruger's barrel. 'I'll just check the cabinet to make sure there's enough ammo.' He opened the door. 'Yeah, here on the bottom shelf, mate. More than enough. Right, let's get out of this cupboard before I collapse with heat stroke. The extraction fan isn't quite up to the job.'

With nothing else to do for a while, Skelter retreated to the boat to hold court with his little, fat, green friend. *'Well, Buddha? Have I missed anything? What about Jane, don't suppose she would approve, would she? Well, yes, I guess trying to reunite Maria with her daughter, but she was never comfortable with violence. She hated guns. I hope she won't think too bad of me. I can't let Mitch down, you can see that, can't you?'*

21

Match Day

Florida
Sunday, October 24th 2004

At 2.30 Stan arrived in a rented box van. Skelter brought him up to speed with the plan and ran through the ground phase.

'All clear, Stan?'

'Sound so far.'

'Good, you say it will take us an hour and forty-five to get to the airstrip?'

'Probably less, just making sure we have slack in the system. Airstrip is not quite what I would describe it as. Never mind, you'll see. Have you weighed the kit and the guys?'

'As you asked, got the figures here. Bathroom scales, no idea how accurate they are but the numbers are within the limits you specified.'

Stan looked them over and seemed satisfied. 'Well, best get your kit loaded then.'

'Back it up and I'll open the garage. Okay boys, time for some exercise.'

'The chutes are in the van. Here are your jump suits, lads,' said Stan handing out four navy blue overalls. 'Hope they fit. Yours might be a bit roomy, mate.'

Turbo smiled as he took the suit. 'What else is new?'

They were ready in fifteen minutes.

The men set off late afternoon with Stan at the wheel and Skelter up front with him. The others rode in the back with the equipment. Stan drove South, then East along the Tamiami trail for a few miles, before turning onto an unsigned dirt road that wound into the forest. After half an hour, the road ended in a clearing about thirty metres across. There was nothing to see but scrubland. The stretch of close grazed, possibly mown grass running across their line of sight did not look like a runway to Skelter. 'This is it?'

'This is it,' said Stan, banging on the bulkhead behind him. 'Time to let slip the dogs of war.'

Skelter was still scratching his head when Stan leapt out and opened the back. The three passengers climbed out and stretched their limbs.

'Okay boys,' said Stan, 'we need to check the ground for any obstacles, debris. We've got forty minutes, so let's crack on.'

In line abreast, the four men walked the grass, searching for issues. They dragged two rotten tree branches from an otherwise clear landing strip and returned to the van.

'He's due in ten,' said Skelter. 'Get the kit ready.'

The lads pulled on their overalls and claimed their Bergens and parachutes.

'Okay for a smoke?' said Brick.

Skelter nodded. 'Sure, fill your boots.'

Turbo rolled up the legs of his oversized overalls, the sleeves too. 'If I'd known in advance, I could've altered these to fit.'

'Turbo was an apprentice tailor before he joined up,' explained Skelter, to a puzzled looking Laz.

'No kidding?'

'Hear that,' said Turbo. The faint sound of a distant aero engine drifted in, getting louder as the source drew nearer.

'Bang on time, H,' said Stan.

'Yeah, hope it's a good omen for the rest of the job,' Skelter said. 'We need all the help we can get on this one.'

'Amen to that,' echoed Brick, through a cloud of tobacco smoke.

'I'll second that,' Turbo said, his eyes fixed on the plane, as it skimmed the trees and drifted in towards them.

This pilot knew his business. He brought the airplane in on first approach, as the sun dropped below the horizon painting the surrounding trees with a rose pink mist. Wheels touched down with a slight bounce, which – given the rough nature of the ground – was better than expected. The plane raced through the scrub, until halfway down the strip, it slowed and finally came to a halt away off to the left.

Stan drove the van forward through the sparse vegetation, to the edge of the landing zone. The aircraft rotated one hundred and eighty degrees and taxied along the close-cropped grass towards them. The Cessna trundled past the onlookers and rotated again. The pilot lined her up for take-off in front of them, applied the brakes and cut the engine.

'Who's the man?' asked the bespectacled freckled guy with a heavy Irish American accent.

'That's me,' said Skelter. 'I was expecting an Indian, Smoke on the Water.'

'It's Smoke <u>over</u> Water. Mother was a Cherokee, but I got my father's genes. Smoke is fine. Yours,' he said handing the keys to Stan.

Skelter raised his eyebrows.

'Only one not wearing coveralls. Besides he looks at the ship like he knows airplanes. Tanks are almost full, no issues. Fuel for a hundred and twenty miles above what you specified. Take good care of her, man, okay?'

'As if she was my sister,' said Stan.

The Irish Indian turned on his heel and returned to the aircraft. He took out a large rucksack and wandered off a little way from the van and he set up his bivvy for the night.

'Okay, Stan this is your shift. What next?' said Skelter.

'Hang fire, while I do my checks. No point in loading until we are ready to go. Rest up a couple of hours and then we'll fit chutes and check equipment.'

'You heard the man, boys. Stand down for now.'

Turbo shook his head. 'Just like the friggin army. Hurry up and wait.'

'You know you love it, Turbo,' said Brick through

teeth clenched around his pipe stem, as a flake of moist tobacco shredded under the heel of his hand.

'Says who?'

'Me.'

'And who the fuck are you?'

Brick stroked his thick moustache and replied in a measured tone. 'To quote John Lennon, and a Yorkshire gnome, I am the Walrus.'

Turbo stuck two fingers up at him.

Skelter shadowed Stan, intrigued to learn what went on and also to keep himself occupied. He watched the pilot walk around the aircraft, manipulating the control surfaces; ailerons, rudder, etc. and then open the engine cover. 'Checking for fluid leaks,' he explained, taking a torch from his pocket, shielding it with his hand. 'All as expected. Can't be too careful in this game,' said Stan with a smile, as he climbed in to run the pre-flight.

Skelter walked back to join the rest of the team, who were fussing over parachutes, other equipment and weapons. They checked and rechecked in the obsessive-compulsive way that soldiers do when preparing to go into action. Skelter cycled through his own rituals, which included a pep talk with the Buddha. All done, he sat down against the front wheel of the van and closed his eyes to offer a small prayer for a safe outcome.

22
Take Off

Florida, Everglades
Sunday, October 24th 2004

'It's time, H.'

Skelter opened one eye.

Brick stood over him with a plastic mug in his hand. 'Coffee, warm…ish,' he said.

Skelter opened the other eye and blinked three times. 'Ta.' He drained the tepid, half cupful in one and handed the mug back. He got to his feet, stretched and went across to his kit. Perched on his Bergen, Laz stuffed the barrel of his AR15 into the pack. The Atchisson shotgun was in there somewhere, in pieces. The men would have to rely upon their pistols, until they could reassemble and load their main weapons.

By the light of the moon, the men strapped on parachutes and checked their equipment. Stan and Laz re-checked each man, including each other, before they heaved the Bergens aboard and climbed in through the large cargo doorway. The door was completely missing. 'This'll make it easy to exit with the kit,' said Skelter. The Cargomaster had no seats, but otherwise, it was much the same as the one they had jumped from at the Silverlakes club. They sat on the plywood floor, backs to the fuselage, two on each side facing one other. Attached to the sides at regular intervals, karabiners hung on webbing straps for the men to secure harnesses and Bergens. Skelter would spend most of the flight up front with Stan, in the co-pilot's seat.

Stan reeled through the cockpit checks, flipping switches and checking dials until, with a final 'brace for take-off,' he wound up the engine. The revs increased until the noise inside made voice communication impossible. The airframe vibration increased dramatically, until Stan released the brakes and the Cessna leapt forward and careered down the rough grass strip. They rattled, bucked and bumped along, the roar of engine echoing in the cabin as they gathered speed. Skelter held the Buddha tight to his chest, soaked in sweat, from the humidity and anxiety. Stan's piloting skill was an unknown quantity and a rough strip in the middle of the Everglades with only moonlight to guide you, well...

The bumping stopped. They were airborne. A loud, collective exhalation of breath from behind him told Skelter he was not the only nervous passenger. He always found it hard to be brave when he had no control over a situation.

The speed was exhilarating. Trees whizzed past in a blur as Stan hugged the ground so close Skelter could swear he heard his own sphincter tighten. He turned and glanced into the back at the faces of Turbo and Brick, grim and determined. *Wonder how I look to them,* he thought, trying hard to find his Bruce Willis face. Not convinced he had managed it, Skelter closed his eyes and withdrew to a safe place, where, for the umpteenth time, he rehearsed what he was about to do. He prayed. A sudden, sharp turn slammed him against the side of the cockpit, jerking him out of his safe zone. He looked forward, out through the windscreen. A dark screen of reeling trees scudded away to the left, as Stan pulled the plane around to avoid colliding with the black mass. Skelter cringed and gripped the seat with whitened knuckles. He stopped breathing as the pilot corrected and aimed for an impossibly narrow gap. Skelter flicked a glance back at Brick and Turbo. The whites of their eyes glowed in the dark. He switched forward just in time to witness Stan barrelling the aircraft through the gap at one hundred and fifty miles an hour. Stan's credentials were no longer in doubt. Skelter wished he'd packed a change of underwear. Flight time, around two hours, at least a third overland, according to Stan. He determined to keep his eyes closed as much as possible. An image of Lucy flashed through his mind. She was wearing her angry face.

'Now for the tricky bit,' Stan said, after forty minutes in the air. 'We're getting very close to homestead air base.'

'Know it,' said Skelter, 'on a job there with Brick in ninety-nine.'

'They have a dedicated anti-smuggling unit, good but under-funded and over stretched, so cross your fingers.'

'Will do,' *and everything else I can muster,* he thought as the pilot eased the plane even lower. *This man's a maniac, he's going to get us killed.* Crushing the Buddha in his fist Skelter prayed for safe deliverance and tried not to vomit. In between the flashes of fear, he was full of admiration for Stan's skill and the size of his balls.

The plane skimmed the vegetation at suicidally low altitude. *This man has serious flying under his belt, Buddha, they must have done some hard-core smuggling, him and Mitch.* Another abrupt manoeuvre slammed Skelter into the seat as they climbed to skip over a belt of pines before dropping down beyond them, leaving Skelter's stomach racing to catch up.

'Coast coming up,' said Stan opening the taps. The engine note changed as the aircraft increased speed to maximum, flashing over Key Largo as it hurtled on its way out to sea.

Skelter breathed a misplaced sigh of relief. A reflex, he knew how hazardous flying low over water was, it being notoriously difficult to judge height. His hand ached from gripping the statue so tight. Relaxing his fingers a touch, he returned to praying. He looked at Stan, but refrained from talking to him. Sweat ran down the pilot's face, the concentration intense, but behind it all, Skelter felt sure the man was having an adrenaline ball.

The change in engine note prompted Skelter to open his eyes. He had all but exhausted his rehearsals of 'what ifs'.

'We'll be climbing soon, H. You might want to get ready.' Stan shouted to the boys in the back above the noise of the engine and the air rushing in through the doorway.

'Roger that.' Skelter climbed over and joined the others. Laz was ready with his Bergen. Skelter nodded, pleased to note the man was switched on. He clipped on his chute and let Laz attach the Bergen to hang behind his knees, a real challenge in a moving aircraft with a large opening in the side. All up Skelter was carrying 45kilos. They all were.

Turbo kitted Brick and checked him, while Skelter crosschecked Laz. The men were ready: goggles on, poised, grim faced and silent. Skelter struggled to hold it together; parachuting had never really floated his boat. His fear of heights went back to being a boy, who never climbed trees as high as the other kids.

The aircraft slowed, as Stan banked to make a climbing turn to starboard, to minimise the possibility of throwing anyone out prematurely. Turbo pulled a piece of paper from his pocket and handed it to Skelter. Written on it in black marker pen: *Changed my mind. You go ahead I'll wait in the plane.*

Skelter laughed aloud with relief. Priceless; the man knew him too well.

Turbo grinned and gave him the thumbs up. Brick nodded.

They levelled off. Skelter looked through the door in the hope he might glimpse something that resembled an island. The moon cast a strong light but all he could see was ocean six thousand feet below, then, as the heading changed, there it was, looking impossibly small. He pointed. Laz picked it up, then Brick. Both thumbed acknowledgement. Turbo latched on last of all. On their feet now, the wind howling through the opening swirled

around, flapping the legs of their jumpsuits. Skelter looked towards the cockpit, at the torches gaffer-taped to the seat. *Talk about make do and mend. Heath Robinson would have been proud.* The thought had barely entered his head when Stan reached across and pressed the switch on the top torch.

'Red on,' Skelter screamed, as Laz took a firm hold on his harness. Skelter's stomach hit the roof of his mouth and his legs turned to lead. The second torch flashed on. 'Green on, green on,' Skelter yelled. He turned, stepped to the door and pitched forward into the slipstream. Training kicked in. He put his arms out and arched his back, reassured by the presence of his expert instructor's grip. Laz looked at him, eyes wide. Skelter nodded and raised his right thumb. Laz winked then looked down, in search of the island. Skelter checked around and up, relieved to see the other pair close to them. He glanced at his altimeter, surprised at how calm he was. *Four-thousand feet.* Way below, the impossibly tiny target started to grow. Laz jerked his harness and indicated a change of heading. Skelter followed his lead and tracked left. A second pull on the harness told him they were on course. *Altimeter three thousand, wind howling, suit flapping, falling at one hundred and twenty-five miles an hour.* Skelter felt light headed. *Breathe, breathe – remember to breathe dammit. Altimeter two thousand five hundred, jerk on the harness, Laz, hand signal away, two-seconds to deploying. One, grip handle and pull. Adrenaline rush, sensation of shooting upwards, two, three, head back, check canopy. Deployed, no malfunction. All round observation, Laz, left arc, check below, two more chutes below right, steer towards target.*

23
Wolf's Lair

Knuckle Key, Caribbean Sea
Sunday, October 24th 2004

Pedro Alvarez was bored. He saw no point at all in patrolling the perimeter of the only house on an isolated island, miles from anywhere. 'I tell you Ernesto, this is a waste of time. We might as well be inside playing cards and watching movies with the others. Why would anyone want to come here? The Bahamian authorities? They get paid big money to leave us alone. Why would they kill a chicken that lays such valuable eggs? Lope is losing it, man, too much coke has scrambled his brain.'

'Are you crazy? Do you know what he will do to you if he hears you talk like that?'

'I'm not afraid of him, he's on the way down, man, seriously.'

Ernesto gripped his companion's arm and looked up

to the starlit sky. 'Listen.'

'What?'

'Airplane, I heard an airplane.'

Pedro stopped, looked up and strained his ears. 'You're imagining things, amigo, just the sound of the surf on the sand, that is all. You know the crazy thing is, the beach is beautiful. White sand, palm trees – just like in the holiday brochures. Americans pay a fortune to vacation on an island like this and we are paid to be here, not a great deal but...'

'What is it with you? Why you always complain? You gonna get yourself in real trouble one day soon. Lope will cut your balls off, I swear.'

'Lope is too busy with his pleasures to notice, using too much stuff. He is losing his grip.'

'That was a plane, Pedro.'

'Well, if it was, it has gone now, so forget it and let us carry on this pointless patrol.'

The two men walked down the side of the building towards the rear, Rifles casually slung across their shoulders. They turned past two enormous galvanised steel tanks, one of which held rainwater collected from the roof. The other stored waste water and sewage, most of which was recycled into water for flushing the toilets. It was impressive and expensive engineering but a far cry from what Pedro remembered.

'Remember the old days, when you could stand in the shower all day? Two years ago we all lived in luxury in the islands. Bars and music and girls, lots of girls. He had that beautiful yacht.'

'He still has the yacht,' said Ernesto.

'Maybe, but he'll never sail her again. Lope will end his days on this rock in the middle of nowhere. Too many enemies, I tell you the vultures are circling, amigo. Soon, one of them will take his place.'

'Think you can do it?'

'Keep your voice down, damn you. No, I do not.'

'I don't believe you, you have big ideas, Pedro, but a brain the size of a pea and even smaller balls.'

Inside the house a middle-aged black woman stood by the stove, preparing a meal while her daughter laid the table for two.

'This gas bottle is almost empty,' said the woman.

'Shall I fetch one from the store?'

'No, I'll get one after they've eaten. Almost finished, just enough gas left, I think. You can tell him it will be ready in five minutes.'

'Me? You want me to tell him?'

'Yes, child, and be sure to knock. And do not go in unless he asks you to,' she added. The teenager looked nervous. 'Go now, he won't bite you.'

The girl left the kitchen and made her way up the pinewood stairs. A sound like a rutting stag came from the farthest room at the back. She knocked nervously upon the wooden door, but got no response, so she knocked again, louder, then again louder still.

'Go away,' said an angry voice.

'Supper is ready,' said the young girl, before she fled downstairs and ran into the kitchen.

'Steady child,' said the girl's mother, 'slow down, what is the matter with you?'

'He shouted at me, told me to get lost. Why is he always so angry?'

'Never mind him, he will be fine when he has filled

his belly.' The woman handed her daughter a tray with a plate of red snapper and Spanish rice. 'Take this through to Martin, I'll be along in a moment, when Lope comes.'

Wolf got out of bed, picked up a fine Cuban cigar from the dressing table and sliced off the end with a razor-sharp butterfly knifes. He stepped onto the balcony, leaned on the rail and began blowing smoke rings, watching as they wafted skywards on a breeze too gentle to cool his skinny, sweating frame. Back in the bedroom, a dark haired girl sat by the bedside cabinet, working a line of coke on the glass top with a credit card. The intimate scent of her young flesh lingered in his nostrils, despite the smoke. With a wry smile, he bent to pick up the shorts discarded earlier in his lust for her and pulled them on. Lope slipped his feet into a pair of espadrilles and went to look for a shirt. 'Take it easy with that stuff,' he said to the girl, wasting his breath. In spite of himself, he liked her. Young and pretty, she was an enthusiastic student in the art of pleasing the Wolf and he meant to keep her, for a while at least.

24
Landing

Knuckle Key, Caribbean Sea
Sunday, October 24th 2004

Seven hundred feet below Skelter, the smooth waters of the Caribbean glistened silver in the moon glow. Ahead and a mere fifty feet below, Laz steered into wind to run parallel with the target beach. Skelter followed the example. The harness tugged at his shoulders as he slowed down.

No sign of life, wonder if they have dogs? All that planning – you forgot about dogs. You're slipping mate.

Laz corrected again, heading for the beach at speed, three hundred feet up. Skelter steered after him, then as Laz made the final turn into wind at two hundred, Skelter swallowed hard and followed. He tripped the hooks to release his Bergen. The load fell away and a second later, a harsh jerk told him it had reached the end of the fifteen-foot retaining rope. Skelter observed Laz's Bergen swinging below his partner as he pulled down over the narrow strip of white moonlit beach.

Skelter turned into the wind again, what there was of it, then it all happened at once; the thump as the Bergen grounded, slack rope, splash, wet arse, brief humiliation followed by relief. The beach was only metres away. Skelter stood up to his calves in water, wet but happy. He collapsed his chute and reeled in the rucksack. Thirty feet away, Laz was similarly engaged, but on dry land. Skelter dragged the canopy onto the sand and reached into the Bergen for the Steyr. Sliding the barrel onto the receiver, he locked it with a twist, slotted a magazine into the housing and drew back the bolt. He pulled a large nylon bag from the side pocket and stuffed the chute inside before pulling the drawstring tight.

Laz hauled his kit across as Skelter cocked his pistol and pulled on his ops vest. They stashed the bundles at the base of a brace of palm trees.

Further down the beach, the shadowy figures of Turbo and Brick beavered away at their tasks.

'Looks sweet,' said Laz. 'Guess we got away with it.'

'Sure hope so.'

Brick and Turbo trundled in, weighed down with kit, and cached their chutes with the others. Turbo had already assembled his Atchisson and had the Ruger on a sling around his back. The Colt hung by Brick's side.

'Ok, let's bury these chutes and get moving. Watches, boys. Time check, midnight thirty-three in 5 4 3 2 1... Set.'

Brick and Laz hastily scraped a couple of holes in the sand to bury the kit while Skelter and Turbo covered the approaches. The night was warm, humid and quiet, only the sound of the surf and the palm fronds rustling in the breeze blowing off the sea.

That's a bugger, Skelter thought, any dogs and they'll get our scent right off the bat.

The team followed Skelter along the edge of the trees until they ended. There was no cover, other than very sparse, low vegetation for several hundred metres. Skelter and Laz crept forward at a crouch covered by the other pair. They went to ground after forty metres and took up firing positions as the others sprinted up to and past them. Skelter watched Brick with admiration. A pipe smoker pushing fifty-five and he moved like a panther. Skelter braced to move, glanced at Laz. The American acknowledged with a tilt of his shotgun barrel.

Red team hit the dirt. Skelter jumped to his feet and advanced swift and silent, Laz a metre behind and left. The leap frogging continued until they reached a small patch of scrub within sight of the main house. Here the four men went to earth together. Skelter took out Mitch's binoculars and scanned the house and immediate surroundings. No sign of anyone. He spotted a camera, above the porch. *Should have seen that coming.* He carefully checked every inch of the target visible from his position. He noted three more cameras. One on each corner and another, sneakily placed under the steps, at ground level.

'Right boys,' he whispered, 'cameras everywhere. Stealth is out. When the time comes, speed, aggression, surprise. For now, we backtrack and give this place a wide berth. We'll take the beach route and hook round to the barracks. We must assume cameras there too, so be ready to go in hard and fast.' Nods all round. 'Okay, let's move.'

Skelter led the way towards the trees, then turned for the beach before heading back towards the far end of the island and the barrack hut. The delay cost them twenty precious minutes. Skelter looked up at the moon glowing in the tropical night sky. *Hang in there Stan, keep circling. We'll get this done.*

They made it to the hut without incident, and crawled forward to a point a hundred metres away to the side with their backs to the sea. Skelter checked out the building. *Not a camera in sight, no dogs. So far, so good. Windows open, no air conditioning unit. Cheapskate. That's going to cost you, Wolfie.*

Skelter waved Brick and Turbo off and hooked his hand to signal them to circle right. He and Laz would close in from the left in the classic pincer move. His pulse was up. Adrenaline – which had been on drip feed, now surged, forcing the valve open, pumping like Black Sabbath's bass drum. On the balls of his feet, Skelter hissed, through clenched teeth. 'Remember, no dead people, ours or theirs.'

Turbo and Brick sprinted away. Laz leapt forward so quick that Skelter raced to catch him up. Still no reaction from the barracks. They reached the building, crouched against the wall and pulled on their respirators. The words of Paddy Mayne, famous founder member of the SAS, flashed through Skelter's mind. *'When entering a building, shoot the man nearest to you first – he is in the best position to harm you, then shoot the first man to move. He is switching on and has begun to react to the threat.'*

Skelter pulled on his respirator, jerked the pin from a

CS grenade and held it up to Laz, who was similarly poised. He nodded. *Release lever, 2, 3, – post through the window.* Crack, crack, the grenades detonated, fizz, fizz, the gas belched out into the confined interior, thick white fumes filling the space within seconds. Fits of coughing broke out, men cursing and yelling.

The pair raced around to the other side as Turbo and Brick crashed through the door. Bodies choked and spluttered in the thick smoke, blundering into gloved fists, boots, rifle butts. It was difficult to see anything because of the gas, but Skelter clocked one figure reaching for a weapon lying on a bed. Before he could take action, Brick's rifle cracked, the muzzle flash bright in the dense fog. The weapon smashed onto the floor, its magazine ripped from the housing as a slug of copper cased lead tore through it. To add to the mayhem a bed had been set on fire by a grenade.

The men subdued the disorientated bodyguards in less time than it takes to tell. There were only five of them. All cuffed, gagged, bagged and dragged outside while Turbo threw the bedding onto the floor and set about stamping it out. Laz and Brick gaffer-taped the men's ankles together and then to each other's, while Skelter collected their weapons.

25

Alarm

Knuckle Key, Caribbean Sea
Sunday, October 24th 2004

'Mother of God, Pedro, what the hell are the idiots playing at? If they're drunk again, Lope will go crazy.'

'He'll cut them up, the stupid bastards. They got a death wish or what? We better go see.'

The two men jogged towards the accommodation hut. Sixty metres short, they both pulled up. 'It's on fire.'

'Quick, we must...' Ernesto stopped dead this time. 'Something's wrong, amigo...'

Wolf ran out onto the balcony at the sound of the shots. Unable to see anything, he spun around and darted back inside to grab a walkie-talkie from the bedside drawer.

'Get dressed,' he said to the girl in the bed, who seemed oblivious to his sense of urgency. 'Now, Eva.' He reached into the wardrobe, took out an automatic rifle and hurried along the landing, up the stairs, to the rooftop terrace. One glance told him serious trouble was brewing. What he didn't know, was the exact nature of it. He saw the smoke rising from the accommodation building. Wolf shone a searchlight at the building and pressed the switch on the radio.

'Ernesto, are you receiving?'

'Investigating, boss, not sure... Jesus, Mary and Joseph.'

Wolf heard several bursts of automatic gunfire. 'What's happening? Speak to me. Ernesto?'

Pedro and Ernesto unslung their rifles as they doubled forward to check out the commotion 'This is not stupid drunks, Pedro. This is serious. Something bad is going down.'

'I told you I heard a plane. Now do you believe me? Look at the smoke. We are under attack, man.' Pedro raised his weapon and fired a burst in panic. His aim was high, the rounds passing over the roof.

'Pedro, stop. Are you loco? You will shoot one of our boys. We got to get close, find out what's going on. Wait.' Ernesto spoke into the radio. 'We are on it, Boss. Looks like someone got on the island, DEA maybe, wait, we'll call back.' In his excitement, Ernesto had forgotten to press the transmit button. 'Let's go, Pedro.'

'Good job, boys,' said Skelter, as he pulled off his

respirator when the gas had dispersed, 'these are going nowhere. Let's get on with it.' He went through the door, straight into the blinding glare of a powerful searchlight. The crackle of small arms fire split the night air. He hit the ground and rolled back into the cover of the building. 'Shit.' He fought his instinct to return fire. The shooting stopped. 'With me,' he yelled, leaping to his feet and legging it towards the beach, keeping the barracks building between himself and the house. Skelter stopped at the water's edge, turned and collided with Turbo. Had it been Brick, he would have been kissing the surf.

'Ernesto, what the fuck is going on? Ernesto come in, answer me,' Wolf cried, trying to focus the searchlight with one hand and operate the walkie-talkie with the other, without letting go of his rifle. One of his bodyguards joined him on the roof. 'Keep the beam on the fire,' he ordered, handing over the searchlight. He charged down the stairs and burst into the bedroom. Eva had pulled a dress over her head and was looking for her shoes. Lope grabbed her wrist and despite protestations dragged her downstairs. 'Martin, the airplane, pronto,' he yelled, barging past the black woman and her daughter.

Martin Neumann jumped up.

'They are here,' said Wolf, eyes wide, his voice pitched an octave higher than normal.

Martin's eyes registered understanding. He followed his boss across the hallway into the kitchen and out through a side door.

'What is it? What's happening, Wolfie?'

Eva got a sharp shove in the back. 'The plane, now. We have to get off before…'

The sharp sound of distant shooting spurred Eva into action. She sprinted barefoot to the Cessna. Martin Neumann reached the plane first, wrenched the door open, dived in and made his way forward to the cockpit. Eva was close on his heels, propelled by fear instilled by the rattle of gunfire.

Wolf climbed aboard and closed the door, ignoring Eva as he clambered into the co-pilot's seat. Martin checked dials, flicking switches as if his life depended upon it.

'Move it, damn you,' Wolf said, in a voice like that of an excited woman.

Neumann worked as fast as he could, without compromising safety any more than necessary. He was an old pro, he had every intention of growing older.

Wolf was verging upon hysterical.

The engine started to turn.

26

Contact

Knuckle Key, Caribbean Sea
Sunday, October 24th 2004

'Work around to the sides. Brick, Turbo, left flank. Laz we're right. Clear? Let's move.' Skelter set off at a trot, hands gripping the Steyr, safety off, ready to go lethal. They had not covered more than two hundred metres when a sound reached Skelter's ears, which caused him to curse in spades.

'Oh fuck, no, please…'

'Hear that, Chief?'

'Too fucking right, come on, move it.' Something told Skelter they were going to be too late. The noise increased and as they reached the edge of the airstrip, the plane thundered past in a cloud of dust and sand. Seconds later, it roared into the night air and disappeared.

Skelter screwed his eyes shut against the swirling dust. 'Bollocks.'

'That's ballsed it,' said Laz, staring after the fleeing aircraft.

As the dust settled, Skelter opened his eyes to see fresh bursts kicked up in front of him; two, three, like puffs of smoke. He pushed Laz to the ground. 'Incoming,' he yelled, pointing to the house. A figure, silhouetted by searchlight. 'Aim high.' Skelter bounded forward, as Laz fired a couple of short bursts over the man's head. He dropped to one knee and fired six rounds rapid. Laz sprinted through like a lurcher. It was enough. The incoming firing ceased. The figure disappeared. They made it to the house unscathed, at the same time as Brick and Turbo appeared from the opposite direction and burst in hard and fast. Skelter dived through the open door to the first room, rolled right, covered by Laz. *Movement in the corner, screaming, Laz sweeping left. The kitchen, two women huddled together, hysterical.* Skelter put a finger to his lips and lowered the rifle. The two men carried on, cleared their half of the ground floor and started up the stairs, Turbo and Brick following.

They found one man on the roof, cowering in a corner. His rifle lay several feet away. Turbo cuffed him. 'All clear, H,' Brick announced after a quick sweep of the area.

Skelter ran downstairs and out the front, Laz hard upon his heels. He took a flare from his pocket and set it off. The crimson fireball burst high overhead. 'Lights, we need runway lights.' He darted back inside and upstairs to the searchlight.

Skelter directed the light onto to the airstrip. *Could have been made for the job. Idiot, it was.* He looked along the beam, saw a figure knelt at the edge of the strip, a flicker of a flame. The man ran a few yards. Skelter recognised Laz – flicker, flame, a dash across to repeat the process on the other side. Turbo cottoned on and ran ahead to light more of the flare path pots. *Of course. How else would they land at night? Should have realised.* Skelter held his breath. They'll never do it in time.

The thought hit Skelter's brain just as the throttling sound of a high revving petrol engine met his ears. A quad bike appeared below hammering full belt for the far end of the runway, quickly swallowed by the darkness. As the sound faded, another engine note drifted in on the wind. Stan, winging his way in. It would be close. The red flare fizzed its last, as first one, then another flame, flickered at ground level in the distance. Now, two more – on the opposite side. The engine noise grew louder, twin bright white landing lights low, drifting right, left, right again, lining up. More flames on the right, creeping closer, Turbo and Laz heading towards Brick's quad, the plane almost kissing the farthest pots. *For fuck's sake keep your heads down, boys.* The bright whites shuddered and bounced. Stan was down. The Cessna ran on into the searchlight's beam and rattled to a halt, thirty yards from the house. It swung to the left as Laz and Turbo legged it to the plane. Skelter left his lofty perch and galloped down the stairs two at a time, burst through the door and sprinted to join the others at the aircraft.

'Well done, boys,' said Skelter, slapping Laz's back as he reached the Cessna. Stan thrust his head out of the window. 'Turn us round,' he shouted, above the noise of the engine.

Skelter nodded. 'You heard the man.'

They set to, pushing the tail over to swing the aircraft in line with the strip for take-off. Brick arrived in a cloud of dust and gasoline fumes. 'Fetch the chutes and kit. Turbo, lend a hand.'

Brick gunned the motor and roared off with his partner clinging on like a limpet, as the four wheeled death trap bounced across the rough ground.

'Birds have flown,' said Skelter.

'Tell me about it,' said Stan, 'almost wiped me out, mate. Nearly went in the water, fuck knows how I missed him. So what now?'

'Can't catch 'em. We're fucked.'

'We know where they're going.'

'We do?'

'The distribution centre, only option Wolf has. Where else?'

'Can we get to it?' Skelter asked.

Stan screwed his face into a crooked frown. 'Fly back, take the van and we rent a couple of airboats. That'll take us close. We'll have to think on our feet from there. Too noisy to go all the way with those big fans.'

'Are you serious?'

'Sure I am.'

'What's this we shit, I thought…'

Stan tilted his head to one side, shrugged, grinned and arched his eyebrows. 'You never really get it out of your blood. One last adrenaline ride. You wouldn't deny me?'

'You're a bloody diamond, Stan.'

'Laz, check the prisoners and scavenge what weapons and ammo you can find, looks like we're gonna need them this time.' Skelter shook his head at the empty sky. 'What a cock-up. We should be flying back now, all sorted.'

'Don't worry, Chief, you'll get the job done.'

He checked his watch. 01.34. 'Listen, Laz, you've fulfilled your contract, but stick with us, I'll make it worth your while.'

'I'll take it. What about the prisoners, Chief?'

Skelter looked at the trussed up triggermen squirming in a heap in the corner. 'They'll be fine, work their way free in a few hours. Grab some of these,' he said, as he picked up a brace of rifles by their barrels. He had already slung one over his shoulder. Skelter staggered out under the weight of the additional hardware. 'I'm getting too old for this pack horse crap.'

'Ok, your call,' said Laz, as he followed him out towards the plane, laden with weapons.

'Going to start your own war?' Stan asked, as the men loaded the confiscated weapons.

The sound of the quad bike announced the return of Brick with Turbo grimly hanging onto a mountain of bags.

Stan hopped from one foot to another as he pretended to check the aircraft.

Skelter grinned at the animated pilot. 'C'mon boys, let's get loaded, we need to get out of here, before Biggles blows a gasket.'

Everyone pitched in and, in less time than it takes to tell, the men had climbed in and grabbed the retaining straps ready for take-off. Skelter sat up front watching Stan wind up the engine until the airframe shook fit to split. He glanced across at the pilot. Stan's face was a mask of concentration. Skelter ran through the sequence in anticipation – brakes off, open the taps. On cue, the Cessna surged forward and raced down the strip between the twin lines of the dying flare pots. The white foaming water of the breakers loomed out of the gloom as Stan hauled back on the column and the aircraft lifted off.

27
Going to Ground

Everglades
Monday October 25th 2004

Wolf pounded his fist into the seat. 'Bastards, bastards,' he cried, over and over. 'They will pay for this. When I find the man who sold me out, I will cut out his liver.'

Martin Neumann was too busy trying to plot a course and keep the aircraft level to take any notice of his employer's tantrums. Despite the bright moon, flying over water, under the radar, demanded total concentration, even for a flyer with twelve years' experience in the US Navy to draw on, not to mention six years as a bush pilot in Alaska.

'Who did this to me? Who? I cannot go back to the island now, everything there is finished. The staging post, we go there,' he said.

172

Neumann shook his head briefly. *Where else, moron?* He thought. They had no choice, it was the only place they could land without the risk of getting caught by the authorities. Landing in the dark with no runway lights would be a challenge. Thank goodness for the moon.

Martin Neumann was fast losing patience with Wolf. He needed all his concentration to fly the plane and he could do without being subjected to the near hysterical rant about his losses, who would pay and what he was going to do to them. Such graphic detail took away the threat's impact, the way constant repetition of the F-word does. Landing on the unlit airstrip was not as tricky for him as it might be for many a pilot. It was a stable platform, unlike the pitching deck of an aircraft carrier in a force six. That said, the ear bashing was making things unnecessarily difficult. As he turned onto his final approach, he lost it. 'If you want to get down in one piece, I suggest you keep your mouth shut.'

Wolf pushed the barrel of his rifle into the pilot's cheek. 'Show some respect, gringo, or I teach −'

'Shut the fuck up,' Neumann interrupted, 'before I crash the damn airplane.'

Wolf looked through the window at the trees flashing past, their crowns higher than the wings. The reality check calmed him a little. 'You know what I do to those who disrespect me?'

The pilot was not listening. The airspeed dropped as he deployed flaps. Seconds later, the wheels hit the dirt and promptly rejected it. The airplane bounced twice more before a final bone-cracking crunch, followed by an erratic high speed run as the Cessna careered through the darkness. Finally, Neumann brought the plane to a screeching, skidding halt.

Wolf glared at him as he shut down the systems and prepared to exit the aircraft.

'What a rush,' said Eva, leaning over the seat, hooking her arms around Wolf as she kissed his neck.

He shrugged her off. 'Eva!' He climbed out of the seat and pushed her away as he opened the cockpit door and jumped out. She followed close behind him.

'I have to go,' said Eva, hopping from one foot to the other. She ran off into the trees.

'Where is everyone?' Wolf marched off towards the shelters, just as bodies tumbled from their pits, freshly vacated hammocks swinging wildly as he approached. The sorry looking bunch that stumbled out to greet him did nothing to improve his mood. 'Drunken, lazy, pigs,' he screamed, waving the Armalite around with alarming disregard for safety. Wolf smacked his rifle butt into the nearest man, splashing bright, red blood from his nose. Wolf ignored his screams, as he sank to his knees. 'Get out here, all of you,' he screamed. 'Now, you worthless bags of dog shit. Now, I said.' He kicked an empty rum bottle. It skittered across the floor and shattered on impact with an old steel ammunition box.

Martin Neumann kept his distance. Wolf, eyes wild, waded into his crew, slapping heads and threatening them at gunpoint. Without warning, he turned on Neumann. 'You worthless piece of shit, you don't disrespect the Wolf, you hear me, gringo?'

Neumann stared back at Wolf with contempt in his eyes. Wolf lowered the weapon and shot the pilot through his right foot. Martin Neumann yelped, fell to the ground and rolled in the dirt clutching at the bloody mess that had been his big toe.

'You bastard, Jesus, my foot, you fucking lunatic.'

Wolf turned his attention back to the hung-over crew. 'Get this airplane out of sight.'

They sobered up and set to with fear-fuelled enthusiasm.

'And clean this place up,' Wolf yelled after them.

Martin Neumann removed his bloody shoe and wrapped a handkerchief around the stump of his toe. He moaned in pain and hobbled across to the aircraft in search of the first aid kit.

Eva came running out of the trees. 'I heard a shot. Are you all right Lope?'

'An accident,' he said. 'Martin has hurt his foot. Do not concern yourself, Eva. It is only a scratch.'

Eva frowned.

'The gun went off, that is all. Don't worry, he can still fly.' Eva looked at Wolf and then at the men, all of whom avoided eye contact.

Wolf's men pushed the aircraft under the camouflage awning and cleared away the evidence of their drunken revelry. Wolf took Eva into one of the shelters. 'I'm hungry, make some food,' he said.

Eva looked around at the hammocks and cheap plastic garden furniture. 'With what?'

'Under the stove, you will find everything you need. Go. I have to kick some culos.' Wolf went off in the direction of the plane to make sure they carried out his orders.

Eva turned the knob on the cylinder, lit the gas and filled two large pans with tinned meatballs and mac and

175

cheese. She opened vacuum packed tortillas to serve with the concoction. No one complained. After the meal, Wolf led Eva away from the others and into the other shelter. He got a stash of coke from under the sleeping platform and they snorted a couple of lines apiece through rolled up dollar bills.

'What's wrong, Chicquita?' he asked, when she failed to respond to his advances.

'I'm tired. I need sleep,' she said.

'The cocaine will wake you up,' he said, 'come on, let's have some fun.' Wolf started to paw at Eva.

'Please, not now. Later, promise.'

Wolf grunted, got up and went outside.

28

Improvise and Adapt

Everglades
Monday, October 25th 2004

Hair-raising at times, particularly the last leg over the Everglades, the return flight proved otherwise trouble free. As they closed on the final destination Stan announced.

'You might want to brace yourself, H, this could be tricky by moonlight. Pray if you want, I won't object.'

This did nothing to steady Skelter's nerves, already stretched like guitar strings.

He's winding me up, the bastard. Skelter shot a quick glance at Stan. His face told the story. *Oh, shit… Our Father, who art in heaven…*

'Brace yourselves, lads, landing imminent,' Stan shouted to the passengers.

All Skelter could see were flashes of dark green scrub and swampland, punctuated by an occasional glimmer of silver moonlight reflected in black water. Almost on the deck, no sign of the strip. His sphincter ached from over tightening. *Forgive us our trespasses as we forgive...* Something struck the base of Skelter's spine, solid as a nine-pound hammer. He screeched and opened his eyes. The hammer struck again, Stan's face was a grotesque contortion of anxiety and concentration. The aircraft kicked right, bounced and rattled along the dirt and grass runway as all three wheels finally remained in contact with the ground. The interior grew dark as the black mass of the tree line thundered towards them. 'Holy...' Skelter put his arms across his face and leaned back from the screen. The Cessna skidded, lurched to the right and shuddered to a stop.

Stan killed the engine. Uncanny silence reigned for several long seconds until Stan broke it. 'Piece of piss,' he said.

A sweat-soaked Skelter looked him in the eye. 'You lying bastard.'

'What's up, we're here aren't we, and in one piece?' Stan twisted around in his seat. 'All right in the back?'

'I think I might have broken a nail,' said a camp voice.

Skelter exhaled, laughing. Typical Turbo, always there to take the piss when it got tense. He offered a short silent prayer of thanks for their deliverance. The waiting ferry pilot appeared out of the darkness and rapped on the window.

'She's sound. No damage,' said Stan.

The man nodded and proceeded to examine ailerons, wing struts, tyres.

'Laz, fetch the van and start transferring the kit,' said Skelter. 'One thing, Stan, where the hell are we going to rent an airboat at this time of night? And how are we supposed to get all the weapons aboard without causing suspicion?'

'Got you this far okay, haven't I? Trust me.'

Skelter hated not being in total control but he had no choice and, to be fair, Stan had delivered in spades so far. There was something about him, an air of quiet ability.

Stan handed over the airplane. Skelter paid off the pilot, then got stuck in with the others, unloading and loading. As soon as they finished, Brick, Turbo and Laz jumped into the back of the van while Skelter climbed in beside Stan. They trundled off along the dirt trail, lights off, towards civilisation.

'Don't look so worried, H,' said Stan, 'it's all under control.'

'Well, you've done a great job so far. Can't fault it. We've been lucky, too.'

'Funny, that,' said Stan.

'What?'

'More I practice, the luckier I seem to be. Strange, don't you think?'

'Shush, smart arse, don't tempt providence. You're right, mind,' said Skelter, before he retreated into himself to figure out what to do next. His hand found the Buddha nestled in the depths of his cargo pocket amongst the indigestion tablets, mint humbugs and boiled sweets. He caressed the bald head and drifted into planning mode. *Suck it and see. No intel, no recce, don't know for certain Wolf's even there. What do we know? Well...Stan says he knows the where and he reckons he can get us there. Airboats are*

179

noisy. Canoes. Canoes we need. At least for the final approach. Wonder if Stan's been into the place or just flown over it? He's real deep. Him and Mitch; a right pair. God knows what they got up to together.

Skelter came out of his telepathy session with the green figurine as the van reached the highway and Stan turned east towards a distant Miami.

'Twenty minutes,' said Stan.

Skelter looked at his watch: 04.23. It would start to get light around 06.45. 'Any chance we can get our hands on some canoes, Stan?'

'No problem, mate, many as you want.'

Skelter breathed out and relaxed a little. The immediate future was full of uncertainty but they were making progress. *What do you think fat man, we gonna pull it off?* The green God's silence was as deafening as it was disappointing. *Stay positive, focus, you can do this.* Skelter's internal battle raged on as Stan pulled off the road alongside a pair of red painted, single storey wooden buildings. Next to them, a large sign towered above the reed thatched roofs. "Arnie's Air Boat Rides. Canoes for Hire. Hot Food. Cold Drinks." He backed the van down the side of the nearest building, close to the water at the rear.

Skelter jumped down and let the boys out. Brick had lit his pipe, almost before his feet hit the gravel. Behind the building, a cleared channel five metres wide held a number of airboats alongside a wooden jetty. 'So, we just help ourselves?' Skelter said.

'Yep,' said Stan, 'Soon as I get the keys.'

Skelter turned to the team and shrugged. 'Wait here.' He followed Stan to the rear of the building, startled momentarily by the floodlight they had triggered. He tapped Stan on the shoulder and pointed to the burglar alarm. He just grinned and turned his attention to the ten-digit electronic lock, stabbed his stubby finger at the buttons and opened the door. Once inside, Stan's finger worked its magic on the intruder alarm keypad, on the wall, just inside the door. He switched on a small lamp and sat behind the counter.

'Your face, H. Wish I had a camera. I'll explain later. Let's just say, you can call me Arnie.'

'This is yours?'

Stan took a set of keys from under the counter. 'Fifty percent.' He scribbled a message on a note pad and left it on the counter.

'You just keep on delivering, boy. We'd have been stuffed without you on the team.'

'Piss off, we all throw what we can into the pot. That's why we're a team, man.' Stan picked up a bunch of plastic bottles from a shelf and from beneath the counter produced a GPS, which he put into his pocket. 'We can load up now,' he said. 'I just need a map from the front office.'

Skelter found the three men behind the van talking in whispers.

'What's the crack, H?' said Brick, as all eyes turned to Skelter.

'We're going into the swamp with a couple of airboats. Stan knows where this Wolf hangs out.' He paused to let it sink in. 'They won't be expecting us.'

'They weren't expecting us the first time,' Brick replied.

'No,' said Turbo, 'but he was off pretty smartish.'

'Look, I understand your concern but not here, not now. Let's get loaded up and away before it gets light. We'll raft up when we're clear and off the tourist run. You can have your Chinese Parliament then. If anyone wants to back out, all I ask is you lay up long enough for me to get in and finish the job.'

Laz looked at the others, 'I'm cool with that.'

Turbo and Brick looked like they would need some convincing.

Stan passed around the plastic bottles. 'Mozzie repellent, slap plenty on, lads.'

Skelter opened the van's rear doors and climbed in to get his kit. He exchanged his rifle for one of the weapons confiscated from the gang and stuffed his pockets with full magazines. The next twenty minutes were a busy blur, transporting weapons and other kit to the airboat. Laz stashed as much of the gear as he could in a large aluminium locker spanning the beam in the bow. While this was happening Stan found two fibreglass canoes and tied them to the stern.

'Ready to roll,' said Stan, at last. He climbed into one of a pair of elevated seats, perched six feet above the deck. 'H?'

Skelter accepted the invitation and climbed into the second high-seat.

'Here,' said Stan, offering a set of ear defenders.

'Cheers,' said Skelter, putting them on.

The others took the two bench seats on the deck.

Laz stepped forward and cast off as Stan started the engine. Thanks to the ear defenders, the noise made less impact than Skelter expected, despite the propeller being directly behind his head.

29

Airboats and Canoes

Everglades
Monday, October 25th 2004

The airboat pushed forward into the channel, slow and steady, guided by the light from twin spot-lamps mounted at the sides of the elevated seats. Skelter looked down at the illuminated dials in the console, between himself and Stan, and noted the built in GPS. He breathed a little easier.

By the time the first wisps of dawn kissed the horizon, they were deep into the swamp. Cypress trees rose out of the water to tower above them. Stan negotiated a way along a bewildering series of creeks and channels then slowed to idle speed at a fork in the channel allowing the boat to drift into a clump of young trunks. He cut the engine and tied up. 'This do you?' he asked.

Skelter nodded, lowered the ear defenders to his neck and climbed down with Stan to join the others. 'Okay boys, this is what I plan to do. Get close as we dare then switch to canoes. Laz stays with the boat, while we go in and recce. Stan's GPS can get us bang on. He knows the place.'

Turbo frowned.

'Don't ask,' said Skelter, reading the man's face. 'From there, we play it by ear, adapt like we always do. It's what we're good at, second nature.' He stopped and looked for a reaction.

'You used to be a better salesman than that,' said Turbo. 'You're slipping, mate.'

Laz remained upbeat. 'Looks okay to me, so far.'

'Brick?' said Skelter.

The big man leaned back and stroked his moustache in silence.

'What is it?'

He sucked on the stem of his unlit pipe. 'We're civilians. Chances are that we could wind up in jail. The bad guys are going to fight. We are going to hurt people, maybe kill someone. What about the police, the FBI?'

'If you want out, fine,' said Skelter. 'I understand the argument. You're right, we're not in the army any more. This is criminal, but I have to do it. You know why. I don't expect any of you to share that and if it means I carry on alone, I will. I know what the odds are. I have to do this.'

'I'm not backing out, H, I want to steady the ship. We need to understand the possible consequences of what we're going to do, that's all.'

Skelter let out a long slow breath. 'So, you're in?'

'I'm in.'

'All in?'

The faces, stern but upbeat, gave Skelter the answer he'd hoped for. 'Okay. How far, Stan?'

'Another forty minutes and we'll take to the canoes, then an hour to get close enough to recce.'

'Better get cracking, then.'

The bewildering maze of channels through cypress swamp, lily and waving sawgrass left Skelter's head spinning, as Stan skilfully negotiated the twists and turns at speed. After half an hour he slowed down to a crawl with a dramatic drop in decibels. The aluminium hull glided over the carpet of green vegetation covering the black water, with ease, leaving no apparent damage to the plants. White egrets and grey herons stalked the shallows in search of food while, high in the cerulean sky, hawks traced slow circles on the rising thermals. It was a beautiful place.

Stop gawping and focus. Serious work ahead. Deep in his pocket Skelter's hand found the Buddha, fingers traced the round head and smooth belly. He thought of Jane, wondered if she would have approved of his mission. His focus flipped to the present, to Lucy. She would not be happy at all. He had promised to give up the life of violence – meant it too – but circumstances conspired against him. Not how she would see it, though. He considered the possibility of failure and of injury, or worse. *We really are getting too old for all this,* Skelter's fingers stroked the fat green Buddha. *For God's sake, stop being so damn negative. So far, we have climbed over, under or gone around every obstacle. It'll be fine, won't it, Buddha, buddy?*

The speed dropped again to a crawl, as the boat

nosed towards a group of cypress growing in the shallows. A big alligator lay motionless in the water watching the boat glide by, the fan blades humming hard in the still, warm air.

'Five minutes to holding point,' said Stan.

Brick went forward and unlatched the locker. He flipped back the lid and passed the weapons and vests back to Turbo and Laz. He put his on and popped a couple of smoke grenades into his pockets.

'I'll take a couple of those,' said Skelter.

Brick tossed him two. 'Catch.'

'Cheers.'

Turbo passed Skelter's ops vest along with an Armalite.

Stan nosed the boat into a dense area of cypress and killed the engine, letting the forward momentum carry them to a fallen tree with a matted patchwork of roots that formed a small dry platform. 'Tie us off, Laz,' he said.

'Roger that.' The former officer jumped onto the shelf and secured the mooring rope.

Turbo chuckled. 'Well behaved for a Rupert, in't he?'

Brick smiled, but said nothing.

The men untied the canoes and pulled them alongside the bow. Like the airboat, they drew almost no water, ideal given that the depth at their present location was less than eighteen inches.

'We'll take the shotguns, with both ammo options in addition to your personal choice, of course. Otherwise, take your pick. CS will be no use out in the open so leave it and ditch the respirators. Stan will lead, with me as crew. Brick, you follow with Turbo. Laz, mind the store, as you Americans say.'

Laz looked disappointed but resigned. 'Okay, Chief.'

'We'll get near as we can, then I will go forward to do the recce. Based on what I find, we'll work out a plan and once we agree, we'll go in. Any questions?'

Complete silence.

'It is a bit thin right now, I know, but we have surprise on our side'.

A chorus of low murmurs, coupled with a twinge of arthritis in Skelter's knee, served only to remind him that – if not over the hill – he had reached the summit. *I swear if I come back from this, I will quit for good, Lucy. On Mam's grave.* 'Let's get loaded.'

'Great idea,' said Turbo, 'soon as the job's done and you can pay, H.'

'Comedian.'

They filled two canoes with weapons, ammunition and water.

'Make sure you top up your mozzie repellent lads,' said Stan.

The men climbed in, cast off and, with Stan and Skelter in the lead, they paddled into the watery hinterland. After a while, the cypress gave way to mangrove, the roots arching into the shallow, brackish water like the grotesque claws of alien creatures. The channels became narrower and the trees closed overhead, their branches interlocking with their cousins on the opposite bank. Skelter watched a water moccasin casually swim across their path. The snake showed no sign of concern. Why would it? They were in her back yard – aliens, invaders. He glanced behind, reassured by the sight of the others paddling silently a few metres astern.

'Give it another five and take a breather, Stan, okay?'

'Roger that, H.'

Skelter swivelled in his seat and held up his hand, fingers spread. Turbo nodded.

When they stopped, Turbo and Brick drew alongside.

'How are we doing?' said the former.

'Stan?' Skelter asked.

'Sound, not too far now.' He checked the GPS.

Skelter removed the magazine from his rifle, checked the free movement of the spring and replaced it. The others took the cue, the sound of metal against metal jarring in the silence of the mangrove tunnel. It felt like another planet.

Getting close now. 'Silent routine from here,' said Skelter, after Stan confirmed the location with the GPS. He reached out and grabbed onto a mangrove root and as soon as Stan was ready, he pushed off to the middle of the channel. It was almost narrow enough to reach out and touch either side. Skelter dipped the paddle into the water and, with practised ease, stroked rhythmically, driving the vessel forward with barely a ripple. It had been clear from the outset that Stan was no stranger to a canoe and they melded well. One less thing to worry about. The channel gradually narrowed until the only practical way to progress was by gripping the roots and pulling the canoes along. Then just as it opened up again, Stan stopped and signalled that they were close to the end of the line. Ahead of them lay the mouth of the tunnel and a stretch of open water, the other side of which a dense concentration of mangrove dominated the view.

Stan used hand signals to indicate that the camp was to the right of their position, two hundred metres away. They could hear muffled sounds of activity, difficult to get a bearing on in the terrain. Stan held up a hand. Skelter signalled to the other canoe to stay put.

The metallic sound of a sliding bolt from Stan's seat in front told Skelter it was time to cock his rifle. He applied the safety, laid it at his feet and took up the paddle. The canoe glided noiselessly through the thick overgrown mangrove tunnel and nosed out into the open water. They steered sharp right, to keep tight to the edge of the trees, slow and steady. Skelter took his cue from Stan. After a few minutes Stan raised his hand and stopped the canoe. Without a word, he climbed out into the swamp. It barely reached his knees. Skelter followed and they pushed the craft out of sight into the mangrove and tied off to a root.

The sounds of voices drifted across the water. Skelter tapped Stan's shoulder and pointed to the canoe. He nodded and climbed up onto the mangrove roots and settled down next to the vessel, his Armalite across his lap. Skelter reached into the boat for the binoculars and slipped the strap over his head.

30

Recce

Everglades
Monday, October 25th 2004

The confused web of roots and the need for silence made
progress through the mangrove swamp laborious. The
slightest noise carried a long way over water. Skelter
considered himself fortunate that he did not have too far
to travel and in spite of the bewildering tangle, as long as
he kept sight of the open water through the vegetation,
he would not get lost. Half an hour of lifting his knees up
to his chest and holding them while he found a gap in
the roots to step into, left Skelter knackered. He
calculated he had covered less than three hundred
metres. Humidity must be near ninety percent, he
figured. The good news was, that, despite the dense
mangrove, the sound of voices and other human activity

meant he was close; real close.

Skelter stopped for a breather, resting against a twisted and stunted trunk. He stared into the tangled timber but saw nothing. His hand sought solace in the pocket that held Buddha. Just touching the smooth hard stone slowed his anxious breathing. *What the hell was I thinking, fat man? What possessed me? Finding Eva in this place is a big ask but getting her out… I must be crazy. If I ever get out of this, I will go straight. No more playing commandos. I swear I'll ask Brick to help me choose a pipe to go with a pair of fleece-lined slippers.* He unzipped his fly and took a leak, careful to piss on the bark to keep it silent. Ok, gripe over, time to go.

Skelter moved forward with infinite care. He made no sound detectable above the ambient. Less than five minutes later he claimed his reward. The trees thinned out a fraction, just enough to provide a glimpse of buildings. Time to get down and dirty. Low and slow gets you in the know. Ten uncomfortable minutes crawling through eighteen-inch-deep, brackish water brought him to the edge of the clearing. The most difficult part was keeping the binoculars clear of the water. The weapon didn't matter; it would work wet.

Skelter slid forward like an alligator on the hunt, mouth tight to keep out the foul water, face screwed up at the smell that wormed its way into his nostrils. He eased himself into a place from where he could look into the camp. From his low position, only the tops of buildings were visible. He could clearly make out the tail of an aircraft, beneath a palm frond covered camouflage net.

Can't get eyes on from here. They can't see me, then. Must get higher. As Skelter rose to his feet, a chill ran up his back.

The hairs on the back of his neck prickled. Instinct told him he was not alone. He slipped the safety catch and tightened his grip on the rifle, heart playing a drum solo as the adrenaline kicked in. He froze. Had he not just emptied his bladder, he might have done so there on the spot as his eyes met those of the half submerged alligator. The five-foot reptile remained absolutely still. Skelter felt like an item on a menu. Without taking his eyes from the creature, he climbed up into a mangrove tree using his left hand to guide him by touch alone. He kept the weapon trained on the alligator until he reached a point six feet above the water. Here Skelter stopped and clung, shaking, to his perch. *Slow down, slow it down, easy boy, that's it.* It took several minutes before his heart rate returned to near normal and he managed to breathe without gulping. He eased the safety back on. From his elevated position he had a fuller view of the buildings, which appeared to be little more than reed-thatched shelters tucked beneath trees. He climbed further and worked his way up, twelve feet into the crown in order to get the best possible view. The only sign of humanity was a solitary figure beneath the wing of the plane. Skelter thumbed the focus wheel and zoomed in on the man. He was sitting cross-legged on the ground, a rifle across his knees. Skelter scanned the ground for possible approach routes but stopped every few minutes to wipe the sweat from his eyes and clear the lenses with a soggy handkerchief. Perspiration poured from him.

He took a swig rom his water bottle. *Got to keep hydrated Buddha, deadly out here.*

The gang had chosen their spot well. Only one possibility presented itself. Skelter searched for an alternative way out, but found no workable exit route.

After an uncomfortable hour perched in the treetop, there was no still sign of Eva. He had caught brief glimpses of movement in the shelters, but nothing concrete. Time was marching on, past noon and his stomach was rumbling. *Why didn't I bring something to eat? I could murder fish and chips. I'd settle for a Mars bar. This is not going well, Buddha. What if she's not here? Even if she is − I'm not sure we can get her out − if we locate her.* He shifted his weight to preserve his circulation. *I don't remember OP work getting this uncomfortable so quick. Definitely a young man's game.*

Skelter swept the camp with the binoculars. *Nothing − the boys will be getting worried. No radio. How did I make so many basic mistakes?*

Skelter's chin dropped onto his chest as he let the binos hang loose. He rubbed his eyes and let out a long breath. *Not looking good, Bud, is it?*

He braced himself in his perch and lifted the binos once again. They felt heavy, or maybe it was his arms. He checked out the shelters and searched the tree line but saw nothing, then a figure emerged from the plane, dressed in light grey slacks and a loose fitting white shirt. The man with the rifle jumped up. He nodded at the man as he spoke to him. White shirt turned back to the aircraft. Skelter followed him to the boarding step. Jackpot. Framed in the fuselage doorway; Eva, it had to be. A younger Maria, couldn't be anyone else. The man in the white shirt climbed into the fuselage.

Skelter did a double take. *What the f… That's a turn up.*

White shirt disappeared from view.

Skelter took out a ziplock bag from his ops vest and removed a notebook and pencil. He made a sketch map of the camp layout and resealed the book in its waterproof home.

Skelter climbed down from his perch and backed away into the swamp, eyes locked on the alligator which showed no inclination to move. Skelter fought the urge to rush, careful to keep noise to an absolute minimum. *Wonder how thick an alligator's skull is, how many rounds it'll take to kill one.*

He made it back to Stan without incident and the two men launched the canoe into the edge of the open water. They paddled in silence until they reached the creek where the others were waiting and drew up alongside their canoe. Both men looked relieved to see them.

'Any luck?' asked Brick.

'Some,' said Skelter; 'good and bad.'

'Sounds ominous,' said Stan.

'What's the age of consent in this country?' Skelter asked, responding to Stan's remark.

'Varies, twelve in some states, eighteen here in Florida, I believe.'

Skelter exhaled smiling. 'Thank God for small mercies.'

'You seen her then,' Turbo said.

'She's here, but she didn't look unhappy about her situation. Looks like she's playing hide the salami with Wolfie.'

'That's awkward,' said Brick stroking his moustache. 'What about opposition?'

'I saw one rifle but there are two shelters in the trees. Might hold at least a dozen. I made a sketch map.' He showed them the notebook and went through all of what he had seen. 'Only one route in and it's far from perfect. The exit is a real problem. Unless we can secure all hostiles, we'll be sitting ducks, with an unwilling prisoner of our own in tow.'

'What about the plane, could you fly us out, Stan?' Brick asked

'If there's enough fuel in the tanks. Should be able to land at our strip. No vans waiting for us this time though and it's a bloody long walk.'

'What about your cell phone?' Skelter asked.

'Who can I call? Not like ringing a cab now is it? There's Laz as well, don't forget.'

'He'll take the boat back if we don't show up by midday tomorrow. His money is safe with Mitch, he knows that.'

'Still doesn't solve the problem of who to call.'

'Maria,' said Skelter. 'No brainer, it's her daughter.'

'Don't suppose Laz has a cellphone with him,' said Turbo.

'No signal out here and I don't have his number with me.'

'Okay, it's not perfect, but we're here now so show us the route in,' said Brick, chewing the stem of his unlit briar.

Skelter took a pencil to an empty page in his notebook. 'This is us, here. The edge of the mangrove curves to the East, like this. At a point just before we have eyes on the camp, we stash the canoes in the mangrove and wade in. The water is around two feet deep close to the swamp, but dry ground is only twenty feet away. This dead ground of shallow water is the only option. We crawl in the shallows to this point where there is cover on the dry land. A belt of scrub running thirty metres into a tree line. We can follow this to the back of the camp on the landward side. From there we approach the aircraft and the shelters under cover of the trees.'

'What distance?' Turbo asked.

'Sixty, sixty-five metres.'

'We'll be hidden from view but badly exposed to fire crawling through the water. Why not move through the mangrove?' said Brick.

'Not practical, look around - you can see how difficult it is. Four of us with assault equipment? They'd be bound to hear us.'

'So, two by two,' said Turbo.

'Sure. I'll go first with Brick; need to keep our pilot back until we know the score. You two cover us in, then we return the favour.' Skelter handed the sketch plan over for the men to scrutinise and slumped in his seat. He pulled a rifle cleaning kit from his pack and stripped the Armalite. Before the members of his team had reached consensus the reassembled weapon lay across his knees.

Turbo nodded to the other two who reciprocated. 'We're in.'

Skelter felt his heart lift and his body relax. 'Thanks, boys, I owe you, big time.'

31
Wolf's Will

Everglades
Monday, October 25th 2004

Wolf found Martin Neumann sitting beneath the wing of the aircraft, his foot heavily bandaged. 'How is it?'

'Like you give a shit, you fucking psychopath.' Neumann's tone matched the look he gave Wolf.

'Be careful, Martin, I have many more bullets than you have toes. Lack of respect by my workers will not be tolerated. Those with ideas above their position will be eliminated to protect the business, whatever it takes. It is nothing personal.'

The colour drained from Neumann's face.

'Let us begin again, Martin,' said Wolf placing a hand upon his shoulder, as his black eyes bored into Neumann's skull. 'Come,' he said, moving the hand to

Martin's elbow to help him up. His right hand held the rifle in a firm grip.

'Where are you taking me?'

'Somewhere more comfortable.'

'I'm okay here, really.'

Wolf shook his head. 'I insist,' he said, indicating the way with the barrel of his Armalite.

Neumann hobbled towards the shelter where he saw Eva lying in a hammock listening to a transistor radio through headphones. Wolf spoke again. 'What happened to your foot, was an accident. Eva knows this. If I hear anything from her that suggests otherwise…' Wolf tapped the rifle and smiled at Neumann.

The pilot did not return the smile.

'Eva, I think we should let Martin rest here. He will be more comfortable. It is the least I can do after such an unfortunate accident. Come, Chiquita, bring a blanket. We should leave Martin to rest in peace,' he said annunciating the last three words for the pilot's benefit.

Wolf led Eva to the Cessna where he laid the blanket on the floor of the cabin and invited her to join him.

32

Advance

Everglades,
Monday, October 25th 2004

Stan and Skelter in the lead, followed by the others fifteen feet astern, paddled strong and steady. They hugged the mangroves, Skelter's skin pouring sweat in sticky, humid air, the sun beating down on his bush-hat. Sweat ran down the nick of his arse. His crotch itched and chafed but discomfort was par for the course and no stranger to him. It was overridden by the joy of full support from his team in what they all recognised as a flawed enterprise. He was moved.

After paddling for what seemed like ages, Stan and Skelter allowed the canoe to drift into the edge of the mangrove and float to a stop. The others pulled alongside and, without a word, all four men disembarked and pushed their vessels into cover. They pulled on ops vests, checked weapons and equipment, went through individual, silent, pre-action rituals and psyched themselves up for the task ahead.

'Ready?' said Skelter.

Three heads nodded. Skelter placed a hand on a shoulder of each of the men in turn, then waded out of the trees to the edge of the swamp. Closely followed by Brick, he moved though the shallows, eyes glued to the edge of the mangrove as the dry land appeared across the open water. Skelter slowed, waded a couple of steps, stopped, listened and looked hard. He swished slowly forward again, stopped and lowered himself into the water, holding the binoculars aloft. He raised his head cautiously and put the binos to his eyes. He could just make out the roof of one of the shelters, beyond the edge of the mangrove trees. A white egret stood sentry duty at the top of the canopy. He could see no sign of life. Skelter stuffed the binos into a plastic bag he had scrounged from Turbo and settled down in the water. He turned to signal the second pair and then prepared to begin the crawl into no man's land.

The adrenaline tap had been opened a quarter turn and Skelter's heart pounded like a bass drum. His mouth was bone dry as he made like an alligator – elbows, knees and feet through the shallows. The weight of weapons and ammunition made progress difficult and uncomfortable in the dank atmosphere, as he struggled to fill his lungs with air and not brackish water. He gritted his teeth and inched forward. *Don't look up, stay low, stay low and keep moving.* Fighting the urge to take a peek was a major challenge, but he managed to keep his focus. *Not too far, Buddha. Look out for us, boy, we need all the help we can get right now.*

The foul, salt-slicked water sloshed against his chin as Skelter elbowed his way, tight lipped, through the muddy detritus of the swamp, towards the point where the scrub line kissed the shore. He was tiring. Only twenty-five metres to go. Might as well be twenty-five hundred. He had to catch his breath and stopped long enough to suck in several huge lungful's of air before Brick tapped on his ankle. One last gulp, then mouth shut and he dug his elbows in. Adrenaline drove him forward until, with shaking legs and aching arms, he clawed his way to the exit point. Skelter turned to look back towards Turbo and Stan, but he was too low to see them. Hauling his tired bones onto dry land he slithered into the low scrub.

Skelter could not see Brick, but he was aware of his presence close behind and cautiously raised his head. The aircraft's tail was less than twenty metres away. Beyond it to the right, hidden in the trees, were the two reed-thatched shelters. The guard remained beneath the wing, sitting on the ground with his back to Skelter. He looked beyond the man, towards the spot where they had left Turbo and Stan. *Shit, too low.* Skelter looked around for somewhere he could get to his feet without the risk of being seen. *It's all going to rat shit.* At that moment, Brick crawled up alongside him, sweating heavily under the cumbersome weight of equipment. He had a shotgun in his hands and an Armalite slung across his back. He pointed to where they had left Stan and Turbo, placed the shotgun beside Skelter and pointed to his eyes, then the point where they had crawled out of the water. Skelter nodded as a wave of relief relaxed his facial muscles. Brick slid away. He would retrace far enough to have eyes on the others, without exposing himself. All Skelter had to do was stay put.

The next several nerve-wracking minutes left Skelter feeling vulnerable. No escape route, no cover from fire, only enough for concealment – no idea of enemy strength or capability. His heart hammered into the dirt, sweat ran down his back and steam began to rise from his shirt and pants as the hot afternoon sun dried the cotton twill. *Hadn't thought of that. You are really slipping boy.* He itched in every crease and cranny but daren't scratch. He risked a quick look around. Still no sign of anyone, other than the man under the wing. No sound above that of the local wildlife. He inched his body into a position where he could turn his head to face the route they had taken from the water's edge.

It seemed like a lifetime before he spotted a slight movement in the vegetation. Brick was back. He crept alongside, reclaimed the shotgun and inched his way into a position to cover the shelters. The next fifteen minutes stretched to eternity. Skelter was burning adrenaline with the brakes locked on, lying like the coiled spring of a cocked rifle, waiting for someone to squeeze the trigger.

At long last he caught a flash of movement at the edge of the water. The boys had arrived. He detected further movement at the edge of his peripheral vision. The guard was on his feet – on his feet and heading his way, weapon in hand. The man was fumbling with his zip. He found what he was looking for as he reached the edge of the canopy covering the aircraft. He stood relaxed, rifle in the crook of his arm and began to relieve himself. The relaxed stance lasted only seconds. The man stiffened, craned his neck and advanced a few paces towards the point where Stan and Turbo were about to exit the water. He stopped, raised his rifle and shouted something in Spanish. Whatever it was he didn't get to finish it. Three rounds from Brick's quick fire Atchisson saw to that. The dense plastic baton rounds struck the man centre mass. He jerked backwards with a gasp as he and his rifle hit the ground.

The spring holding Skelter in check had been released, the trigger squeezed. He leapt to his feet and ran to the plane and reached the door as Wolf's head poked out. The man's face was off the scale in the surprised stakes – he froze. Skelter's eyes registered the pistol in the man's hand, the message reached his brain, bounced back and fired along his sinews to hands that smashed the steel barrel of his rifle onto Wolf's wrist. The scream stopped as Skelter slammed the butt into the man's gut, knocking him back into the fuselage. Skelter leapt after him and swept the interior with his weapon. Eva screamed, cowering in a corner clutching a T-Shirt to cover herself. It was only then that Skelter registered that the winded Wolf was also naked.

Brick appeared in the door. 'Okay, H?'

'Yep. The guard?'

'Cuffed and ankled. Shall I do this one?' he said looking at the wheezing nudist.

'Please.'

Brick grabbed the man's wrist. He started to resist but a bone jarring backhand changed his attitude.

Eva screamed. 'Stop, stop it. Who are you?'

'Get dressed, and shut your mouth,' said Skelter.

Brick completed his task in seconds. He did not respond to Eva.

A burst of automatic gunfire erupted outside. Skelter jumped out and hit the dirt.

Turbo sprinted up to join him. 'Just keeping their heads down,' he said, the rifle still smoking in his hands.

'Where's Stan?'

'He's behind you,' said the man himself.

'Oh no he isn't,' mimicked Turbo.

'Pack it in, Widow Twanky.' Skelter turned to Stan. Too late; the man had already disappeared into the aircraft.

33
Take Off

Everglades
Monday, October 25th 2004

There was movement in the nearest shelter but no incoming fire.

'They'll not be too keen on shooting at the plane,' Skelter said. 'They won't want to hurt Wolfie. Just keep an eye out until Stan can get us away.' Skelter jumped back into the Cessna.

'What about laughing-boy?' Brick asked.

'Just watch him for now.' He went forward. The sound of the engine turning over killed his question to Stan.

'All aboard,' the pilot said.

Skelter raced back to the door. 'Turbo.'

'Roger that.' Turbo stood up, fired a burst of

discouragement into the roof of the shelter, then jumped aboard.

Skelter grabbed Wolf by the ankles. 'Brick.'

The big man nodded and grabbed the prisoner under his arms. Together they heaved him through the door. They had already started to move when Brick swung the door shut, and sat on the bare cargo floor, grinning like a maniac. 'That was easier than I expected.'

Skelter dashed forward and threw himself into the co-pilot's seat.

Stan lined up the plane and opened the throttle wide. The airframe shook and rattled as it strained against the brakes. 'Hold on,' he yelled, not that it was necessary. He released the brakes and the plane kicked forward into the growing blizzard of dust and fine plant debris. They gathered speed and rocketed down the strip.

Eyes glued to their flight path, Skelter offered a high-speed prayer, his white knuckles gripping the seat and Buddha. The end of the strip drew nearer and nearer and still Stan held the stick perpendicular. Sweat streamed down Skelter's face. Fear of losing control of his bladder flashed through his mind. The water beyond the strip expanded to fill the windscreen of the vibrating cockpit. The scariest Disney World ride ever – for real.

'We're not going to make it,' Skelter said, his words drowned by the engine noise, as Stan hauled back on the stick. With inches to spare, they lifted off, the blast from the prop whipping up spray from the water. Skelter's heart hammered like a machine gun with a runaway belt. *Buddha, Buddha, Buddha...* They were not clear yet. Smack in their path, a majestic line of tall swamp cypress stretched towards the heavens.

The plane clawed skywards in slow motion, while

hurtling forwards like a bullet towards the tree line. Frozen in concentration, Stan's face streamed with sweat. The muscles in his forearms at tearing point as he pulled at the stick with every ounce of strength he possessed.

Skelter squeezed his buttocks together, prayed louder and faster, as he gripped Buddha for all he was worth. He felt a thump as the undercarriage whipped through the wispy top of one of the trees. They were over. He let out a huge sigh, tears of relief cutting through the grime on his cheeks. 'Great job, Stan boy, brilliant. Way better than expected. Piece of piss. Yeah.' Skelter punched the air, hitting the cockpit ceiling. 'Sorry,' he said. They dropped below the tops of the tallest cypress and Stan throttled back as far as he dared.

'Need to climb in a couple of minutes to get my bearings,' he yelled above the engine.

Skelter's reply never made it past his throat. The aircraft jerked, as if it had been hit by anti-aircraft fire. The windscreen exploded in a cloud of white, peppered with crimson. Stan grunted as the egret smashed through the windshield into his the face. The plane nosedived.

The silence confused Skelter, the complete absence of sound. Unable to move, he struggled to make sense of what little he could see. They were moving very slowly upward. Water, water everywhere. Water above his head, wetting his hair. *Holy shit. We're upside down, sinking. Where's the buckle? Where's the bloody buckle? Don't panic. Steady does it. Follow the strap. That's the way. Got it.* The seat belt fell away, and he dropped headfirst into the swamp water, surfacing a nano-second later as Stan disappeared into the murky green. Skelter fumbled for the belt and found the buckle. He yanked the quick release and pulled the unconscious pilot clear of immediate danger. Noises from behind. 'Everybody all right?'

'Just about, fanks. Brick's got a shiner. Lass seems ok.'

'Gimme a hand, Stan's out cold.'

Brick appeared behind and above Skelter, sitting on the roof on the inside of the fuselage, legs braced against the remains of the bulkhead. Skelter pushed while he pulled, aided by Turbo. With considerable difficulty they dragged Stan into the back as far as the door. The tail was at thirty degrees to the horizontal and above the water.

Eva was in shock, eyes vacant, clutching a cargo strap with both hands, as if her life depended upon it.

'What happened?' asked Turbo.

Skelter pulled something from Stan's shirt front. It was a mess of soggy white feathers. 'How's that for shit luck?'

Stan began to stir. His eyes opened 'What the f… ?'

Skelter waved the feathers.

'Bastard.'

'Can you move?'

Stan nodded. 'Think so.'

'Let's get you out of here. She's settled on the bottom, I think. Not deep. Help him out. I need to get my weapon.'

'Where are you taking me?' said Eva.

'To your mother. Do as I tell you and don't cause trouble.'

'I don't –'

'Shut it, or I'll tape it shut.' Skelter said as he turned to climb down the slope into the submerged front. He lowered himself into the mangled mess that had been the cockpit, took a big breath and pulled himself below the surface. Visibility was zero because of the mud and debris. He fumbled and felt amongst the twisted wreck. He came up for air three times without success. On the fourth attempt, he located and successfully retrieved the weapon.

Outside the plane, knee deep in swamp, Skelter took in the surroundings and assessed the situation. They had crashed near the edge of open water. Ahead was more of the same, behind them – a thin line of tall cypress trees. More cypress to the left: smaller, closer and more dense. The most promising option. Skelter checked Stan out. The pilot appeared much improved and more aware. The egret had left him with an egg-sized lump on his temple and a badly bruised cheek.

'Got your GPS, Stan?'

'He held out his hand. And it's working. What do you reckon?'

'Less than two hours of daylight left. We'll not get far. Need to hole up for the night, look for the canoes in the morning. Best we can do.' Skelter took his water bottle from his vest and shook it.

'Arf a bottle,' said Turbo.

'Bit less,' said Brick.

'Bout the same,' said Skelter, 'back up in the canoes. How far from the camp?'

'Under two miles,' Stan said, checking the GPS.

'Right, let's get moving before the bad guys turn up. Couldn't find your weapon, Stan, sorry.'

'Take this,' said Brick, handing him the Colt. 'Here.'

He handed over the spare magazines.

Stan took the rifle and slung it over his shoulder. 'This way,' he said.

They waded off in single file. Stan in front, with the GPS. Turbo, then Eva, tucked in the middle. Brick brought up the rear.

'Correct me if I'm wrong,' said Turbo, 'but isn't this swamp full of alligators?'

'Nah,' said Stan. 'If it were full, there'd be no room for the snakes.'

'Cheers for that. Rubbish landing by the way,' said Turbo.

'Thanks a bunch, you can drive next time.'

They had travelled no more than a few sluggish paces when Skelter stumbled and tripped over an obstacle hidden beneath the swirling sediment thrown up by their feet. He struggled to his feet. 'This is no good, can't see where I'm treading. Change to arrowhead.'

Stan remained on course, Brick moved two paces right, Turbo left. Skelter grabbed Eva and dragged her behind and left of Turbo. 'Keep this line so you can see where you're putting your feet.'

She complied in sulky silence.

Skelter moved right to wade behind, and right of Brick's path. The clouds of muddy water that billowed up to obscure the bottom were now less of a problem. The undisturbed water to his right was shallow and clear enough to see the bottom. Clear enough to spot the alligator lying motionless under the surface a few metres away. He kept a close eye on the three-foot reptile but said nothing, for fear of causing panic.

34

Hunters and Hunted

Everglades
Monday, October 25th 2004

Lying in the dirt at the edge of the airstrip, his skin a mass of bloody grazes and lacerations, Wolf was incandescent with rage. The dust storm from the backwash of the propeller stung his eyes. What hurt him most, though, was his pride. He tried to get to his feet, but instantly realised that would not be possible until he could untie his feet. A scream of frustration died in his throat, behind the duct tape covering his mouth. Wolf reached for it with his cable-tied hands and tore it from his face. 'You will die for this, gringos,' he screamed at the sky. 'Whoever you are, I will find you and make you pay.' He tugged at the Velcro strap around his ankles, oblivious to the pain.

Wolf heard the engine pop and stop, followed by a crash, as the plane ploughed into the swamp. He immediately looked, but there was no sign, no smoke, wreckage, nothing. They must have gone in beyond the cypress trees. Not much over a mile away. After a minute of frantic tugging, he freed his legs and stood up. He hobbled towards the shelters, his bare feet burning from the heat of the dirt. The sound of a commotion somewhere inside reached his ears and, as he drew near, he called out. A chorus of replies came back. Men came running out, brandishing weapons, but they were a sorry-looking bunch.

After a couple of minutes, someone found a knife and wire-snips and cut the cable ties. 'Water,' he demanded, 'get me a gun.'

Two of the men offered their rifles. Wolf grabbed the nearest one and staggered into the building to look for water. One of them thrust a bottle at him. He gulped a big swig, swilled his mouth, spat it into the earth and then gorged himself. 'Wait here,' said Wolf, as he ran across to the shelter to grab a pair of shorts and a T-shirt from a makeshift washing line. He pulled them on, then trotted back to the waiting men. 'The boats, get the boats, quick now. Follow me.' Wolf led the way, fuelled by the fire of adrenaline, stoked with desire for retribution. 'If they did not die in the crash, they will wish they had.'

Not all of Wolf's men shared their leader's enthusiasm, but he was oblivious. Some, however, were up for teaching the interlopers a lesson. They pushed the boats into the swamp and piled into the flat-bottomed craft.

'Over there, make for the trees,' said Wolf, pointing at the grey-bleached cypress trunks rising out of the still water. 'Paddle, you lazy bastards, paddle, faster.'

The men put maximum effort in, most driven by fear of Wolf's unpredictable violence. No one wanted to wind up like Martin Neumann. He was the pilot. Wolf needed him. The rest of them were expendable. The boats scudded across the flat open water, nosing through the dense mass of lilies and water hyacinth, towards the cypress line.

Now that Skelter could see the bottom, progress picked up – it needed to. He fiddled with Buddha, as he waded forward. *Thanks, Bud, for getting us out in one piece. Stay with me, I'm going to need you. Those guys are bound to have boats and they'll be well pissed off.*

Less than three hundred metres away, the trees teased them with the promise of sanctuary within the dense vegetation that fought for space amongst grey cypress trunks. Rafts of floating plants peppered the surface, slowing progress and obscuring the bottom until, with one hundred and fifty metres to go, the rafts fused into a contiguous carpet as the water became shallower. Soon it was less than calf deep. This made things much easier as they were able to step clear of the swamp and increase their stride. Every half-dozen steps or so, Skelter looked back towards the crash site and beyond it, to the line of cypress trees, for any sign of Wolf's crew. They made it into the trees without incident and climbed over a fallen cypress, onto relatively dry land. The men went to ground, instinctively facing the area of perceived danger.

Eva flopped in the sawgrass at the base of a dwarf fan palm. 'I'm thirsty,' she said.

Skelter offered her his water bottle, but kept a firm grip on it. 'Just a sip, we don't have much.' He put it to her lips, and she took a swallow. It was all she got. Skelter ignored the hostile glare.

'He will come for me,' she said, 'and when he does…'

'He'll wish he'd stayed at home,' said Skelter, turning away to confer with the others. 'We'll stay put for now, boys. We can watch the approaches from here. If they come,' he checked himself, 'when they come, we can either use them for target practice, withdraw to the interior or both. Remember we're civvies, so try not to kill anyone, just put enough rounds in to sink whatever boats they have.'

'We on overtime, H?'

'Fuck's sake, Turbo.'

When his boat reached the tree line, Wolf saw the tail of the aircraft sticking out of the water. 'Slowly now, there may be survivors. No one shoots unless I say so, you hear?'

A rippled 'yes, boss,' issued from a wave of nodding heads, accompanied by a chorus of rifle bolts driving live rounds into empty chambers.

Wolf knelt in the bow, looking at the mangled airplane through the sights of his rifle, finger twitching over the trigger.

Skelter watched them break through the trees. Two flat-bottomed craft, six in each, four men paddling, two with weapons at the ready. Skelter followed them through the binos as they approached the wrecked aircraft. As they got close to it, Skelter could clearly see Wolf kneeling in the lead boat, a rifle tucked into his shoulder.

'Get alongside,' Wolf ordered the man at the helm. 'Manuel, inside.'

Manuel took a pistol from one of the crew. He hesitated.

'Inside, I said.'

Manuel cocked the weapon and released the safety catch.

'What are you waiting for,' said Wolf, jabbing him with the barrel of his rifle.

Manuel stuck the pistol through the doorway, thrust his head in after it and jerked it out again. He repeated this twice more before he climbed in to explore. Wolf followed close behind.

The sound of automatic gunfire ripped through the peaceful surroundings, sending a flock of birds squawking skywards. Wolf tore the magazine from the weapon, replaced it with a fresh one and emptied that into the cockpit in a few seconds

'Someone's pissed off,' Turbo whispered in Skelter's ear, as the antagonists swarmed around the plane like angry ants. One man disappeared into the wreck, followed closely by Wolf.

'Good boy, Wolfie,' said Skelter with relish, 'any minute now.'

'H?' said Brick.

'I told you he would come,' said Eva.

Manuel slid down the plywood floor towards the cockpit. He yelped as something caught across his throat. A loose wire from somewhere. A taut wire in fact. He heard a sharp crack, but its significance did not register. Wolf heard it too. Like Manuel he had no idea what it was, not, that is, until the grenade detonated four seconds later.

Turbo put a hand to his mouth to stifle the laughter as clouds of white smoke billowed through the door of the fuselage. It seemed ages before the two men emerged, hands to their mouths as they stumbled blindly and tumbled into the water. They staggered around, clawing at their faces as the CS gas did its itching, blinding work.

Eva gasped 'What… You bastards.' The last words Eva would utter for some time. Brick clamped a hand over her mouth and Turbo strapped her wrists together with a cable tie. He finished the job with a strip of duct tape across her mouth.

'Nice one, H.'

'Cheers, Turbo,' said Skelter.

Wolf convulsed, coughed and retched, still wheezing and clawing at his eyes twenty minutes after the booby trap had sprung. The air was blue with expletives. The men became agitated and anxious. Wolf's continued humiliation made him volatile, liable to lash out at any unfortunate soul within range. When he recovered, he ordered them to make towards the nearest patch of forest, reasoning that that was the most logical place to start the search. Manuel tried to reason with Wolf. 'We should move away from here. If we go after them, they will kill us all.'

'You yellow snake. We go now.'

'We're sitting ducks out here, Lope.'

'Coward, I will shoot you myself.' Wolf ranted, his eyes ablaze with hate.

Despite the threats, Manuel persisted with his old friend. 'These are bad asses, boss, pros, mercenaries. If we leave, we can come back along the tree line where they cannot see us. They are watching us. I can feel it. They have us in their sights. Make them think they have scared us off. We will have the advantage.

Wolf was fuming, but he wasn't stupid and Manuel had been his friend for a very long time. He trusted him. Decision made.

The boats left the crash site and headed away, parallel to the shoreline. After half an hour, they switched course for land and made it to the edge of the forest, just as the curtain of darkness fell. Wolf put Manuel in charge of the lead vessel. Wolf was no fool. He wanted to wreak vengeance upon these mysterious mercenaries, but he had no intention of dying in the process. He waited until Manuel had put twenty feet between them before he ordered his crew to paddle. They hugged the shoreline the way a tight dress clings to a supermodel.

35
Swamp Rats

Everglades
Monday, October 25th 2004

Skelter watched the hunters through his binoculars as they paddled away to his left, parallel to the shoreline. He followed them until they disappeared beyond the curve of the forest's edge. 'They know we're here,' he said, 'my guess is they'll hook around and tuck in tight to the tree line and try to sneak up on us. They won't risk coming ashore, too noisy in this jungle.'

The others nodded in agreement and they all went into a huddle. 'Brick, Turbo, take the shotguns, deploy five metres apart. Stan, move up ten metres beyond them. Take a torch, it'll be dark in twenty minutes. Flash a light now and again, give them something to focus on. If we're lucky, they'll think that's where we are. I'll be

218

ten down from Brick, waiting for them to pass me. Brick, you and Turbo initiate the ambush. Hit the crews with plastic bullets. I'll follow up with flash bangs, so be prepared. After that, just wade in. Stan, soon as it goes noisy, feel free to join in.'

'Cheers, I accept your kind invitation.'

'They'll come up close to the shore and they won't be using lights, not when they think they've got the drop on us. We'll only get one shot and they will be switched on. Questions?'

'Prisoners?' said Brick.

'Disarm, disable. Cable ties, duct tape – wrists only. We'll leave them to find their own way home. That it? Right got a torch, Stan?'

'Yep.'

'On your way, then.'

Skelter checked his pockets for cable ties – half a dozen and a roll of tape. He dropped two flash bangs in his right side pocket and the one remaining CS gas grenade in the left, then checked his weapon and magazines. After a slow steady crawl to the water's edge he slid his feet in as the others faded into the tangle of undergrowth behind him. Wading into the swamp, he followed the course the boats had taken. Visibility over the water was excellent in the moonlight, forcing him to keep in the shadows, close to the trees. Eyes trained on the distant shadowy vegetation for signs of movement, Skelter crept from one cypress trunk to another. Rifle at the ready, palms sweating, he prayed he would not need to use it. After sixteen paces, he climbed out of the water onto a stump with a rotting toppled trunk still hanging onto it by a shred of timber. Skelter settled behind it to watch. Soaked with sweat and swamp water, he stank like a sewer. Hunger gnawed at his stomach. He pictured Lucy working away to bring order to the chaos of cardboard boxes and tea chests in their new home and could smell the tikka masala takeaway. He reached into his pocket and fondled Buddha's bald pate. *How will she react when she discovers what we've had been up to, buddy? Best not to worry, eh? Just focus on getting everyone back in one piece. You know the chances of getting away with this without law enforcement sticking their oar in is fading fast, don't you?* Skelter looked up to the sky and gave himself a brief reality check. *Should I be worried about you, Buddha, buddy? Are you becoming a bit too real? What would Judith make of our relationship do you think?* Skelter sighed aloud. *Maybe my time with Judith isn't over after all.*

Stan's light flashed, flickered and died. A minute later, it flashed again. Just for good measure the sound of swearing rippled across the swamp. Pure theatricals, no way he had a problem. Skelter could only wait for a reaction.

Manuel knew the men they hunted might still hold the initiative, lying silent somewhere in the undergrowth, ready to slaughter them at the touch of a trigger. Perched right up in the bow, eyes and ears tuned into the sounds of the night, he was not happy. Wolf would get them all killed before he would give up.

The crew dipped their paddles with infinite care, scared of making a sound, as the boat glided along the line of the cypress grove, Manuel's the only finger on a trigger. Silent and slow they might be, but they were not invisible. They were the sacrificial lamb. The moonlight made them perfect targets. Manuel prayed hard for clouds. To make matters worse, discipline had gone to the dogs in Wolf's boat.

A flashlight beam flicked on and off, accompanied by low cursing.

After forty-five minutes lying in the dark, ears and eyes strained to snapping point, Skelter began to doubt the plan. He squeezed Buddha with his left hand and prayed. *C'mon, you arseholes. Where are they, Buddha? This has to work. Without the boats, we are well and truly buggered.*

Stan's torch had flashed a few times since, no doubt to give them a better chance to pinpoint his position. He made a fair bit of noise splashing and cursing. Skelter hoped it was part of the pantomime. *Don't overdo it, Stan, for fuck's sake, don't want them twigging it. Why would we risk giving ourselves away? They might...* A sound − faint, different; not natural. Almost lost, swallowed up by the chorus of night creatures. Water slapping against... A boat hull? Skelter tuned his ears to the noise, filtered out the collective clamour of nocturnal wildlife. Most of his military career had revolved around small boats. That unmistakable sound. He gave Buddha a quick squeeze for luck, took his hand out of his pocket and pulled a flash bang from his ops vest.

Excited by the sight of the light waving ahead, Wolf's crew were sure they had the upper hand. Driven by his desire for blood, Wolf also let his guard slip. He focussed on the intermittent beam, salivating at the prospect of revenge. Soon he would teach these gringos a lesson. In his excitement, he uttered an oath aloud.

Manuel cursed Wolf under his breath. His boss was a liability. Shut them up, mother of Jesus. Madness, sheer madness. He was almost beside himself, torn between straining his eyes and ears for the enemy and turning about to confront Wolf and his noisy crew.

The cussing dropped to a whisper as the searchers closed on the light flashing intermittently over the water. Ten minutes passed. Skelter slid as far forward as he dared. He spotted the silhouette of a boat, low to the water, indistinct at first, then the edges sharpened in the moonlight. Whispers floated over the water. He shrank back deeper into the undergrowth and turned around to see or, rather, not see the dense wall of vegetation. A curtain of darkness greeted him, his night vision temporarily lost from staring at the flashlight beam. He groped his way into the massive tangle of logs and roots. The searchers got closer. Skelter's heart rate soared as the adrenaline pumped and anxiety gnawed at his gut. To move at all was difficult enough, doing it silently – an almost impossible task. Aware of the closing hostiles, he burrowed into the web of roots and foliage, covered his face and lay still, no more than ten feet from the water's edge.

The sound of the paddles. He held his breath, and tightened the grip on his weapon, almost deafened by the thump of his own captive heart, beating against the bars that were his ribcage.

They wanted blood but, to Skelter, they were about as frightening as a boatload of blue rinsed tourists. He might have felt sorry for them, but for the circumstances. If the gloves had been off, they would be toast, but they were not. These men would kill without thinking, to protect their business, and he could not afford the luxury of meeting fire with fire. He had to defeat them with guile and cunning and plastic bullets.

What's new, Buddha, boy? We've been here before. Belfast, Bogside – baton rounds against snipers and bombers. Rules of engagement that might have been written by the IRA. Threat of court martial hanging over us like Damocles' sword, and no one holding the reins on the Provos. They never had gloves to hamper them.

36
Ambush

Everglades
Monday/Tuesday, October 25th/26th 2004

The seconds ticked away. The first boat glided across Skelter's eye line, less than twenty feet away. He counted seven heads silhouetted against the moonlit water. The second craft slid by three hull lengths astern. *Perfect, bloody perfect. Any moment now – ten, nine, eight.* He shifted from his prone position to peer over the fallen trunk, instead of under it. The second boat was still visible against the water, with the lead craft's outline merging to form a single silhouette. *Four, three,* Skelter pulled the pin from the flash bang and steadied himself.

The hairs bristled on the back of Manuel's neck as an icy shiver ran down his spine. Inside his chest, his heart pounded like a piston.

Wolf nearly wet himself with excitement, convinced he was minutes away from unleashing an orgy of violent vengeance upon his tormentors. Alive with adrenaline, he gripped his rifle so tight, he almost stopped the circulation in his fingers.

His world exploded in a blast of noise and blaze of blinding, orange muzzle flashes.

Screams joined the noise of gunfire, as the tightly packed crews buckled under a hail of dense plastic bullets pouring into them at over 300 metres a second from point blank range. In less than eight-seconds, forty solid plastic batons smashed into the bodies, with devastating results.

Something thumped the fore-stock of Wolf's Armalite slamming him into one of his men, pitching them into the bottom of the boat with a violent thud. Men yelped and cursed as baton rounds blasted many overboard into the swamp. Others fell on top of Wolf in the deafening chorus of sustained gunfire.

Skelter lobbed the stun grenade into the convulsing mass aboard the nearest vessel. Screams, splashes as men floundered in the water. He yelled 'grenade' and shut his eyes tight. The white magnesium light still penetrated his eyelids, and the bang rendered him deaf, as he knew it would. Eyes open again, he jumped into the swamp and ploughed into the now silent chaos, grabbing the nearest man by his hair and pulling the unfortunate wretch under the water.

Before Wolf could react, the grenade's bucket of instant sunshine blinded and deafened him. His brain seized; he ceased to function.

Manuel found himself without a weapon and in danger of drowning. His shoulder burned with a sharp pain from the impact of whatever had smacked him overboard. Survival instinct kicked in and propelled him forward as, gripped by panic, he splashed away from the chaos. Seconds later, a figure loomed out of the darkness bang in front of him.

The instant the ambush triggered, Stan leapt into the shallows and waded towards the mayhem. The flash of a grenade threw up the silhouette of a figure blundering towards him. Stan slammed his fist into the man's face knocking him off his feet with a splash. He dragged the body from the water and taped the man's wrists behind his back, before he could recover.

The boys swarmed over the dazed victims, yelling and brow beating, cable-tying wrists at pistol point, dominating and subduing the disorientated enemy before they could recover their wits. It was quick and brutal.

Once trussed, the boys crammed the sorry-looking bunch into the lead boat. Skelter counted nine men. For good measure, they stuck duct tape over their eyes. They collected the weapons and put these in the rear boat, along with all the ammunition. The subdued gang members huddled together, shocked and dazed – all except Wolf. Skelter dragged him to one side and made him kneel in the swamp, cuffed and blindfolded. As soon as he was sure that the boys had everything under control, he dragged Wolf away to the spot with the log from where he had watched the boats. He pushed the man onto the land, taped his mouth over and forced him to roll under the log. He pressed the muzzle of his rifle into the man's cheek. 'Stay put if you want to live, amigo, comprende?'

Wolf said nothing, didn't even react.

'Poor bastard, you can't hear a bloody thing, can you? Near blind too, I'll bet?' Skelter waded back to the others.

'Brick, fetch the girl, will you, soon as you're done?'

He nodded and said something. Skelter stabbed a finger in his ear and waggled it in a vain to hasten the return of his hearing. *It'll come, patience, boy, at least the ringing's stopped.* Turbo slapped him on the back. The little man's grin dissected his face. Skelter flashed his happy face at him, relieved that no one appeared to have been too seriously hurt, a strange and bizarre addition to his combat experience. *We did it, Buddha, boy. We did it.*

Stan splashed in, dragging a terrified looking Manuel. 'Caught this one trying to leave.'

'Cheers, Stan,' said Skelter.

Brick appeared, dragging the girl. Eva's eyes were wide and staring. 'What have you done? Where is Lope? If you have hurt…'

'Somebody tape it shut,' said Skelter. Brick obliged. 'Get in the boat.' The look he gave her got a result. She climbed aboard.

'Get them ashore,' said Skelter. Stan, Turbo and Brick hauled the prisoners out and bundled them onto dry land. 'Stan, how long will it take them to get back to camp.'

'Bit of a squeeze in the one boat, but couple of hours at most, I should think, once they've worked themselves free.'

Skelter thumbed off the safety catch. 'Without the boat?'

'Most of the day,' he said, 'if they're lucky.'

Skelter raised the Armalite, switched the fire selector to automatic and emptied the magazine through the floor of the hull. Thirty high velocity bullets tore through the aluminium like a hot meat skewer through cooking foil. 'Perfect,' he said, the acrid gun smoke stinging his nostrils as the water poured in through the peppered aluminium skin. 'Time to go.'

Skelter's boys had retrieved a total of five paddles from the boats, but he did not think it wise to trust Eva with one. They also found two flashlights in their boat, and, crucially, two bottles of water. When they had paddled beyond earshot of the gang members, Skelter passed the water around and cut Eva's restraints. She ripped the tape from her mouth without a murmur and sat in stony silence.

'Don't suppose we got much chance of finding Laz in the dark?' said Skelter to Stan.

'No, but he'll be fine. He knows to go back and wait twenty-four hours with the van. I left a note for my partner about the boats in any case.'

Skelter turned to Stan, who, by default, was elected navigator. 'Home, then. Good work, boys, smooth as a well lubed dildo. No trouble?'

'Only the one that Stan lamped, he kicked off a bit,' said Brick, 'Must have been the only one who didn't take any hits. Stan gave him another smack and he got the message.'

With the GPS, all they had to do in theory was follow a compass bearing, but the terrain would not allow it. They knew where they wanted to be, but had to deviate every few minutes to circumvent stands of cypress trees, dense tangles of mangrove and the odd bit of land here and there. When they reached an area remote from any islands or patches of dry land, Skelter told the men to stop paddling and strip the confiscated weapons and scatter the parts into the swamp. After a couple more hours paddling, they pulled into a patch of cypress and, taking it in turns to keep watch, they at last managed to snatch some sleep.

The sky lightened in the East and the trees morphed from black silhouettes into three dimensional colour. Progress became easier and quicker.

'How are we doing, Stan?' Skelter asked.

'Half an hour, forty minutes, might get there before Gerry opens up.'

'That your partner?'

'Yeah. Don't worry, he knows how to keep his mouth shut. Ex 82nd airborne, he's sound.'

'Looking forward to seeing the wife, Stan?' said Turbo, as he dug his paddle through the floating vegetation.

'She'll be pissed off big time. But with luck, she'll let me live.'

The remark raised a chuckle. Things were settling down. The end was in sight.

37
Howling Wolf

Everglades
Tuesday, October 26th 2004

Humiliated in front of his men, for the second time in a few hours, by a bunch of strangers, had Wolf seething. Who were these people? Didn't they know who they were dealing with? He struggled to stand, trying in vain, to free his hands from behind. He succeeded only in inflicting pain as the cable ties cut into his wrists. He scraped his cheek across the rough bark of the fallen cypress trunk to remove the duct tape from his mouth. After several painful frustrating minutes, he rolled back a corner. Once he had, it was not long before he cleared the gag from his bloodied and bruised lips

'Miguel, Manuel, Bernardo,' Wolf called out, as he

staggered into the swamp to make his way back.

'Is that you, Boss?'

'Si,' he replied 'where are... Manuel.' Wolf greeted the man who emerged from the dense vegetation at the edge. 'They have gone?'

'Yes, Boss.'

Wolf struggled from the water. 'Cut these handcuffs off me,' he demanded. The men lying in the vegetation were in no position to help, being handcuffed, not to mention battered and bruised from plastic bullets and concussion grenades.

'Does nobody have a knife? What was the shooting? Who did they shoot?' The men looked scared for good reason. Wolf's short fuse had been getting shorter since he sampled his own merchandise.

'The boat.' A man nodded to where the sunken craft was just visible below the surface.

'Bastards.' Wolf stamped his feet and kicked out. He went berserk with the inevitable result for a tired, battered man with hands secured behind his back; he fell over, onto his face. The short ripple of ill-advised laughter died, but Wolf's renewed tantrums just made matters worse. His authority had all but evaporated. He had to regain control. Summoning every ounce of his willpower, he got back up, went into the water and climbed aboard the sunken boat. He sat in the middle up to his chest and sawed the cable tie on his wrist backwards and forwards, on the side of the aluminium seat. It took a while and it hurt, but the result was worth it, for in the land of the blind, the one eyed man is king. Wolf intended to reclaim his crown.

'What we gonna do, Boss?' Asked Manuel, as he climbed into the boat to follow Wolf's example.

'Do? Do? We going to find these bastards and slice them into pieces; little tiny pieces.'

'But how…'

Wolf stopped the man in his tracks with a look. By now, eight sorry-looking bedraggled specimens in cable tie handcuffs stood before him.

'What boats are left at the camp?' A murmured discussion followed a short silence. 'How many boats?'

'Two,' I think, said one.

'You think?'

'Canoes. Two small canoes is all, Boss.'

'Move it, back to camp. Now.'

There was a general reluctance to move among the demoralised men. Three had sustained significant injuries in the ambush, a few were still in shock. Wolf could feel his authority slipping further. 'I said move.' His voice sounded camp, the result of swollen lips. He had no gun to threaten them with. He could not shoot someone's toes off this time. 'Stay here and die then, pussies.'

Wolf waded out in the general direction of the camp. Just five men followed him, the rest – exhausted and injured from baton rounds and rifle butts – stayed put.

Wolf and his followers splashed and crashed through the swamp, more likely to scare away alligators, than attract them. It was less hazardous than it appeared as alligator attacks upon humans were not common, and snakes rarely bite unless threatened.

Mosquitos plagued them for the five hours it took to get back and drag their exhausted bodies ashore and collapse on the ground.

Skin covered in bites and blistered from the sun, Wolf's first thought was for water. He drank his fill from the store in the shelter and went to check the boats. 'Where is the other canoe? Where are the paddles?'

'The paddles are here, under the tarp,' said Manuel, lifting the green woven plastic sheet. 'The canoes were together.'

Wolf looked at the kayak. There were blood spots beside it in the dirt. 'Martin Neumann.' Wolf spat at the ground. 'Manuel, you will come with me in the canoe.'

'Yes, Boss. Now, Boss?'

'No, eat first.'

'I make food, yes Boss?' It was Miguel, little wiry Miguel, with a face like a rat.

Wolf nodded. 'Yes, do it, I'm hungry. I need to find clothes.' He walked away towards the second shelter, the one reserved for himself and Eva, or whatever woman he had at the time. There were three hammocks for sleeping – complete with mosquito nets – a plastic table and four chairs and a raised platform, with a mattress, for not sleeping. Under the platform, was a crude, wooden cupboard with twin doors. Wolf dialled the padlock combination and opened the doors. He took out lightweight cotton trousers with a leather belt, a T-shirt and a pair of rubber-soled boots. An old biscuit tin contained two cell phones with a charger each, a Colt .45 automatic and half a box of ammunition. He tucked the Colt into his waistband and tipped the dozen bullets into his pocket. He tried the phones, but both batteries were dead. The T-shirt was large and baggy, but he doubted the weapon would go unnoticed amongst his crew. From the back of the cupboard, he pulled out a waterproof money belt and strapped it around his waist.

When he returned to the others, the smell of hot food made him salivate.

'Soon be ready,' said Miguel.

'Manuel, start up the small generator.'

'Okay, Boss.'

'Charge these,' said Wolf, handing over the charger and phones.

The first sighting of Arnie's Airboats lifted Skelter's spirits like a thermal under a buzzard's wings. Half way along the approach channel, he breathed a sigh of relief as he spotted the van alongside the building. 'No sign of Laz,' he said.

'The airboat's back,' said Stan, 'he won't be far.'

Skelter glanced at his watch. It was seven fifteen and the yellow blush of imminent sunrise glimmered in the East.

As soon as they bumped the dock, Skelter leapt out and sprinted to the van. The back door was unlocked. Laz was pleased to see him, despite the rude awakening from his sleep.

'How was it? Anyone hurt? I heard gunfire.'

'We're fine and we got the girl. We need to get the kit aboard and ship on out, pronto.'

'Okay, Chief.'

Laz stepped out and doubled to the dock to help with the unloading. In less than fifteen minutes, they were ready to roll, just waiting for Stan to lock up.

'Just leaving a note for Gerry,' said Stan, climbing into the front with Skelter and Laz.

Laz shoved the shift into drive and pulled away across the gravel and onto the highway. 'Boy, am I glad to see you guys, you had me worried for a while.'

'We had us worried, too,' Skelter said.

'What about the bad guys, did you…?'

'Slapped 'em around a bit, that's all, nothing serious,' Stan said. 'They'll have some lovely bruises, but they'll get over it. Can you drop me at my office, Laz?'

'Sure, buddy.'

Wolf stuffed himself with tinned chilli and boiled rice along with the other five men. He was still fuming over the turn of events, but he had his thinking head on again. 'Manuel and me will take the canoe, get an airboat. We will come back for you.'

'What about the others?' Miguel asked.

'Fuck them, useless bastards,' said Wolf.

Manuel looked across at Miguel with narrowed eyes and pursed his lips.

Miguel got the message and concentrated on filling his stomach. He did not pursue the matter.

38
Coming Down

Sanibel Island
Tuesday, October 26th 2004

The van pulled up a few yards shy of the main entrance
to Stan's real estate business. As he climbed out, Skelter
noticed something in his eyes he had not seen before.
For the first time in the entire operation, Stan was
scared. 'Good luck with the missus, mate,' he said.

'Cheers pal, I'll need it.'

'Let's go, Laz, next stop Mitch's, give Maria her
daughter back. Wish her luck, she'll need a shed load.'

'How come?' said Laz.

'Of course, you don't know, do you?' said Skelter.
'Maria's little Eva and Wolfie have been playing hide
cthe salami together.'

'No shit?'

'No shit,' said Skelter.

Skelter jumped out of the cab. 'Back up to the garage. I'll open up.'

He entered through the side door and pressed the button for the roller door. While it was rising, he went into the house and called out for Maria. She ran in, eyes frantic with apprehension. 'She's fine, give us a minute to get the van in and close up. Mitch?'

'Sleeping,' she said, brushing by.

Skelter caught her arm. 'Go back to Mitch. I'll be along in a minute. Please, Maria, you must trust me. Eva's fine, not hurt, now go and let me finish the job.'

'But I must see her…'

'Five minutes, Maria. Five minutes.'

'No, now.'

'Maria, I need to tell you something first. Eva, he did not hold her against her will, Wolf…'

Maria looked shocked. She shook her head, tears forming in her eyes. 'No, not my Eva. Who says this?'

'I saw them – together. I'm sorry.'

Maria pushed past Skelter and charged into the garage. Skelter withdrew. He found Mitch with the nurse in attendance. 'It's fine, mission accomplished. It's Maria letting off steam,' he said, to explain the fearsome row going on between mother and daughter. 'Eva's fine, but she's taken her mother for a ride. She and Wolf…'

Mitch looked dumbfounded. 'So sorry, laddie.'

'Save your strength, she's back now. Let them sort it out. At least her brother can stop feeding information to the gang now.'

Maria walked in, dragging her daughter by the arm. 'Eva has something to say to you.'

Eva remained tight lipped at first and then screeched, 'you're hurting me, Mama.'

'Hurting you? Hurting you? Lucky I don't kill you, bringing shame on your family, making your brother do bad things to protect you and all the time you laugh at us. You are a stupid, selfish, child and you will apologise to these men who have risked their lives to bring you back. Now do it, before I forget myself and whip your worthless hide.'

Eva screamed in reply. 'I am not a child.'

'Then stop behaving like one.'

Skelter sat down, embarrassed. 'Maria, there's no need...'

'Okay, I'm sorry, I'm sorry, now let go of me.'

Maria looked at the girl with contempt and released her grip. She turned to Skelter. 'You look awful, H, she has put you through this,'

Maria finally accepted that the grudging apology was the best she was going to get. Eva's eyes told Skelter the contempt in her mother's voice hurt far more than the bruise blossoming upon her arm. Maria frogmarched Eva out of the room and Skelter turned to Mitch, who, despite the commotion, had slipped into sleep.

'It's the morphine,'

Skelter looked up in surprise. He hadn't noticed the nurse sitting in the corner.

'We finally persuaded him,' Lena said. 'The pain stopped him from enjoying Maria's company. Poor man. Rock and a hard place.'

'Sorry about just now, Lena,' said Skelter.

She placed her hands over her ears, then eyes, and

finally her mouth. 'Seen it all before, I'm a pro, H. Pros don't tell.' She screwed her face up. 'You could use a shower.'

'Think so?' he sniffed the armpit of his swamp soaked T-shirt. 'Reckon you might be right there. On my way,' he said with a grin that shone through the grime. Skelter went up to his room, stripped, emptied his pockets, and put his filthy clothes in a bin liner, scrounged from the kitchen and tied it shut.

The warm water citrus shower gel breathed new life into him. He towelled dry, pulled on a pair of shorts and a T-shirt and made his way downstairs in time to catch Shawna coming through the front door.

'Morning.'

'Morning, H, you smell nice and fresh.'

'You should have been here an hour ago.'

'And why is that?'

Skelter held the kitchen door open for her. 'Oh nothing. Morning, Turbo.'

Turbo raised his coffee mug in salute. 'Morning, mate.'

Through the French windows, Skelter could see Brick strolling over the lawn, exuding clouds of blue/brown smoke, looking at peace with the world.

'How many for lunch today?' asked Shawna.

Skelter did a quick mental head count. 'Seven, including you.'

'Eight,' corrected Turbo. 'Laz is in the garage, sorting gear out.'

Skelter grabbed a coffee and made himself a cheese sandwich. He took them through to where Mitch lay semi-comatose, Maria beside him. 'Eva?' he asked.

'Asleep in my room.'

Skelter raised his eyebrows.

Maria put her hand into the pocket of her Capri pants and pulled out a key. 'I locked the doors to the balcony, as well.'

'How is she? Physically, I mean. Not sick at all?'

'Withdrawal, you mean. I am not a fool. I know she will have taken drugs. That animal will have made sure of that. It is how it works. I will get her checked by a doctor, Lena gave me a number for a clinic in Fort Myers where I can take her.'

Skelter placed his hand upon her shoulder and gave it a gentle squeeze. He walked over to the desk. 'Got a minute, Lena? I need advice. Fancy a walk outside?'

'Sure, fresh air is good for body and soul.'

'I'll come straight to the point. Mitch is fading fast, isn't he?'

'It's accelerated. That's why he gave up on fighting without the morphine. Everyone has their limits. He pushed it much further than I could have imagined, but now…'

Lena reached out and took Skelter's hand. She looked into his eyes, eyes welling with tears. 'It's a balancing act.'

'I understand. I just don't want it to happen so soon. Selfish I know. It's going to be very soon.'

'We can't say for sure,' Lena began.

'I have watched men die, Lena. It will not be long.'

After lunch, Brick, Turbo and Laz crashed out to catch up on missed sleep. Skelter had a phone call to make.

'Mark, how are you? Is everything okay? I've been frantic. You didn't call and…'

'Lucy, Lucy, listen, stop worrying I'm fine, honest.'

'Thank God. You're sure?'

'Absolutely, totally fine, just tired. Late night, last night.'

'Hungover are we? Well, serve you right.'

'How's the move going?'

'That's it, change the subject.'

'Tell me,' he said, 'I've got news.'

'What news?'

'What do you think of Scotland?' he asked. 'Ever been to Speyside?'

'No, but my little brother used to stay on an estate up there, during school holidays. Friend of Daddy's. Loved it, never stopped talking about the place. Why do you ask?'

'I wouldn't worry too much about unpacking all the boxes, Cariad. Wait 'til I get back.'

'Stop talking in riddles, Mark. Tell me what's going on.'

'We might need to consider relocating. I'll give you the full story when I get home.'

'And when will that be, you infuriating bastard?'

'Mitch is on his way. I can't leave just now.' His voice trembled.

'Mark, you okay? Look I'm sorry, take whatever time you need. I'll let work know.'

'It won't be long now, Cariad. A few days at most I reckon. Look I need a kip, I'm shagged. I'll keep you updated on Mitch.'

39
Endex

Sanibel Island
Tuesday, October 26th 2004

When Skelter woke, it was dark outside. He dressed and went downstairs, barefoot. Mitch was asleep, Maria too. Outside in the garden, Brick puffed on his briar, beer in hand, talking with Turbo and Laz.

'All right, boys? See you've started without me. Back in a mo.' He went in through the French doors and straight to the refrigerator, grabbed a bottle and rejoined the others. 'Well, here's to a successful job,' he said, clinking bottle necks. 'Well done, boys.'

'Yeah, we got away with it.'

'Don't be so surprised, Brick,' said Turbo, 'we are the best, remember.'

'I'm not used to trying not to kill the enemy.'

'A first for all of us, I'm sure,' said Skelter, looking at Laz.

'Roger that, Chief, totally new concept.'

'You came through with flying colours. If we can do a quick debrief, I'll go and sort out the pay parade. Nothing to say beyond 'well done'. We need to organise returning the kit, getting everyone home.' Skelter turned to Turbo and Brick. 'When are your flights?'

'Tomorrow, late afternoon.'

'I could take the guys and return the weapons on the way to Miami?' Laz offered. 'Take the van to Stan and leave any refund on the gear with him. If you'll trust me to.'

'Think I might manage that.' Skelter said, with a smile.

'We trust you,' said Turbo. 'We know where you live.'

'Sorted then. I'll arrange the money transfers soon as I finish this beer. It's already set up, just a phone call.'

After he made the call, Skelter sat with Maria and Mitch for a while. The woman looked washed out, knackered. The fire within, all but snuffed out. 'Why don't you get some rest?' he asked, 'you look beat.'

Maria looked at him with eyes bloodshot from recent crying. 'There will be time for that soon enough,' she said, looking at Mitch's emaciated body. His shallow breathing as he slept barely making his chest rise. 'Too soon. I should have gone with him the first time he looked at me. It is hard for me to say but in my heart I know it. The church says I must stay with the man I first lay with. Am I so bad for wishing to be with the one I love? How can this be right? A man with love in his heart, a man like Mitch... How? I do not understand.'

'Maria, religion is something I will never really understand, even though I am a Christian and I pray to God. So much misery and destruction is imposed upon innocents in the name of religion, it is a wonder I don't denounce God myself. I am sorry that you did not take the chance, but it is done now. Don't be so hard on yourself.'

Mitch stirred and a low moan escaped his lips. He opened his eyes and reached out to Maria. She grasped his trembling hand and held it, her grip firm but gentle. He tried to speak, she leaned closer to kiss his cheek, changed her mind and kissed him on the lips. The smile upon his ravaged face shone like a beacon. His head sank back into the pillow and he expired. The time for tears had come.

Maria looked at Mitch, then Skelter. Lena got up from her desk. Skelter hung his head. Maria slumped across Mitch's chest and wept in silence.

Skelter stared at his friend through moist eyes. He felt exhausted. It was the end of an era. Life had changed much in the last six years. Some good, some bad, some dreadful. Another link with his past life severed. He thought about his impending birthday. *Fifty, how did that happen?* He took the little green God from his pocket and unselfconsciously addressed it. *'Well, what next, fat boy? We've some adjusting to do, you and I.'*

Lena threw him a strange look as she came over to check for a pulse. He knew there was none to be found, but she had a job to do. She was a pro.

The telephone rang and rang. He'd started to compose a message in his head, for the answerphone, when Lucy picked up.

'Mark, what is it? It's past one o'clock.'

'Sorry, I should have… Mitch… Mitch died half an hour ago. I needed to hear your voice. Selfish of me, I'm sorry.'

'Darling, I'm so sorry, talk as long as you want.'

'I've never lost anyone so close before, except for Mam. The hole is so big, Cariad, so big.' He could feel the tears wet upon his cheeks. His mentor and role model, the mighty Mitch Mitchell, reduced to a memory.

'Mark, you still there?'

'Yes, sorry, just wandered off for a second. I'm adrift, like I've lost my rudder. Right now I wish I could get home and fall asleep in your arms. Sorry, I'm being a real… It's been a lot to take in. The cancer, Maria, Eva…'

'Who?'

'Maria's daughter, she went missing, back now. There's more, Mitch has named me as executor. Shouldn't be too complicated, except I'm not sure which law applies. He has a British passport but lives most of the time over here. Got property in both countries. Only two beneficiaries.'

'That should make it a bit easier. I suppose you will have to stay longer to sort things out.'

'Afraid so, Cariad,' he paused, 'I miss you.' She did not reply but she was still there, 'Lucy, are you all right?'

'Fine, took me by surprise, you don't… Not normally…'

'Doesn't come easy. Wish…'

'Shh, it's fine, really it is, I love you for it.'

'The beneficiaries, Cariad. Mitch had no family. The US assets go to Maria. He wanted her to be secure for her lifetime and she will be, but she will be without him. It makes me realise how lucky I am.'

'That is so sweet. Nice to have something to remember him by.'

'Whisky,' said Skelter.

'A fine malt, I'm guessing.'

Skelter took a sharp intake of breath. 'Are you in bed, Cariad?'

'Where else would I be at this hour?'

'You're lying down?'

'Mark?'

'Not a bottle, Lucy, a distillery. I've inherited a whole bloody distillery, on Speyside – the family business.'

'Are you serious?'

'Perfectly. God knows how I'm going to manage it. The only experience I have of Scotch is as an end user. There's more. The family estate, too. House, tenant farmers, fishing, grouse moors. I'm gob smacked… Scary. Such responsibility. So many people.'

'Oh my…Seriously? Wow, that is a hell of a news bombshell.' The line went quiet.

'I really am at a loss for what to do. Still cant get my head round it, Cariad.'

'Easy boy, we'll manage.'

'I'm lucky to have you, Lucy.'

'We are lucky to have each other.'

40
Farewells

Sanibel Island
Wednesday, October 27th 2004

Over coffee in the garden, Skelter said his goodbyes to Turbo and Brick. They left with plenty of time to spare, so Laz could get back in daylight. Another job ticked off the admin list. The funeral directors were due to collect Mitch's body early afternoon. At three p.m., a doctor arrived to see Eva. Skelter didn't understand why Eva hadn't kicked off – she had to be an addict. That was how sleaze-balls like Wolf worked. Get them hooked and make them dependent upon you. How come she had been so quiet?

Skelter bumped into Lena in the hall. 'Hey, what's

up? Thought you'd finished here.'

'Just tying up the paperwork with Katya.'

The collision jolted the penny free, to drop into Skelter's consciousness. 'How could I be so stupid?'

'What's that?' Lena said.

'Eva? Why isn't she screaming for a fix?' he asked. 'Much morphine left, is there? Should be a fair stash, Mitch refusing it for so long.'

Lena glared at him.

'Don't get out your pram, I'm on your side, just couldn't believe she'd be clean. I'd have done the same in your shoes.'

'I don't know what…'

Skelter smiled and poured himself a coffee. He walked outside and wandered along to the dock. The sun was warm and bright. A heron stood perfectly still at the water's edge, staring into the canal. The bird made no attempt to move when Skelter approached and he slowed down in deference, as he stepped aboard the boat. With his head revolving like the barrels of a Gatling gun, he sat in his favourite spot, as recent events whirred around his skull.

Skelter sat with a mug in his right hand and Buddha in his left. *'Well, my little friend, I suppose we should be grateful we're still here. It nearly went tits-up any number of times. No need you trying to tell me I should pack it all in now, eh? Not the way things are. Life's never going to be the same. Imagine me taking over from the Laird. Who'd have thought? Hope I don't let Mitch down.'*

Skelter drained his mug and made his way back to the house. *Time to say farewell to Mitch.* 'What time are they coming for him, Katya?'

'In about half an hour. Should I leave you?'

249

'Please.'

The nurse got to her feet and went towards the kitchen. Skelter perched on the edge of the recliner, leaned forward and touched Mitch's cold cheek. 'I'll try to be worthy, old friend. You put a lot of faith in me. Scares me a bit to be honest. You always understood how much you meant to me and I will always be grateful to you for believing in me. This is another challenge you've set me, only this time you won't be here to guide me. I'll do my best to make you proud. Rest in peace now, old friend.' Skelter got to his feet, leaned over and kissed Mitch's forehead. This was unplanned and surprised him. He felt lighter in his heart, having done it.

He wandered into the kitchen. 'Katya, do you know where Maria is?'

'In her room, with her daughter. I would not interrupt them just now. Not a good time, I think.'

'Oh, okay.'

Skelter stood beside the fountain with a beer, watching the sunset, when Lena approached him looking perplexed.

'Have you seen a cell phone lying around, H? Mine's disappeared.'

'Where did you last see it?'

'Yesterday, when I was here. When I got home, I looked in my purse and zip, no phone. I must have put it down it somewhere. Can I use yours to call my number?'

Skelter reached into his pocket. 'Here, help yourself.'

'Thanks.' Lena tapped the numbers in.

Skelter grabbed the phone from her hand.

'Hey!'

'Did you give Eva anything yesterday?'

'Now wait a…'

'This is important, Lena, I need to know. Tell me.

'You think Eva might have taken my phone?'

'Well, could she?' Lena's face gave him the answer.

'Come,' said Skelter, 'quietly now.' Lena followed him up the stairs. He stopped outside Maria's room and handed Lena his phone. She dialled the number. A ringtone sounded inside the room. Skelter made a motion with his hand across his throat and she cut the call. He retreated downstairs with Lena. 'I want to keep your phone for now. I appreciate it's a lot to ask.'

'I need my phone, H.'

'Not as much as me. You can use Mitch's for now,' he said.

'Just what is going on here?'

'Not quite sure yet, it's complicated. I'll get back to you.'

'When exactly?'

'Give me an hour.' Skelter went to his room. A broad smile lit up his face as he retrieved the cell phone he had picked up from the side of Wolf's bed on the island. He checked for messages. There were six from the same number – Lena's. The smile broadened. He pocketed the device, went to Maria's room and knocked on the door. 'Maria, you in there? It's me, H.'

The door opened.

'Can I come in?' he asked.

'Of course, what is it?'

'Eva. I must speak to Eva.' The girl was sitting on the bed staring out of the window. She looked wasted.

'Lena's phone, Eva, and don't give me any bullshit, it rang in here ten minutes ago. I called it.'

'Ain't got it.'

'She tells the truth.' Maria offered the phone to Skelter. 'I took it from her. I was going to return it.'

'Thank you, I will take it to her as soon as I check what calls your daughter's made.'

'No one, I called no one.'

Skelter checked. No record of outward calls in the last two days. *Smart kid, erased the log.* He checked the messages. Same result.

'Tell Lena I am sorry,' said Maria.

'I'm sure she'll understand. Maria, a word outside please.' Skelter led the way onto the landing and out of earshot of Eva. 'She will try to contact Wolf. If she succeeds, that will be bad news for everyone. Watch her.'

Maria nodded, the strain of recent events engraved upon her face. She seemed to have aged in the two weeks since he had first met her.

'Best get Eva away, Maria, as a precaution,' said Skelter.

He walked down the stairs fingering the little green God. *She doesn't deserve all this shit, Buddha, buddy. All the big houses in the world would not compensate for the loss of a daughter, but money might provide a private clinic to fix the problem. Good luck with that, Maria.*

.

'I won't go,' said Eva, 'you can't make me.'

'What is wrong with you, child?' Maria said, exasperated.

'I am not a child. You hear me? I am a woman.'

'To become a woman takes more than periods,' said her mother. 'You have a long way to go. Sleeping with a loser like Lope won't get you there. Why do you cause me so much pain? Don't you care about your family? Your brother could go to jail, you selfish brat.'

'Sorry, Lena,' said Skelter, 'I need to hang on to your phone for a few days. You'll be well compensated, I promise.'

'That's no good to me. All my numbers are in there and my friends, they...'

Skelter held up his hand. 'How about we drive to the mall and buy a new one, top model, pick whatever you like? We can copy the contacts to the new phone.'

Lena's eyes narrowed like slits in a pillbox. 'What the fuck's going on?'

'I'll throw in a bonus if it will quench your thirst for answers. Shall we say fifty bucks?'

Her face softened.

'Okay,' said Skelter, 'one hundred dollars and a new cell phone, no questions. What do you say?'

'Deal.'

He held on to Lena's phone and kept Wolf's in his pocket, aware that Eva would not give up, and he needed to keep one step ahead. 'C'mon, then, let's go get you a new toy,' he said, picking up the keys to Maria's pickup.

When he returned from his shopping trip, Skelter took a bottle of mineral water from the fridge and sipped from it as he walked down to the boat. An osprey flew low over the canal. Skelter watched it's lazy graceful wing-strokes and marvelled at how effortless the bird made flying look, as it skimmed across the dark, rippled water.

A light breeze stirred the palm fronds with a low soothing, swishing sound. He checked Lena's phone for any reply from Wolf. *'I know it's a long shot but chances are in his line of work, he'll have more than one phone. Maybe she texted another number as well. Worth a shot. Well, fat guy, this has been some trip. Don't know about you, but I was not expecting to walk into this kind of shit storm. Hit the jackpot, didn't we, buddy?'* Skelter took a drink from the bottle. *'Still, we haven't had the law sniffing around, although to be fair, I'm surprised. We got away with murder. No wonder these dealers can move drugs around so easily.'*

The warm sun and clear blue sky helped bring a sense of calm to Skelter, something lacking in the past few days. He fell asleep.

41
Out of the Wilderness

Everglades
Wednesday, October 27th 2004

Wolf woke early, confused at first by the foreign objects in his hammock. Then he remembered picking up the two remaining paddles and wrapping his arms around them as he fell asleep with his hand on the Colt.

The first to stir, he yawned, climbed out of his pit, stretched, walked over to the rustic table and put a match to the camping stove. Two inches of water in a plastic bowl sufficed to swill his face, a grubby towel to dry himself. A cup of instant black coffee passed for breakfast. Half way through it, Manuel appeared from the other shelter carrying a small cotton sack.

'Buenas dias, Lope.'

Wolf nodded.

Manuel emptied the sack onto the table. Two bottles of water, two packets of beef jerky, two cell phones and two chargers. 'All charged up, Boss. Any time for coffee?'

'Make it quick, I'm going to pick up a bag.'

'Gracias.' Manuel grabbed a mug, touched the side of the aluminium kettle with his finger and soon withdrew it. Hot enough. He made himself a brew.

Wolf walked across to the other shelter and opened the cupboard under the sleeping platform. Reaching right to the back, he pulled out a black, nylon sports bag. He locked the cupboard and re-joined Manuel, who had downed half of his scalding coffee. Impatient to be on the move, Wolf steered him to the canoe. Before anyone else had stirred, they were on their way, Wolf in the rear seat. Things had changed of late and he had to be more conscious of personal security. Manuel had been with him longer than anyone, since their schooldays in South Miami, playing in the same mean streets, but he could no longer take anything for granted. His empire was under threat. Physical damage he could fix with cash. Damage to his credibility and reputation was a different matter. Sharks were circling, they smelled blood.

After paddling for almost an hour, both men grew tired, neither being used to such strenuous exercise. Manuel dug deep, but his breathing had become laboured.

'Make for the trees up ahead, take a break,' said Wolf, blowing hard.

Much relieved, Manuel managed a nod and altered course towards a cluster of close grouped cypress trees, stopping between the nearest two. Both men drank from their bottles, shirts plastered to their backs in the humid air. It was still early, but already very warm.

Wolf took out his cell phones and tested each for a signal, but with no luck. Masts were not allowed in the national park. 'I'll try again next time we stop. Better move on before the sun gets too hot.'

Manuel nodded, picked up his paddle and with a decided lack of enthusiasm, pushed away from the tree.

It took much longer than Wolf had expected, to get within striking distance of the long arrow-straight highway between Miami on the Atlantic and the Gulf City of Naples. It was almost noon before, after frequent stops, two weary canoeists heard the sound of traffic and paddled into a bed of dense reeds to take a final breather. Wolf checked his cell phones. A single bar. Not enough to make a call but sufficient to accept incoming text messages.

The list was long, but the most recent got his attention. He read it twice and then a third time. A huge smile creased his olive skin, as his right hand strayed to the butt of the Colt tucked in his waistband. 'Let's go, Manuel,' he said, digging his paddle into the water with renewed enthusiasm.

Taken by surprise at the sudden turn of events Manuel dropped his paddle. 'Watch it,' said Wolf.

Manuel fumbled and just caught the handle, before he lost it overboard. He recovered and joined in. Twenty minutes hard paddling later, they pulled up at the water's edge at the bottom of the bank below the road.

'Okay, I think I can get a signal from here.' Wolf

tapped in the numbers with his bony fingers, and clamped the cell phone to his ear. He ran his left hand through his long, black matted hair, his face relaxed now he could hear the dial tone. He pictured a motel room a hot shower and fresh clothes. It rang for a long time before someone picked up. 'Hey Jimmy, it's me, Lope, man. How's my sister? You taking good care of her?'

'Cut to it, Lope, what do you want?'

'Hey, Jimmy, you too smart for me. I do need a favour, had a little accident, stuck on the highway. Can you pick me up, take me to Miami?'

'So, where are you exactly?'

'A mile east of the Turner River road, on the Tamiami trail.' The line went quiet. 'Jimmy?'

'That's two hours away. I got a business to run, Lope. It's gonna screw the rest of my day.'

'I'll cover any expenses. I wouldn't ask if I didn't need it real bad, man.'

'Can you walk?'

'To Miami? Are you crazy?'

'To the river. There's a rest stop next to Turner River road, meet you there in two hours.'

'Gracias, amigo, gracias.'

'This I do for Lola, not you, Lope. Comprende?'

The line went dead.

'Need to hide the canoe,' said Wolf. 'Rest stop a mile up the road. If we carry the canoe across the road, the channel runs alongside the highway all the way to the river. Let's get onto the bank and take a look.'

The two men dragged the fibreglass vessel out onto the dry land and climbed the short slope to the top, ten feet above the waterline. The road was empty, most people who wanted to cross the Everglades used the interstate further north.

They carried the canoe across the single carriageway and stepped across the only obstacle – a low metal crash barrier – with ease.

'Get her in the water,' said Wolf, as he slid down the bank, his hand gripped onto the bow line. In a few minutes, they were paddling along the canal, between the highway and the dense forest.

'We'll take her close, then hide her in the reeds.'

One hour and forty-five minutes, give or take, since Wolf made the call, his brother-in-law arrived at the rest stop. Wolf and Manuel were sitting at one of the picnic tables, chewing beef jerky and nursing their water bottles, which they had topped up in the restroom. The place was basic, parking bays, toilets and a dozen picnic tables. Jimmy did not appear pleased to see them, but he opened the door to the truck and let them in.

'What in the name of God happened to you? You look like you been swimming in a sewer.'

Stony silence.

Jimmy shook his head. 'Where in Miami?'

'We need a Walmart and a place to stay tonight. I need a shower and clean clothes, and a car, truck, anything with wheels. You have something at the garage, yes? Nothing fancy.'

Jimmy rolled his eyes heavenwards. 'Anything else?'

'Swear to God, that's it.'

'Tell you what, I'll take you to the garage and you can use the courtesy truck Take off and find a motel.'

'Okay, okay. I'll bring the truck back in a couple of days. I owe you, Jimmy.'

42
Making Plans

Sanibel Island
Wednesday, October 27th 2004

Skelter took a mug of coffee up to his room and called Lucy. 'Hi, Cariad, just checking in with HQ. What's the weather been like?'

'Glorious autumn day. Warm too for this late in the year. Getting dark early now, though.'

'Been great here, but there's a storm on the way, according to the weather girl on NBC.'

'Do you know when the funeral will be? I assume it will be there, not being flown home is he?'

'No it's local. Not confirmed yet but looks like next week. Friday, probably. How's the house coming on?'

'Fine but since you dropped your whisky distillery bomb, I'm not sure where I am. Are you sure a move to Scotland is a good idea?'

'To be honest, Cariad, I love Hereford, but I see great possibilities on Speyside. We both have to want this or it's a non-starter.'

'My roots are here, Mark, but I have moved around a lot over the years. Daddy is my only close family here and my baby brother has close ties to Scotland.'

'You said Simon used to stay with a school chum in the holidays?'

'Chum? Mark Skelter are you taking the piss?'

'No, honest.'

'Pull the other one. Yes, well remembered, his friend Gordon, the family had an estate near Loch Laggan, close to Speyside. He waxed lyrical about the place, always banging on about the scenery and how it was a stone's throw from the skiing at Aveimore.'

'Does that mean you'll consider it?'

'Might be nice to make a fresh start together. I can work from anywhere. And you can learn about farming and whisky.'

'Don't know what to say, Cariad, I was expecting you to be against moving.'

'Never try to predict a woman, darling. There isn't a man on the planet up to that job.'

'I love you, Lucy Ryder.'

'Of course you do. I'm irresistible.'

Skelter laughed out loud. 'Is that so?'

'Absolutely, and you will follow wherever I lead, as long as you wanted to go there in the first place, that is.'

'You make me laugh, Cariad, and laughing makes me happy.'

'Bless you. You are okay, aren't you, Mark?'

'Why wouldn't I be?'

'Oh, nothing, just asking. Anyway I need the loo, so bye for now.'

'Okay. Speak to you soon, sleep well.'

'You too, love you.'

'Love you too. Bye.'

The Oriole Motel in Homestead, South Miami was stuck in a 1980s time vault. It was, however, anonymous and functional and the staff were discrete. Wolf had used the place before. He and Manuel pulled up outside reception at dusk, bags full of shirts, shorts, tequila and toiletries. Wolf checked in, paid cash in advance for three days and collected the key to a room on the ground floor. After a shower and change of clothes, while Manuel sluiced the swamp from his body, Wolf opened the tequila and poured a large one in a hi-ball tumbler picked up at Walmart. When Manuel had dressed, he joined him, drinking from a throwaway plastic cup.

'Tomorrow, I'll rent a van and an airboat. Take the van, get the boat and collect the men from the camp. Got a cellphone?' Wolf asked.

'Lost in the ambush.'

'No problem, use my spare. Bring them back here, okay?'

'Sure, Boss.'

'Call me when you are half an hour away, understand? I will talk to them and then you take them to Miami. From there, they can find their own way home until I need them again. I see you here at the motel. Tell the men I pay them off when they get here, understand?'

'Yes, Boss, they will get paid when you speak to them. Clear, Boss.'

'Good.' Wolf took a mirror from the wall and laid it on the bed. He emptied a small packet of white powder onto it.

Manuel lit a cigar. 'I'm hungry,' he said. 'I'm going for something to eat.'

Wolf ignored him, too wrapped up in the clacking of his credit card chopping a line on the glass.

Sitting in quiet contemplation on the patio, Skelter filtered thoughts of the future into some semblance of order as they whirled around his head. Feeling relaxed, he watched the germ of a plan begin to grow behind his eyes.

'Hello, H, you look pleased with yourself.'

'Hi, Maria, everything all right?'

'Eva, how she could be so stupid, H. What did I do wrong?'

'Nothing, Maria. You did nothing wrong. Eva is young, and naïve. She will grow out of it. With good treatment and your support, she'll come through.'

'You really think so?'

'Trust me, Maria I understand all about drug addiction,' he said.

Genuine surprise registered on her face. 'I had no idea.'

'More years than I care to remember,' said Skelter. Okay now, thanks to Lucy and a great therapist.'

Tears welled up in Maria's eyes.

'Me and my big mouth,' said Skelter.

'Please. It's okay. Without you, Mitch would have died alone. I have some precious memories to keep because of you.'

The telephone rang.

Maria walked inside and returned moments later, phone in hand. 'For you, H. Stan.'

'Stan, I thought you'd be in intensive care, boy, what can I do you for?'

'Me and our lass were wondering if you might fancy a change of scenery. How would you like to come over for lunch on Saturday? I'll fire up the barbecue.'

'Wow! Not only has she let you live, she's still feeding you. You must do a brilliant line in bullshit.'

'Don't worry, she has many ways of making me suffer. Come to lunch and watch her at work.'

'Honoured. I'll bring beer.' A flash of doubt hit Skelter's brain. 'I smell an ambush. Your missus is there holding a gun to your head. She wants to put my balls through the mincer for leading you astray.'

'Crossed her mind, but she's a very forgiving woman. Anyway, don't be a wimp. Pick you up at six-thirty.'

'Fair enough, mate, look forward to it.'

43

Revenge

Miami
Wednesday, October 27th 2004

Alone in the Oriole Motel room, Wolf scrolled through the calls and messages on his phone. Eva had given the address. With a map his brother-in-law had left in the cab of the pickup, he studied the area. It looked likely that he might access the place from the water, but he needed a more detailed map to be sure. That aside, he was confident an approach by boat could work. The main problem was security. Neighbourhoods like Sanibel often had private security patrols and cops. CCTV cameras, dogs maybe? He would need doped meat. These people had screwed up his business and humiliated him. They would pay. But who were they and how many? Time to find out.

The cell phone rang, the unfamiliar ringtone taking Skelter by surprise. It had stopped by the time he twigged. He flipped open Wolf's handset and scrolled through to messages and pressed 'ok'. 'Relax sweet meat, I come for u help me cameras? dogs? guards? send me all you can. W.'

A broad smile creased Skelter's tanned face. 'Got you, you bastard', he whispered, and took his notebook from his pocket to compose a reply. He sat and chewed the end of his pencil. The figurative shoes of a seventeen-year old Latino girl pinched his feet. Way out of his comfort zone, he needed help. He needed Maria. Eva's mother was eager.

'I want to see the dirt-bag in jail,' she said.

'Let's see what we can do,' he said, with a smile.

Over the course of the next couple of hours, Wolf exchanged text messages with who he assumed to be Eva. Skelter dictated to Maria, who paraphrased them into Eva-speak, to try to convince Wolf that she sent them. They described the security provision in place at Mitch's.

Sat chewing the end of his pencil, Skelter stared at the empty page in his notebook. His face a creased mask of concentration, he searched for the right words. The pencil scrambled across the plain, white surface like a fire ant on acid. 'Okay, Maria, try this.' She listened to him read what he had scribbled, took the pencil and refined the text. The result: 'They take me to rehab Friday morning boat from landing back of house.'

Maria nodded, and he sent the message. The reply came as a single 'W'.

Skelter used the house phone to make another call. It went to voicemail. 'Laz, It's H. Call me back soonest, please. Got a few days' work, if you want it.'

Wolf couldn't pinpoint it, but it just felt wrong somehow. The vibes were not coming through and, in spite of telling himself this was normal, the nagging doubt in his head remained. He didn't know who to trust. Someone sold him out and he had no idea who, or who to. He faced a huge dilemma. How to salvage his empire? Money was no object, but contrary to popular belief, not everything can be fixed by throwing greenbacks at it. A new pilot and a plane were top priority. The longer he left his men stranded on the island, the greater the risk of dissent and of rivals moving in to take over. The loyalty of those men worried him. If one of them had sold him out, he might already be too late. It was only a matter of time before somebody spotted the crashed aircraft and he would be forced to abandon the Everglades airstrip as well – and the camp. Finding another facility would be difficult. A shot of tequila hit the back of his throat and he refilled the glass. It did not remain full for long.

Wolf poured another tequila. The bottle was half empty and Manuel had only drunk two shots before he went out.

Right on cue, Manual walked through the door. 'Everything okay, Boss?'

Wolf nodded. 'Sure.' Sharing his thoughts might help

and he had to trust somebody. Manuel was the obvious choice.

'Manuel, I need you to do something for me tomorrow, when you go to the camp.'

'Whatever you say, Boss.'

'Take the canopy down and use it to camouflage the plane wreck. Do a good job. We must hide it before some flyer sees it and tells the authorities. Keep your wits about you, amigo, trust no one, there are snakes in our midst.'

'I understand, Boss, don't worry I will be very careful.'

Skelter was slumped in front of the TV, stuffed full of Shawna's cooking when the call from Laz came in at 8.10. 'Thanks for getting back so quick, Laz. I have a little problem you can help me with. Can you come over in the morning?'

'Nothing better to do Chief, I have some cash for you anyway, from the deposit on the goods we returned.'

'Cheers, I appreciate it. I'll brief you on what I need and you can let me know if you're interested. Say ten, ten thirty?'

'I'll be there.'

'Thanks, see you then.'

44

Planning a Surprise

Herefordshire, England
Wednesday/Thursday, Oct. 27th/28th 2004

Lucy Ryder called from the bottom of the stairs. 'Wilkins, whatever it is you are doing, leave it and come down. I've put the coffee on.'

'Very well, Miss Lucy.'

Lucy went into the kitchen, negotiating around a pile of deconstructed, flattened cardboard boxes. Wilkins walked in minutes later, rolled down the sleeves of his shirt and took the cup of coffee offered by Lucy.

'You have done more than enough for today, bless you.' She smiled and looked out of the window. 'I'm going away on Friday, Wilkins.'

'Are you going to see Sergeant Skelter?'

'Yes, I have booked a fly-drive to Miami, to surprise him. I should be there to support him at the funeral.'

'If you think so, Miss Lucy.'

'You don't sound sure, Wilkins. What do you think?'

Wilkins frowned. 'If you feel you should be there, then that is where you should be.'

'But?' said Lucy, scanning his face for clues.

'In my experience, Miss Lucy, it's the ladies that like surprises. We men don't always appreciate the uncertainty so much.'

'Are you saying I might catch him up to no good if I arrive unannounced?'

'Not at all. Your husband is a decent man, but I doubt he will like surprises any more than I do.'

Lucy sipped at her cup, deep in thought.

'Is there anything else you need?'

'Thank you, Wilkins, but that's it for today. I really appreciate the help. I couldn't have managed without you.'

'Pleasure, Miss,' he said picking up his jacket from the back of the chair. 'I'll see myself out. Same time tomorrow?'

'That would be great, thanks.' Lucy sat down at the table and made a list of stuff to take on her trip.

Lucy rose early and showered. Still in her bathrobe, excited at the prospect of seeing Mark, she took her suitcase from the wardrobe. She was not used to her married status yet. The final set of illustrations had gone to the publisher two weeks ago, and she was now between jobs. A few days in Florida might compensate for the postponed honeymoon.

Lucy picked out a black lightweight trouser suit and a silver-grey silk blouse for the funeral and then worked through the packing list. Passport, driving licence, credit card... Everything laid out on the bed methodically. You can be proud of me Mark, all ready for inspection. Her father's influence surprised her. She did not remember the brigadier being around much when she was young enough to be influenced.

Lucy checked the tickets. The doorbell rang. The clock beside the bed read 8.55. When she reached the stairs the bell rang again and she hurried down as fast as her slippers would allow. 'Sorry, Wilkins, I've been packing and I lost track. '

'That's quite all right, Miss Lucy, you carry on. I've plenty to do. The brigadier says if you need a lift to the airport, he will drive you.'

'That would be brilliant, but it's an early start.'

'He's used to those,' said Wilkins with a grin. 'Right then, I'll get on upstairs and sort those bookshelves out.'

45

Planning the Trap

Florida
Thursday, October 28th 2004

Skelter, opened the front door. 'Laz, come right on in. Coffee?'

'Coffee would be good, Chief.'

'Let's get a brew and take a walk,' said Skelter, as he led the way through to the kitchen. 'Cream, no sugar, right?' He filled two mugs.

'On the nail.'

The two men went into the garden and down to the landing. Skelter had become very attached to the classic Chris Craft. He found it an inspirational and productive place. He brought Laz up to date with recent developments and the threat that Wolf posed.

'So what's the plan, Chief, where do I fit in?'

'He'll take the bait and come for Eva on Sunday. He will try to take me out. She's ID'd me as the mastermind behind her recovery, so he is going to be seriously pissed off.'

'Guess we did him a lot of damage.'

'That, Laz, is some understatement. He might struggle to recover. What I need is for you to move in here and help me to keep watch. I can't do it alone. If he does what I expect, he will make a move when I'm out on the water fishing. He expects Eva and Maria to be with me. I'll be alone.'

'What about the police?'

'They'll ask questions and Maria could end up being deported. Her son will probably go to prison. God only knows what will happen to Eva. I realise it's a really big ask. I appreciate the risk I'm taking and I expect you to be sensible and turn me down. The last thing you want is trouble with the law. The reward should reflect the risk. Ten grand, tax free.'

Laz showed no reaction. 'Suppose he takes the boat out with something heavy, like a rocket? This is the USA, the home of deadly weapons. You can get anything for a price, with the right connections.'

'And our boy fits the profile,' said Skelter, 'I said I'd be alone, I did not say I intended to be on the boat.'

'Go on,' said Laz.

'Anchor the boat, set a dummy up with a rod, and scuba over the side.'

'Laz looked sceptical. And just where will you get a dummy…?'

Skelter nodded to the fibreglass fisherman at the end

273

of the dock.

'If he does use anything like a rocket, I'll just fade away and let him believe he's won.'

'No offence, Chief, but you're not thinking this through. The police will investigate, Coast Guard too, maybe.'

'It may not go that extreme. He might...'

'Might what? You don't have a workable plan, do you?'

Skelter leaned forward and ran his hands through his hair. 'Guess not. After all these years, the well's finally run dry. *What now, my little, fat friend?*'

'Excuse me?' Laz noticed the little statue in Skelter's hand's.

'Sorry, Laz,' said Skelter, 'we've been through a lot together, this little fella and me. I tell him my problems and he helps me find solutions, only I guess his well's dry too. Look: forget I called, I'll handle this.'

Laz looked nonplussed. 'H, you got away with a lot so far, my advice is don't push your luck. The way I read it, you have two choices. One, you pack up and clear out, get the girl away somewhere and lie low until it's time to fly home. Two call the cops. Whichever, don't go to the funeral.'

'Won't work. This boy won't give up until one of us is dead.'

'So do as I suggest, tell the cops. Anonymously if you must. Let them deal with it. Sorry, but that's good advice, and you know it.'

'Whatever happens, I have to be at the funeral, I can't let Mitch down.'

Laz shrugged his shoulders. 'Sorry, H.'

'It's okay. Thanks for coming over.'

Laz got up to leave. 'Think about it. Would your friend want you to risk putting yourself in danger? What about your family? What about Maria?'

Skelter nodded slowly and looked down at the green Buddha in his hands.

Laz got up. 'Sorry, Chief,' he said, patting Skelter on the shoulder.

'What a mess, eh, boy? What are we gonna do? Not like The Regiment, is it? Not sure I can hack this stuff in civvy street.' Skelter shivered suddenly, despite the heat. *'It's like being back in Northern Ireland, hands tied with red tape, while the players get away with murder, literally. Unless we come up with a plan real quick, we'll have no choice but to contact the cops.'*

After a long time of solitary brain-storming, Skelter finally surrendered. He could not see a way out. Time to tell the troops. He went to the house. Shawna was in the kitchen.

'Maria upstairs?' he asked.

Shawna nodded.

He sprinted up the staircase and knocked on her door.

'Yes?' called a voice from within.

'It's me, Maria, H, can I have a word?'

The door opened. 'What is it?'

'Can you come down to the kitchen, please?'

'Of course.' She went into the room, spoke briefly to Eva and then stepped onto the landing and locked the door. 'There is a problem?'

Skelter took her arm and led her to the stairs. Half way down he stopped. 'You need to leave here soon as you can. Take Eva. Find somewhere safe and keep below the radar until I call you.'

'Wolf?'

'I need to tell Shawna to take time off.'

'He's coming for Eva.' It was a statement of belief, not a question. 'What about you?' said Maria.

'I'll handle it,' said Skelter.

'This awful mess is all my fault. You are a good man, H, and now I fear for you. I have brought so much trouble to you.'

Skelter put up a hand. 'Enough, now go and pack. I need to see Shawna.'

Maria embraced him. 'Be careful,' she said.

'You, too.' He went downstairs.

Leaning on the worktop, deep in conversation, Shawna held a credit card in one hand and her cell phone in the other.

'Sorry,' said Skelter, and he left the room. A couple of minutes later, she called out. 'I'm done, H, you can come in. I'm only ordering some flowers for my mother,' she said. 'It's her birthday, Saturday.'

'Shawna, Maria and Eva are moving out for a few days. Now might be a good time to take a few days off, spend time with your mother.'

'Really?' she said, her expression laced with scepticism. 'How much time do you have in mind?'

'Up to Tuesday, I can manage fine over the weekend. I'll call you. I'm not sure what the arrangements are, but I will make sure you do not lose out financially.'

'Okay…'

Skelter smiled an awkward, uncomfortable smile at the streetwise Shawna.

'Whatever you say. I've been with Mitch a long time. I know much more than I speak of, H.'

'I'm not going to bullshit you. Let's just say I need some time alone to reflect and leave it at that okay?'

'You're the Boss, now. Anyway, I guess I don't have a job now Mitch is gone.'

Skelter shook his head. 'Enjoy your time off. I'll call you. This is Maria's place, now. She might well need some help around the place. I'll have a word.'

She looked concerned.

'Don't worry, it'll be fine.' He tried hard to sound convincing. Shawna's face told him he had failed. She turned her attention to food preparation.

Hope that's not an omen, Buddha, buddy, thought Skelter. *Damn I feel tired, what is wrong with me? Okay, I know, old age is catching up. You must be hundreds of years old, my fat, green friend. Not the same when you're a God, I expect. I bet you never get tired.*

After speaking to Shawna, Skelter went into Mitch's armoury and selected two semi-automatic pistols – a Beretta and a Glock – and loaded two magazines for each. He also took a small revolver, loaded with five rounds, and slipped it into his pocket. He placed the Beretta in a drawer in the umbrella stand in the entrance hall – the Glock under his pillow.

Next he turned his attention to the phone and composed a short text; 'Fishing cancelled, H sick. Me at clinic, back Sunday. Please come 1st door top of stairs. Maria locks me in. H in last room on right. Battery low. xxx.' He took a deep breath and pressed send. *'Cross your fingers, Buddha, boy. That was our best shot.'*

46
Second Guessing

Florida
Thursday, October 28th 2004

Wolf read the text for the umpteenth time. 'This is not my Eva,' he said.

'What is not what, Boss?' said Manuel, as he stirred and rubbed the sleep from his eyes.

'The Wolf is too smart for them. He sees a trap.' His eyes lit up and a self-satisfied smirk bathed his face. 'They will pay dearly for this, Manuel.'

'Yes, Boss.' Manuel made the right noises but did not fully engage with Wolf. 'What about the men?' he asked.

'Pick up the van at nine. Driving licence?'

Manuel took out his wallet. It had the dead smell of

swamp water, but the licence was undamaged.

Wolf took a bunch of dollar bills from the holdall and pressed them into Manuel's hand. 'For the airboat.'

Manuel nodded and pocketed the cash.

The rental lot held less than a dozen vehicles, all vans. Wolf paid cash, waved Manuel on his way and drove back to the motel, where he got busy on the telephone. In a desperate attempt to find a replacement pilot and plane, he tried every contact. The best he got was promises to call back. The burning desire to get the man that caused him such trouble dwarfed any thoughts of Eva. The mystery man, the one called 'H', had got to him so bad, he ached. Ached to feel the man's throat in his hands. The man would beg Wolf to kill him, to end the pain, but not until he told him why. No one disrespects the Wolf without consequences.

Convinced that the phone messages were not from Eva, Wolf guessed they must be from the man called H. His reply had to be drafted with care. A drink would help. Two shots of tequila left. Without bothering to look for a glass, he picked up the bottle, drained it and threw it at the wall. The plasterboard took a dent but the bottle did not break. He kicked at it and missed. 'Bastard,' he said, grabbing the keys to go in search of a replacement.

Wolf returned with a fresh bottle of tequila and sat down with a pen and paper and a glass. He drafted reply after reply while he drank. To convince the sender he believed them, it was vital to get it right. Eventually, he found a form of words he was happy with. 'Be ready for me

Sunday night.' Short and sweet.

A knock on the door woke Wolf. He reached out in the darkness for the Colt, glanced at his watch − 2 a.m He cocked the pistol and went to the door.

'Lope, it's me, Manuel. Let me in.'

Wolf opened the door and as soon as he closed it again, he switched on the light. Manuel looked shattered. 'I got everything done, Boss.' He sat on the bed and put the McDonald's bag at his feet.

'The plane, you covered the plane?'

'Yes, Boss, all done.'

'Is everyone back?'

'Two missing from the ambush, they took off into the swamp, idiots. I got the rest, including those we left near the crash. They are in the van. They asked about getting paid, Boss.'

'What did you tell them?'

'I said you'd take care of it.'

'Good, you did good, amigo. Come I will speak to the men.'

Bleary eyed and weary, Manuel shuffled out behind Lope to the van. After a short pep talk, Wolf paid the men. Each man got a two-hundred-dollar bonus to keep him sweet. He took the keys and got into the driver's seat. Manuel looked way too shot to drive. 'Go and get some rest,' said Wolf.

Manuel pulled a cheeseburger from the bag and took a huge bite from it. 'It has been a long day,' he said, as he pulled the ring on a can of coke, 'thank you, amigo, I will.'

Wolf closed the door and started the engine.

47

Calm Before the Storm

Florida
Saturday, October 30th 2004

Skelter rose with the lark and went for a run to clear his mind. After forty-five minutes, he jogged back along the narrow lane to Mitch's house and up the drive. *'Well, Buddha, what do you think? Will the Wolf walk up the drive like the mailman or slink in the back by boat? Whichever, buddy, we'll be waiting, won't we? Okay, fat man, time for a shower.'* Skelter keyed in the security code and opened the door.

After coffee and a long, slow shower, he shaved, put on blue linen trousers and matching shirt and went out into the garage and looked at the Maserati. It cried out for a run to the mall.

First call was the liquor store for beer and a large box of chocolates for Stan's wife, in the hope that it might save his balls from the mincer. He returned an hour and a half later and had just put the car in the garage when Stan pulled up in a red convertible.

'Be with you in a minute,' said Skelter, 'soon as I lock up and set the alarm.' He went into the house to the control panel, punched in the code and left by the front door, locking it as he went.

'How's things at home?' Skelter asked. 'She forgiven you yet?'

'Work in progress, mate. Got a bit of grovelling to do yet but she'll come around, I wouldn't have missed it, H. You forget how good it feels when you've been out as long as I have. You did me a big favour.'

'Couldn't have done it without you, mate.'

The smell of charcoal that greeted Skelter came as a pleasant surprise. It seemed Stan preferred the traditional over the convenience of bottled gas. 'Don't see the point, mate. Might as well use the grill in the kitchen, can't beat charcoal-grilled steaks for flavour.'

'I'm with you there,' said Skelter. 'Where do you want these?'

'In here,' said Stan, taking one of the crates as he stepped from the terrace through the wide opening into the kitchen. 'Say hi to Jenny.' Stan nodded to a petite blonde preparing a mountain of salad at the island unit.

'Good to see you, H.'

'And you, my love. Nice place,' said Skelter.

Stan opened one of the twin doors to the giant fridge. 'Wherever we can squeeze them in, mate.'

Skelter loaded the bottles and went out and picked up the box of chocolates from the passenger seat of the car. Five minutes later, he sat swapping stories with Stan and drinking beer from an overstuffed, ice-filled cooler.

'Just what I needed, this, mate. I was ready for a change of scenery.'

Stan clinked the neck of his bottle with Skelter's. 'Hope you're hungry, we've got some great steaks.'

Skelter made an effort to relax. 'Sounds perfect.' He could do nothing more until Sunday evening.

Stan grinned as he placed the big tinfoil platter alongside the barbecue.

'Weren't kidding, were you?' said Skelter. 'Steak? Half a cow more like.'

'Coals are about ready. Another beer?'

'I'm okay for now, ta.'

'If you're worried about driving, forget it, you can crash here.'

'Need to keep a clear head,' said Skelter.

Stan frowned and cocked his head to one side. 'What's up?'

'Nothing, honest, tell me about you and Mitch. Didn't you find him the house?'

'That's right, strange coincidence. He walked into the office one day looking for a place, hadn't seen him for twelve years, not since the Falklands.'

'Fate, mate.'

'Maybe so. Anyway, we picked up where we left off. He was a good bloke, but you know that. Served with him, didn't you?'

'Yes, back in the seventies. Twenty-one when I joined the Marines, took a shine to me, he did. I learned a lot from that man.' Skelter's voice faltered, and he took a big swig from the bottle. 'The rumours about Mitch being a smuggler, how much truth is there?'

The smile that creased Stan's features, raised another from Skelter. 'He had a colourful life, Mitch, especially in the early days here. He spent a fair bit of the mid- to late-nineties sailing around the Caribbean and Mexico.'

'Oh, aye.'

'The rest would just be speculation,' said Stan.

'Of course it would,' Skelter replied, with a smile. 'I don't suppose you might have sailed with him at any time?'

'You don't?' said Stan, picking up a large pair of stainless steel tongs to place three huge steaks onto the grill above the ash grey charcoal.

The meat sizzled and spat as it soaked up the heat, releasing a deliciously smoky aroma that sent Skelter's taste-buds into orbit.

'Any news on the funeral?' Stan asked.

'Not yet, I'll let you know soon as.'

'Cheers.'

48

Darkening Clouds

Florida
Saturday, October 30th 2004

In South Miami, Wolf left the motel and drove the pickup to his brother-in-law's garage. He handed over the keys, then walked out into the almost deserted street. A stiff breeze blew Styrofoam fast-food containers and ketchup-stained papers over the weeds, fighting to reclaim cracked concrete for mother nature. After five minutes, he began to take an interest in the few cars parked alongside the road and soon found a suitable model. He looked around. These mean streets were not for the faint-hearted. This was gang-controlled turf. All clear.

The car was a wreck, not even locked. No matter: as long as it moved under its own steam. Wolf jumped in and hot-wired the ignition. It was noisy and the inside looked and smelled like a dumpster, but it ran fine. Forty minutes later, he dumped it in large parking lot in a more affluent part of the city, near the airport. Ten minutes after that, he drove away in someone's shiny silver pride and joy. The two-year-old Lumina took off with a vee six purr towards the North. The Chevy would blend in with Sanibel's affluent surroundings. He turned onto the Tamiami Trail and tucked in behind a dark grey sedan, sticking to the speed limit. The last thing he wanted was a brush with the law.

British Airways flight 1526 touched down at Miami International at 14.27pm local time, just three minutes late. The pilot taxied to the gate and, as the seat belt sign went out, the cabin erupted like an unearthed ant's nest as passengers rummaged in the overhead lockers for baggage. Lucy remained seated, content to gaze out of the window and wait for the commotion to subside. She never understood why people rushed to stand, clutching their bags in cramped discomfort, waiting for the exit tunnel to be connected and the crew to open the cabin doors.

Lucy left the aircraft, made her way to immigration and stood in line. By the time she had cleared passport control and collected her suitcase, it was well past three o'clock. Behind the professional painted smiles, the rental desk was efficient and fast. The cabin of the two-door sedan was clean but depressingly beige and the cheap plastic and futuristic dashboard offended Lucy's design sensibilities. On the plus side, the seats were supportive and comfortable. The air-con produced a pleasant environment. Lucy studied the map for ten minutes in the parking lot before setting off on what she expected to be a three-hour drive, assuming she didn't stop.

Lucy set the cruise control when she reached the Tamiami Trail. The radio belted out Delta Blues from a New Orleans based station, relaxing her, as she settled in for the ninety-minute drive across the Everglades.

Wolf reached the outskirts of Naples in the late afternoon. He found a small roadside steakhouse and pulled up outside. He put the map in his pocket and walked into the timbered air-conditioned interior. A waitress greeted him. 'Good afternoon, my name is Destiny and I will be your waitress for today'.

She led him to a quiet booth and handed him a menu. 'Can I get you something to drink, sir?'

'What beer you got on draught?'

'Coors Light, Miller –.'

'Coors, please, Senorita.'

'Certainly, Sir,' said Destiny, and she turned and headed towards the counter with Wolf's eyes locked on to her peach-like rear.

Cute little ass, I'll take a piece of that. Wolf turned his attention to the menu. When his beer arrived, he ordered T-bone steak, rare, with chunky fries, onion rings and a side of mushrooms.

After he had filled his belly, Wolf ordered another beer and took out the map. He could not believe his luck. The house should be easier to approach than he expected. It overlooked a nature reserve. There had to be a public parking lot or picnic area. He rubbed his hands together beneath the table and smiled. *Soon you will feel the teeth of the Wolf, you who call yourself H. Not a name, only a small part of a name. You will be lots of small parts when I feed you to the sharks, amigo.*

Shawna called at the liquor store to pick up a couple of bottles of California red. It was there that she missed her credit card. After the initial panic died down, she paid cash and walked out to her car, trying to recall where she had last used it. Relief washed over her as she realised she must have left it at Mitch's while distracted by H, in the middle of ordering flowers for her mother. Annoyed with herself for being so careless, she set off for Mitch's. It meant being late for dinner, but when it's dinner for one so what. A spectacular sunset flushed the horizon with carmine and crimson as she drove across the causeway.

The sunset took Lucy Ryder's breath away as she too witnessed its splendour from the same causeway. Her heart rate climbed the closer she got to her destination. *Was Wilkins right? Should she have warned Mark she was coming?* She would know soon enough.

Wolf parked at the wildlife reserve, under the trees. He took a small duffle bag from the car and slung it over his shoulder and wiped the car of prints with a cloth he had brought for that purpose. He set off on foot, walking along a trail, just as the sun's final glow faded. The track ran parallel to the road until it turned deeper into the trees. Here he moved off into the dark of the forest keeping just inside the edge, close enough to see the road. The open nature of the trees and sparse undergrowth made progress easy despite the dark. Wolf soon found himself opposite the house he believed to be the one he wanted. Eva had described the distinctive turret feature, triple-garage facing the road, and that it was the last house on the lane. It had to be the place. The front door was less than one hundred metres away. He took the Colt from his waistband and pulled back the slide. The heavy, forty-five calibre round, chambered with a satisfying click. No car in the driveway, no sign of life. He moved further along to get a view down the side of the building.

A white glow, from twin porch lanterns, illuminated the entrance, but no lights showed at any of the windows. Wolf spotted a camera mounted on the garage covering the drive. One text said there were no working cameras. How could she know? He did not believe Eva had sent the text. Wolf did not worry too much for he knew that even if the cameras were rolling it was unlikely anyone in the house was monitoring them. They were there to record evidence and to act as a deterrent. Speed was the key, speed and surprise. If his gut was right, the man, H, would expect him tomorrow night. The shrubbery on the right offered cover up to the garage, from where he could climb onto the roof and force an upstairs window. Time to move.

49
Stalking Wolf

Sanibel Island, Florida
Saturday, October 30th 2004

Lucy drove along the Sanibel to Captiva road, looking for the turning. She pulled off the tungsten-bright highway onto a narrow, poorly-lit lane. Hemmed in between the dark forest and unlit, unoccupied holiday homes, Lucy grew apprehensive. Black and forbidding, the last mile added to the sense of isolation, the houses being spaced far apart and set well back from the road. She slammed on the brakes as something leapt out of the dark onto the road in front of her. The deer disappeared in a flash, bounding into the trees. She sat for several minutes, heart racing, fighting the panic rising within her. It subsided and she set off again. There were no cars, no sign of human life at all.

Wolf checked for signs of life. Nothing but trees to the right, extending into the darkness, beyond the point where the end of the road met the water, near the entrance to the drive. He edged his way out of the trees and onto the narrow grass verge. One last check and a sprint across the road into the shrubbery. So far so good. He crawled through the bushes to the corner of the garage where he jumped up onto one of tall, plastic garbage cans. With a smile, he shook his head, pulled himself onto the garage roof and lay flat, eyes wide, ears open. No lights came on, no sign of any response at all. Through the trees, a flash of car headlights coming his way. He froze.

Lucy felt the nervous tension reach her gut as her car headlights lit up a thick belt of trees where the road stopped. A huge sigh of relief escaped her lungs as she read the number on the mailbox at the end of the lane and turned into the driveway.

Wolf hugged the shingles as the twin xenon beams swept across the roof like searchlights. He gripped the Colt automatic and squeezed the butt grip lever to release the safety. Like an overworked piston, his heart forced adrenaline around his body.

Lucy set the selector to park, pushed the brake and got out of the car. The porch lights helped to lower her anxiety level as she approached the front door and pressed the bell. She waited, pressed it again and waited. No response, no sound, no lights, no sign of movement. She looked around. Beyond the tiny oasis of light in which she stood, nothing but black.

Somewhere in the forest, an animal howled, piercing the silence with a sharp shiver that sliced through Lucy like a knife, prompting one last desperate stab at the bell.

Wolf inched his way to the edge of the roof and peered down. He watched the woman fidget, glancing left, right and behind. It looked like she was not expected and no one home. That presented him with a problem. If no one was at home, the alarm would be active, almost certainly with a direct line to the alarm company, and that would trigger an armed response. Something he definitely did not want.

She might know something and her car might be useful. *She'll go for the car any second now. As soon as she turns her back...* Wolf braced himself to spring. A second set of headlights caused him to change his mind. Flattened against the roof, he tried to hide behind the miniscule facia.

Lucy whipped around and put up her hand to shield her eyes. The car pulled up alongside hers. The lights died as the engine stopped. A woman got out.

'Can I help you?' she said.

'Thank goodness, I thought I'd had a wasted journey.

My name is Lucy, Lucy Ryder. I'm looking for Mark Skelter.'

'Shawna,' the woman said. 'Ain't no one with that name here, lady.'

'This is Mitch Mitchell's house?' Lucy asked.

'Yes, but I'm afraid Mitch has passed away.'

'Yes, I know, Mark, my husband has been staying here, they are old friends.'

'You mean H?'

'Sorry, yes of course, no one calls him Mark except me.'

'Come on, I'll let you in. I don't know where H is right now, I'm afraid. Do you want help with your bags?'

'I'm fine, thanks.'

'If you want to get them, I'll turn the alarm off,' said Shawna tapping her code into the lock.

Wolf could not believe his luck. He had hit the jackpot. The woman popped the trunk and took a flight bag, slung it over her shoulder and pulled out a suitcase, which she wheeled to the door.

Lucy's leading foot had just crossed the threshold when a violent blow slammed her face-first onto the hard tiled floor and sent her suitcase flying. She heard the start of a scream, punctuated by the sound of the door banging shut as she gasped for breath. The scream never really took off. Shawna looked terrified. The woman's eyes churned Lucy's stomach as her brain tried to make sense of the situation.

'No noise,' said a low-pitched voice.

Lucy twisted around and almost poked her eye out on the muzzle of Wolf's pistol. From where she lay, it looked like the barrel of a cannon. She tasted warm blood in her mouth and her nose was on fire.

'I only have a few dollars,' Shawna said.

Wolf laughed, 'Don't want your money,' he said.

Lucy looked at the stubbled face and the cold, dead eyes. She shuffled away on her bottom until she hit the wall, drew up her knees and clasped her arms around them.

'You flatter yourself,' said Wolf, his words laced with venom. 'Get up. Kitchen.' Lucy stood up, still shaking, and followed Shawna. She licked the blood from her swollen gums. 'For God's sake, what do you want?' Lucy said.

'Shut your stupid mouth and do as I say. Sit.' Wolf put the duffle bag on the table and took out a roll of duct tape. He handed it to Shawna. 'Bind her wrists.'

Shawna fought to control her trembling hands as she wound the tape around 'I'm sorry, so sorry,' she said shaking her head from side to side as she looked at Lucy's blood spattered face. Lucy tried to communicate calm, but without success. Wolf grabbed the tape and wrapped Shawna's wrists and pushed her into the chair. Lucy flinched as the man grabbed her ankle to tape her legs to the chair. Shawna suffered the same indignity

Wolf made coffee and raided the cookie jar, gorged himself on shortbread, then took a wrap of Cocaine from his pocket. He cut a line on the grey marble worktop, rolled a five-dollar bill and snorted the white powder. He rummaged through the cupboards and drawers for a corkscrew and a carving knife. The corkscrew he stabbed into the cork of a bottle of fine Burgundy from the wine rack. The carving knife he waved at the two women across the table, smiling at them.

'You are the woman of this man who calls himself H,' said Wolf, jabbing at Lucy with point of the knife. 'He took my woman. Now I have his. This is justice, no?'

Lucy's mind switched to spin cycle. She tried to speak but only managed a croak, so dry was her throat. She swallowed hard and tried again. 'Who are you? What do you want?'

'Who? I am Lope, the Wolf. Everyone knows the Wolf,' he said.

Shawna nodded, eyes like organ stops, her body trembling.

'Not me.' said Lucy.

'You are English,' said Wolf. 'H, he is English?'

Lucy managed a nod.

'Why you English come to make trouble for the Wolf, eh? What you doing here?'

'What have you done with Mark, I mean H?'

'We have not yet met, but we will very soon... and then,' Wolf raised the knife and stabbed it into the table-top with a ferocity that drew a whimper from Shawna's lips. He left it quivering in front of Lucy.

Shawna started to hyperventilate. Wolf slapped her hard across the face, rocking the chair almost to the tipping point. The look in his eyes sent a shiver like an icicle through Lucy's heart. 'Your man, disrespected me in front of my people, damaged my business and stole my woman. He cost me much money, He will pay for this with his blood. I am very rich, very powerful, I could have him killed for small change, but this is personal.'

The more Wolf spoke, the less sense he made. He just went into a long cocaine-fuelled rant, listing his assets and achievements and bragging about his sexual prowess. Lucy was frightened and confused. Whatever the hell Mark had got mixed up in, it was clearly more serious than she thought. The man could not be reasoned with, which left only one option: escape. Somehow they had to get away, but the golden hour had passed. The sooner after being taken, the better the chance of success. Mark had taught her that. Schooled her in personal safety awareness, even down to hostage taking, not that she took much notice. Why would she? The chances of her being a victim... How wrong could she have been? Now she wished she had paid more attention. At the time, she regarded him as an over protective old fart and had feigned interest to keep him happy. Her mind whirred at high speed, scouring her memory banks for fragments of her husband's lectures.

50
The Wolf Bites

Sanibel Island, Florida
Saturday, October 30th 2004

Skelter and Sam swapped exaggerated war stories and watched the sunset while they waded through bottles of ice cold beer. Subtle interrogation skills, honed over a long career, failed to draw Stan on his past adventures with Mitch, regardless of how many beers the man consumed. Skelter could not help but be impressed. 'Well,' he said, as the last vestige of daylight dissolved into starry black velvet, 'it's been great, but I think I should make tracks.'

'Been good to see you, mate. You know where we are. You're welcome anytime.'

'Thanks, appreciate it.'

'I'll call a cab,' said Stan reaching for his cellphone.

Skelter had drunk more than he had intended, but only beer, no hard liquor. He needed a clear head for Sunday. When the cab driver turned off the highway, Skelter told him to stop. 'I'll take it from here, mate. The walk will do me good.'

The cab driver looked at him as if he was nuts. 'You sure about that, buddy?'

'Less than a mile,' said Skelter.

The man looked into the darkness. 'Your call.'

Skelter paid the man and set off into the black. An insect orchestra filled the sticky night with its overture. Individual architect-designed houses sat on generous plots well distanced from one another. They were set too far back to see much but he got the impression Mitch's was one of the largest.

The walk helped to clear Skelter's head. As he drew level with the wildlife reserve, he noticed a car parked beneath the trees. *Someone looking for moths? Bats? Possible, but I don't think so. 'Better check this out, Buddha boy.'* He tried the driver's door – locked. The mini torch on his keyring showed a tourist map on the passenger seat. Nothing untoward beyond the simple fact the car was there. With a nagging doubt he walked away into the lane and carried on towards the house.

Skelter stopped dead halfway up the drive and moved into the shadows. *What's occurring here? That looks like Shawna's car. Whose is the other one? Hey, Buddha buddy, wake up and get your brain in gear. Something here is well out of order.* He slid his right hand into his pocket. *Shit, the revolver, in my other shorts. Damn. Steady, boy. Improvise, adapt, overcome.*

Skelter retraced his steps to the lane and made his way to the edge of the wildlife refuge. With instinct, touch and the occasional glimmer of moonlight, he worked his way through the trees to the side of the house and beyond the end of the road. The ditch that separated the trees from the lane was wide here as it opened into the Intracoastal Waterway. He would have to wade across to reach the rear of the house. Skelter reached into his left pocket and stroked his mentor's bald pate. *'If I'm wrong and there's an innocent explanation for this, Buddha, buddy, I'm going to look a right dickhead.* He took stock. *Not going to happen, is it? You feel it, too, I can tell.'*

Wolf snorted another couple of lines and opened a fresh bottle of wine. 'What you do here, woman?' Wolf asked Shawna, 'you no lady, you work for this man, H?'

'I work for Mr Mitchell, only he died just the other day.'

Wolf jabbed his finger at Lucy, 'why you come here?'

'Funeral.'

Wolf laughed. 'That's real funny lady. You gonna have another soon.' He laughed loud and long. 'You kill me lady, you so funny.'

Shawna started to cry. Lucy stared at the knife embedded in the table top, looking for a way out of their situation. Too late she realised her mistake.

Wolf grasped the handle and jerked the blade out of the wood. He stabbed the point at Lucy's face. She threw her head to the side, the tip cold against her skin. 'Bitch, you try that again I cut your throat.'

Shawna made a noise like a rabbit in a gin trap. Wolf

smacked her across the face with a vicious backhand that snapped her head sideways knocking her chair back. Shawna's knees caught the underside of the table and prevented her crashing onto the hard floor.

Skelter found a fallen branch about as thick as a broom handle, but kinked and crooked. He stepped into the canal, testing the depth with the branch. The water, surprisingly cold for such a humid evening, drew a sharp intake of breath as it reached his wedding tackle. That was as deep as it got and he was soon across, following the shore to the bottom of the garden and along to the boat. He looked towards the house. The kitchen lights revealed someone at the table.

Skelter climbed aboard the boat. In the cabin, he opened the cupboard and took out a spear-gun. He hauled back on the spring and loaded the barbed steel mini-harpoon. He also picked up a torch and a heavy diver's knife. With a deep breath, he patted Buddha's head and made for the shrubbery.

Lucy tried hard to remain calm, despite the shock and confusion. She struggled to work out what was going on but Wolf's deranged ramblings made it impossible to make any sense of it. She had to do something, and soon.

Skelter's adrenaline pump hit the panic button when he got close enough to see into the kitchen. He recognised Wolf at once. A second later he realised that the woman with Shawna was Lucy. *How the fuck? You bastard,*

I'll...Stop, boy, wind your neck in, don't lose your cool. You're right, Buddha, buddy, you're right. Be professional. Can't go in gun's blazing. For one, you don't have a gun and he will have, that's for sure. Skelter withdrew and worked his way around to the garage. With the aid of a coconut palm growing close to the wall, he climbed onto the roof and crept across to the wall of the house, treading as lightly as his espadrilles allowed. The window to the smallest bedroom overlooked the roof above the porch. He probed the frame for weakness using the diver's knife. *Easy does it, now, steady. For fuck's sake, keep it quiet. C'mon, you've done this before, what's the matter with you? That bastard is going to die. If he has hurt her, I will cut his balls off...*

Skelter paused and shook his head hard. *Concentrate, damn it. Stay focused.* Breathing steadied, he pushed the blade in level with the bottom catch and levered the heavy steel blade back and forth as quietly as he could. It sprung open with a snap like a gun shot. Skelter stopped breathing, reached down for the spear gun and climbed through the window. Speed was his best chance. He darted out of the door into his room and grabbed the pistol from under his pillow. He pulled back the slide and crouched, facing the door. Heart racing, driving high-speed adrenaline, he fought to control his breathing, licking his lips to counter the dryness. Sweat oozed from his palms and forehead. His internal antenna swept the airwaves as his ears strained to detect any sound.

Remember, Buddha, it's the second noise that gives you away. The first attracts attention. The listener waits for more to confirm their suspicions. If they don't hear another sound nine times out of ten they dismiss the first. Stay silent and you have every chance of getting away with it. Not a sound, buddy.

51

Settling Scores

Sanibel Island, Florida
Saturday, October 30th 2004

Wolf stopped his drug fuelled rant in mid flow, cocking his head towards the door, to the hall. Shawna had heard it, too. Wolf looked unsure. He turned to the women. Lucy looked away, but he leaned across the table, grabbed her chin and stared into her eyes, his hot breath on her face. He picked up the Colt, walked to the door, stopped and listened.

Lucy looked at the carving knife lying flat on the work surface beyond the table. She looked at Wolf. He passed through the doorway and disappeared. Lucy lifted her arms over her head. *God, I hope this works.*

Wolf appeared in the doorway, pointing the Colt at Lucy, his face a puzzled mask. She lowered her arms, trying to keep her breathing even. 'Just stretching, my arms went to sleep.'

He grabbed the roll of duct tape, tore off a strip and he stuck it across her mouth. Shawna winced, wild-eyed with fear, as he sealed her lips in the same fashion.

Lucy could see he didn't believe her but could also see Wolf had no idea what she had been about to attempt.

Wolf went into the hall and across to the foot of the stairs. Despite the silence, he remained convinced someone was up there and backed up into the office, unseen by the women. He left the door ajar by a pencil's width.

After a minute, Skelter moved forward and crouched to listen again. Nothing. He eased the door a fraction and peered through the gap along the barrel of the gun. Still nothing. He stole out onto the landing, crept towards the top of the staircase and lay prone, hardly daring to breathe. With infinite care, he inched his way forward until he could peer around the corner through the balustrade. The hallway below was empty. He rose to his feet without a sound and started down the stairs, nerve ends fizzing, wired for instant response. Movement in the kitchen, the sound of a chair scraping over tiles. Weapon pointed at the centre of the scene, step by nervous step, Skelter advanced, slowly easing his weight to the front foot to minimise the chance of creaking a tread.

Balanced on the balls of his feet, he stepped onto the

tiled hallway, palms sweating, adrenaline in free flow. Skelter took a step towards the kitchen door, licking his bone-dry lips, his heart pounding.

Lucy raised her arms high above her head again. *All or nothing, here goes. Think positive.* It had worked when Mark did it for a bet. Why wouldn't it work for her? He'd told her anyone could do it. Shawna looked on, baffled and frightened. Lucy stood up with difficulty, her ankles being taped to the chair legs. She took a quick, deep breath and brought her arms down in one swift movement. Her elbows slid past her waist and her forearms struck her hips with considerable force. The miracle happened. The duct tape tore through and her wrists were free. Lucy waddled over to the knife and cut her ankles from the chair, her heart banging like a shutter in a hurricane.

Wolf stiffened at the sound coming from the kitchen, in two minds what to do, still convinced there was somebody upstairs. He edged the door a touch to get eyes on the whole of the hallway.

Skelter froze as his peripheral vision registered movement – the office door. He dropped to one knee, squeezed against the wall on the kitchen side and levelled the pistol. Any threat would have to step out to target him. He aimed at the door. It might be Lucy. Skelter saw the muzzle of the Colt through the crack. It boomed twice, in quick succession. Both bullets passed straight through the plasterboard wall beside Skelter's head. He returned fire with a double tap, both rounds right through the inch-wide gap between door and frame. A woman screamed followed by a loud thump, like a hay bale falling off a wagon. The door clicked shut.

Skelter darted forward and kicked it. It moved a couple of inches and struck something solid. Skelter went for the front door, wrenched it open and ran outside around to the office window. He looked in to see Wolf on the floor the Colt beside him.

Skelter rushed back inside to the kitchen. 'Lucy, you okay?' She stood shaking, carving knife held in both hands. He rushed over and kissed her. 'Sure you're okay, now?'

'Yes, yes, that man?'

'He can't hurt you now.'

Shawna screamed and began hyperventilating.

'See to her. Stay in here.'

'Mark.'

'Just a minute' He crossed the hall, pistol at the ready and shoved at the office door, almost falling into the room as it swung open. He jumped to the side in surprise and alarm and flattened himself to the wall. He jerked his head in and out in the blink of an eye, just long enough to see the open window. 'Shit.' He dropped low and rolled in, sweeping the room with the Glock. Empty. Blood on the floor, blood behind the door, and the window sill. He looked through the window. No sign of Wolf. *'Only one place he's going, Buddha, buddy.'*

Skelter nipped out to the umbrella stand for the pistol he had concealed earlier and ran back to the kitchen. 'He's gone out the window. Here.' He cocked the Beretta and handed it to Lucy. 'Car keys. Quick.'

'No, Mark.'

'Car keys.'

Lucy shook her head.

Shawna pointed to her purse. Skelter pulled it open, took the bunch and grabbed Lucy's hand that held the pistol. He held it to her face. 'Safety is on, here, see? Lucy, focus. Press to release, got it?'

She nodded like an automaton. 'We should call 911.'

'No. No police, understand? No police.'

'Mark.'

'Got to go.'

He ran outside, dived behind Shawna's car, zapped the lock, opened the door and slid behind the wheel, his heart hammering. Eyes everywhere, he reversed out fast, tyres squealing as he careered into the lane, swung round, slammed into forward, hit the gas and switched on the lights. He had driven almost three hundred metres when the bright white beams picked out a figure moving erratically in the distance. Skelter stamped the pedal to the floor.

The figure stopped, turned and dived off the road into the ditch. Skelter skidded to a halt, thirty feet from where the figure had disappeared. He jumped from the car, into the ditch. Heart racing, pistol at the ready, he advanced towards the spot where Wolf had disappeared.

Lucy poured two very large whiskies and passed one to a still shaking, Shawna. Lucy raised the glass with her left hand, her right locked around the butt of the pistol.

'What the hell is going on?'

'I don't know,' said Shawna, ashen faced, 'H went to get Eva, Maria's daughter, from that Wolf man. He is evil. H caused him much trouble. He wants revenge.'

'If Wolf doesn't kill him, he'll wish he had when I get my hands on him. He promised me.' Her face was a collage of frustration, disappointment and fury. 'No more he said, never again. He promised.' She knocked back the whisky in one, coughing as she drained the glass.

Skelter stopped, hugged the bank and listened. Nothing but the chorus of night creatures. *Got to stop him reaching the car.* He crawled forward, toes, knees and knuckles, silent as a panther, stopped. No sound from his quarry. Forward again. Stop listen, move a couple of metres. His eyes ached from straining into the pitch dark. Soaked with sweat and swamp water from the ditch, at least he wasn't bleeding like his quarry. The moon disappeared behind the clouds of a gathering storm and darkness fell black as pitch in a tar barrel. Not even starlight to relieve the blackness. Only his ears to work with now. The weight of the pistol reassuring. Skelter was in the eye of his comfort zone.

Wolf lay still in the vegetation at the far side of the ditch two hundred metres from his car. As he shrank back into the dark, thick, waterside growth, he realised his adversary's vehicle was much closer. His left arm hung down, wrapped with his bloody, shirt as best as he could manage. It was still bleeding but the flow had decreased. He bit his lip and gripped his Colt tighter, unable to see a thing through the curtain of darkness. The only sounds to reach his ears came from frog and insect chorus.

307

Skelter moved forward, through the velvet black inch by inch. Suddenly, the heavens opened. He pressed forward, despite the downpour, his body on fire with adrenaline, expecting at any moment to bump noses with Wolf. The rain drummed a deafening tattoo on the vegetation, making it impossible to hear anything but the loudest sounds; like the noise of an automobile engine.

The mechanical growl came from behind. In the heat of the chase, he had left the keys in Shawna's car. 'Shit.' He scrambled up to the road ready to shoot at the vehicle. The engine noise faded into the storm. Skelter broke into a run, oblivious of the rain hammering into his face. 'Jesus, no, Lucy,' he yelled. He screamed her name at the top of his lungs, legs pounding like pistons as he raced after the car.

A sound from outside gave Lucy a start. 'Mark's back.'

Shawna looked full of doubt. Lucy gripped the pistol with both hands, arms extended, elbows locked. As she reached the door she remembered the safety catch and looked down at the gun. She pushed the safety to the red spot and looked up straight into the eyes of the Wolf, staring down the sights of his Colt. Lucy's brain seized. Her entire world funnelled into the black hole about to explode and end her short life.

Twin echoing blasts drowned Shawna's scream.

Wolf pitched forward, smashing face first into the tiled floor, driven by two nine-millimetre bullets slamming between his shoulder blades at 460 metres per second. In the open window, braced against the frame, Skelter stood, gripping his smoking pistol with both hands, pointing it at the body.

He climbed inside and squelched across to Wolf. He kicked the Colt clear and checked the body. Satisfied the man no longer posed a threat, Skelter stepped over the body and into the hall.

'Let me have that, Cariad,' he whispered, as he gently took the pistol from Lucy's trembling hand. 'You don't need it now.' Arms wrapped tight around her, he held her to his chest until she breathed again. 'Don't worry – he can't hurt anyone anymore.'

There were no tears. Later, maybe.

'Cariad?'

Skelter moved her into the kitchen, where Shawna stood deep in shock.

'Deep breaths Shawna, deep breaths, you too Lucy.'

'What is this, Mark?'

Skelter poured each of them a stiff Scotch.

'What about the police, Mark?'

'I told you, no police. If they get involved Maria will be deported and her son arrested…'

'I don't understand,' said Lucy.

'Ok, ok, first things first. Shawna… Shawna, drink the whisky, I need you to focus. Listen, it's complicated. The short edit will have to do for now We've a lot to do before daylight. Shawna, is anyone at home next door?'

'No. Snowbirds, from Ohio. They only come for the winter, December through March.'

'Perfect. Okay, here's the story…'

52

Clean Up

Sanibel Island, Florida
Saturday/Sunday, October 30th/31st 2004

Skelter told the tale of the failed attempt to rescue Eva from the island, the successful Everglades episode, and where Wolf fitted in. He gave the women ten minutes and more Scotch – to help them digest it. 'This is what we are going to do. As soon as I move him, we clean up every trace. The storm will wash away any evidence outside. We clean the office and the hall.'

Shawna clapped a hand over her mouth and pointed to the unit behind Skelter. What appeared to be blood was seeping from the back the cupboard and down the tiles. A smile of relief spread across Skelter's face as he looked inside the cupboard. The shots from Wolf's automatic had passed through the wall and mangled a tin of tomato juice. Skelter removed a few tins and extracted both spent bullets.

'Once we've removed the evidence, put your clothes in the washing machine and get showered.

'What about him?' Lucy said, gesturing towards the door.

'Lowlife like that become statistics every week. He won't be missed. The police would assume it's a gang killing, except I don't intend for them to find the body. Now are you up for this? Shawna?'

She stroked the darkening bruise on her face. 'He got what he deserved and I sure don't want to get involved with the police.'

Skelter breathed a huge sigh. 'Great, stay in here and close the door, start with the cupboard, duct tape, glasses, cups, anything he touched, bag it for me or in the dishwasher. Second thoughts, I'll take the duct tape,' said Skelter, picking up the roll. 'Give me five minutes to clear the hall and I'll let you know when to come out, okay?'

Shawna nodded, Lucy whispered 'yes'.

Skelter found a pack of disposable latex gloves and a tarp in the garage. 'Wear these,' he said, handing the box of gloves to the women. He went into the hall, closing the door behind him. Skelter rolled the body onto the tarp, bound it with rope and duct tape and dragged it to the garage. Wolf was heavy for such a slim, young man. 'No way am I dragging you all the way down the garden, boy.' Skelter walked across to Mitch's ride-on

311

lawnmower. Outside the rain lashed against the house, trees swaying hard in the gale. *'What do you reckon? Better give it an hour, eh, Buddha, buddy?'*

Inside the house, the women scrubbed and mopped the floors. Skelter got stuck into the window through which Wolf had escaped and re-entered. By one a.m., the work was complete, except for the bullet holes in the wall. Skelter filled these with cellulose filler from the workshop and then hung a picture from the office over the repair.

'Okay, all done. Go and shower, I'll finish up.'

'What about…?'

'All in hand, Cariad. Wrapped in his shroud, ready for the boat.'

'Boat. What boat?'

'Mitch has a boat at the bottom of the garden. Tomorrow, Wolf and I are going fishing. Is anyone expecting you home Shawna?'

'No. Can I stay here tonight?'

'Sure, why don't you show Lucy my room and you use Maria's, I'm sure she wouldn't mind.'

Skelter heaved the corpse across the engine cover of the mower and secured it with bungee cords. The wind and rain had eased. *'Now or never, let's get this done, Buddha.'* He opened the twin doors at the back and climbed onto the machine. The engine fired first time and the mower chugged into the fading storm. The machine crabbed sideways down the gentle slope to the waterline, as the balloon tyres fought for traction on the wet grass. Skelter eased the machine to the end of the jetty.

It took longer than expected. He pulled the body off and dragged it along the staging to the boat and hauled it on to the stern. By the time he had skidded his way over the lawn, back to the garage, he was knackered. He walked back to examine the lawn, relieved to find that the damage was slight, then returned and closed the doors. He stripped off, put his things in the washer and set it going.

Lucy was awake when he slid in and wrapped himself around her. They stayed that way until, overcome with fatigue, they fell asleep.

The storm blew itself out during the night and when Skelter woke, Lucy was already up, sitting by the window looking out over the garden and beyond to the water. He got out of bed and walked over to her.

'You okay, Lucy?'

'Think so. Last night, it doesn't seem real. Like something on television.'

'Nature taking over, your body needs respite so your mind blocks out the bad stuff. It will filter through later. Book a few more sessions with Judith when we get home. I'll be here for you, promise. Sorry I dragged you into this mess.'

She looked at him like a headmistress about to read the riot act to a wayward schoolboy. 'You know I love you, Mark.'

'I feel a big 'but' about to smack me in the face.'

She spoke in a soft voice, her words measured, sharp and clear. 'You promised me you had given up all this action man stuff. You lied to me.'

Her eyes bored into his like lasers. He avoided her

313

gaze.

'Don't look away.'

The words stung like a scorpion and a cold shiver slid down his back. The steel look unnerved him. Skelter turned to her, shame faced.

'It's time you grew up, Mark. I will be generous and give you another chance, one you don't deserve. Look at me. Fuck up again and we are finished, understand?'

Skelter felt like a naughty schoolboy, but with the fear of a man about to face a firing squad. For the first time, he realised how precious she was to him. The cold possibility he could lose her struck him like a rifle bullet. 'I won't let you down again. I promise. I've got plans for the future. Plans to proper settle down.'

'I'm listening.'

'Can we get a coffee first?'

'Okay, get dressed, but no stalling, Mark, I mean it.'

'No, Cariad, promise.'

'So, what is this grand master plan, action man – retired?' The emphasis on 'retired' carried a strong and unambiguous message.

'Depends how you feel about living in Scotland.'

'I'll answer that when you tell me your plan.'

Skelter passed her a coffee and sat down on the other side of the table. 'Before I do, let me tell you why I'll never do another job. Last night, I made a mistake, a serious mistake. I let my feelings for you override my professional judgement, and because of that, I put your life at risk.'

Lucy looked blank.

'I didn't check the body. If I had, Wolf wouldn't have got away.' Skelter leaned forward and took her hand in a tight grip. 'Cariad, I almost got you killed.'

Lucy softened. 'I guess that supports the argument that says you love me, then.'

Skelter nodded. 'I'm past it,' he said in a serious tone. 'Time to hang up my spurs for good.'

She smiled, but said nothing.

'So, are you okay?' he asked.

'I think so. I didn't have nightmares last night, if that's what you mean.'

'Good. They may come later, though.'

'I know,' she said, softly. 'So, tell me about the plan.'

Skelter took a swallow from his coffee cup. 'Mitch has left me is an awesome responsibility and I intend to take it seriously. The estate runs successfully in his absence, as does the distillery. The Mitchell house is run as a hotel, with one wing for the family, but they are now all deceased. We could make it our new home. I want to set up an adventure and survival centre for under-privileged kids, as a permanent memorial to Mitch.'

Lucy smiled and placed her hand over his. 'That is a lovely idea, Mark.'

'He gave me the best start and I want to do the same for others. I've got the skills, connections, everything I need. Apparently, there's loads of wild land perfect for the job, rivers, streams, woods and moorland... Sorry, I'm getting carried away.'

Lucy smiled again. 'It's fine, your passion, it does you credit. I'm sure Mitch would be proud.'

'So, we can move to Scotland?'

'No promises, but I will think about it.'

An hour later, while Lucy and Shawna sat drinking coffee in the kitchen, Skelter went into the garage to rummage amongst the shelves and storage. He put a pair of old dumbbells, a heavy brass padlock and two lengths of chain into an old gym bag and picked up a fishing rod.

Skelter cast off and took the boat out into the channel and set course for the Gulf. It would be a long day, but the weather was calm now that the storm had passed. With the throttle set to cruise Skelter steered out into the open water. *'Well, Buddha, this is a rum do and no mistake.'*

After three hours, he cut the engine. The sea was flat calm. Searching 360° with the binoculars, he satisfied himself he was alone and heaved the bundle half onto the gunwale. It was a delicate balancing act. He got the chain around the body and passed it through the centre holes in the barbell weights. The boat listed 30°, threatening to dump Wolf in before he was ready.

'Tricky, this, Buddha, buddy, got to get the padlock on before he goes.' Skelter fumbled with the lock, fighting to keep his feet as the cadaver tilted dangerously towards the deep.

'Fucking hell.' He steadied his feet snapping the lock shut just in time. Wolf slipped over and slid beneath the water in a trail of bubbles, as trapped air escaped the tarp. The boat bobbed and rocked back and forth to settle on an even keel. *'Thank God that's done, eh, boy? We can go home now.'* Skelter looked down at the dumbbells by his feet, *'Didn't have time to tuck these in, buddy, still there's more'n enough to do the job I reckon.'*

The sun was setting by the time Skelter nudged the cruiser alongside the jetty. Lucy stood on the dock looking anxious. 'Like clockwork,' he said to her unasked question. 'No problems. Anything to eat? I'm starving.'

Her face relaxed. She felt the tension leave her body. 'Oh, Mark.'

'Relax, Cariad, it's over now.'

He finished tying up, stepped onto the dock and held her. Arms around each other, they walked towards the house.

'Lasagne in the oven, from the freezer. Might be a bit dry by now, been in on low for ages. I guessed you'd be hungry. Shawna's gone home.'

'How is she?'

'Don't worry, she won't say anything.'

'That's not what I meant.'

'Yes it is. She's okay now, anyway.'

53
Last Post

Sanibel Island, Florida
Wednesday, November 3ʳᵈ 2004

Uniforms stood out amongst the suits and black dresses at Mitch's funeral. Medal-chested US Navy and Marine Corps and a Royal Marine bugler in dress blues mingled with ex-pats, including Stan and his wife. An impressive wreath from the Royal Marines lay alongside a beautiful understated Christian cross in white lilies, with a single red rose at the centre. A card bore a simple message. *'The little we had was my whole world. Maria x.'*

Later, at the wake at the local golf club, in glorious sunshine, Skelter drank a final toast to his much-missed friend. Maria conducted herself with a dignity that would have made Mitch proud, but Skelter knew that behind the mask lay a devastated soul.

'How is Eva?' he asked.

'The doctors say that with good treatment, she will beat the addiction and get well again,' she said. 'Pray to God he is out of her life for good.'

Skelter took both her hands in his and looked into her troubled eyes, 'Wolf is gone,' he said, 'gone for good. He will not,' Skelter corrected himself, 'cannot, hurt anyone again, not ever.'

She frowned. 'How can you be sure?'

'Never, Maria, not on this earth.'

Maria's eyes flickered like small candles, the kind you get on birthday cakes. 'Thank you, H.'

Skelter squeezed her hand. 'Maria.'

She looked a little lighter of spirit and walked with a more positive step.

A chapter in Skelter's eventful life had reached the last page. He looked forward to a new and very different set of challenges, but he did not underestimate the magnitude of the task he faced. He had his rock to steady and guide him – Lucy. He would not screw up this time, she was way too precious.

'What will you do now, Maria?' Lucy asked.

'I am not sure. I do not wish to stop working. Mitch has left me so much, but without work I will be unhappy. Maybe I sell the house but keep the boat. So much it is the soul of my Mitch.' Maria brushed away the start of a tear with her fingers. 'To buy bar or restaurant would be good. Most my life since sixteen years old, I worked waiting on tables and tending bar so I understand the

319

ways of the business.'

'Sounds like a good plan,' said Lucy. 'Will you look here?'

'Oh no, I want to be in Key West. It is my home. The money will help my brother get his own place, which will make me happy. The most important thing is having money to pay for Eva's treatment. Deep in her heart, she is a good girl, but a bad man turned her head. H says Lope is gone for ever.'

Lucy's face took on a serious expression as she nodded confirmation to Maria who, on impulse, took a pace forward and hugged Lucy.

Skelter accepted the beer offered by Stan. 'Cheers, mate, I was ready for another.'

'So when are you off to U.K., H?' Stan asked.

'Monday. Overnight flight from Miami.'

'Mitch had a good send off, anyway.'

'You can say that again. I wasn't expecting so many people. Who are they all?'

'Mitch got involved with a few local charities, committee member at the golf club and the yacht club. You couldn't help but like him, he was that sort of bloke. Shame about him and Maria, they would have been good together.'

Skelter looked across the terrace at Maria and Lucy, who were deep in conversation with Stan's wife. 'Aye, it is a shame. Bloody religion. Anyway, it was good to meet you, mate, let's keep in touch.'

Stan nodded. 'Yeah, we must. If you ever find yourself over here...'

'Don't worry, I'll come and raid your fridge for beer.'

'Anytime, mate. It's been great to see action again,

but don't tell the wife I said that, for God's sake.'

Skelter's smile almost morphed into laughter. Like many men of action, Stan would rather face the enemy than his woman on the warpath.

Later, Lucy and Skelter sat on the terrace and opened a bottle of Burgundy. The early evening was warm and the sky clear.

'Lovely service,' said Lucy. 'Beautiful location, and that golf course…'

'Yes, terrific vista.'

'When did they say you can collect the ashes?'

'Friday morning. What do you think about organising a memorial service up on Speyside when we get back, Cariad?'

'What a wonderful idea, very fitting. I'm sure it will go down well with the people on the estate. Don't know about you, but I'm looking forward to going home.'

'Do you know, I am about to start a new chapter in my life, and for the first time, I can honestly say I am ready for it.'

'What about your addiction?'

The remark took Skelter aback. 'I'm in control of that. Sheila discharged me.'

'Not Valium,' said Lucy, 'You proved you can handle that one. We both know what really lights your fire; you're an adrenaline junkie. Can you give that up? Because, if you can't, then our future together is far from certain.'

The statement rocked Skelter like a playful slap rather than a right hook. He had been expecting it sometime soon. 'Adrenaline is a powerful rush, I don't deny, but I've given it a lot of thought lately. I have a strategy to deal with it.'

'Oh?' said Lucy, 'Pray tell. I am all ears.'

'Passion,' said Skelter. 'Something we Welsh are famous for. I am sure I can replace the adrenaline with the kick I'll get teaching kids self-confidence, showing them they can achieve anything, but it's not just the outdoor stuff. This adventure-training centre will be the best in Britain, and I'll set up a trust fund in Mitch's name to help kids from backgrounds like mine. Give them a leg up in the world.'

'So much passion pouring from my lovely man,' said Lucy. 'Let's hope you've the answer.'

'I can do this, Lucy, but not on my own. I need you with me.'

He looked like a man on a ledge: poised, nervous, waiting for the outstretched hand to help him back to safety. She reached out. 'We will do this together, darling.'

'You're happy to move to Scotland?'

'Maybe.'

Skelter looked at her with affection. 'Tell you what, we have a few days before our flight back, how do you fancy spending a couple in Key West before we go home? You could relax and take time to mull it over.'

'What about work, Mark? You can't leave them in the lurch.'

'Sorted, I called and spoke to Alan. Geordie Spencer's stepped in to the breach.'

'Thought he'd retired?'

'Yes, but he's still up to it, even at sixty, and he understands the system. Besides, it's extra beer money for him.'

'In that case, okay. Don't suppose we can get in at Dizzy's place?'

'Doubt it. What time is it? Six forty-five, let's give them a call, Dizzy could well still be there, we might get lucky.' He reached into his pocket and took out his phone. At first he got the number engaged signal but after a few attempts he got through.

'Key West Bed and Breakfast, how may I help you?' Dizzy's unmistakable accent brought a smile to his face. 'Tell me you're not fully booked right now and make me a happy man,' he said.

There was a slight pause and then. 'Mark Skelter?'

'The one and only.'

'Well, how are you?' she said.

'Pretty good, but Lucy and I need chilling time.'

'Let me see, I don't think we have anything before Christmas, except tomorrow through Saturday – too soon, of course.'

'Brilliant. Sold. We're only up in Sanibel, we can drive down.'

'You have stayed in the Bates room before, I think.'

'Ground, sorry first floor, in your language. Yes, nice room, big.'

'I have written that in the book. Look forward to seeing you tomorrow.'

'You too, bye.' Skelter punched the air. 'Result.' He called the rental company and ordered a car to be delivered to the house at eleven the next morning. 'We are on a roll, Cariad,' he said, clinking glasses with Lucy and taking a slug of red. What say we order pizza to go with the vino?

'Excellent idea. Hawaiian for me, please.'

By the time they made it to bed, they were stuffed

and well in their cups, but neither could sleep, nor did either show any amorous inclinations.

'How does it feel, Mark? How do you feel, I mean, when you shoot someone?'

Skelter sat up. 'What brought this on, Cariad? No one ever asks a soldier that question.'

'But you are not a soldier anymore, are you? Don't you feel anything, taking the life of another human being?'

'He was about to shoot you, for Christ's sake. I had no choice.'

Lucy lay on her side and reached out to touch his thigh. 'Yes, and thank God you were there. I just can't get my head around it.'

'You knew I was a soldier when we met. It is what we do. We train to use deadly force but most of us hope we will never have to and, thank the lord, few of us face making that decision.'

'But you, Mark, you have, more than a few times. You must feel something.'

'Enough, Lucy, all that's in the past. I did what I had to. Wolf was a pussycat compared to some of the evil men out there. If we don't stand up to them, they will impose a rule you could not begin to comprehend. I will not defend doing my duty to anyone.' He got out of bed and pulled on shorts and a T-shirt.

'Mark?'

'I need some air,' he said, picking up the key and his wallet. He walked through the door without looking back.

54

Winding Down?

Florida
Thursday, November 4th 2004

Skelter drove south towards Naples, but Lucy fell fast asleep well before he reached the outskirts. Much to his relief, she slept right the way across the Everglades and onto the upper keys. By the time they reached Key Largo, he was hungry and stopped for food. They sat opposite each other in the diner but exchanged hardly a word. Back on the highway, Lucy dropped off again, dozing most of the way to the lower Keys, which suited Skelter better than the awkward silent routine. The radio played country music at low volume; the sun shone down from a cobalt sky and he was in the mood for his own company, and Buddha's, of course. Skelter consulted his mentor through the medium of thought waves. *Got her knickers in a real twist this time, eh, fat man? What did she expect me to do, let him shoot her and then tell him what a bad boy he was? Bloody women, what the hell is up with them? What planet are they on, for Pete's sake?*

Lucy opened her eyes but she could not bring herself to speak. Her husband's eyes were fixed on the road, as much to avoid eye contact as anything else, she realised. They were on a bridge, turquoise water stretched away to the horizon on each side. Ahead a sign answered her unasked question. Marathon – around an hour to go. Unable to cope with the awkward silence she feigned sleep, her head awash with unwanted images and unresolved questions. The stark reality of her husband's work had been a severe culture shock. Lucy questioned her future with a man who killed for a living. He had to put it all behind him for good, right now, to give their marriage a fighting chance. The pain in her gut cut deep and she turned to the window to hide the tears forming in her eyes. She opened them again as they pulled up at traffic lights on North Roosevelt Boulevard at the junction with Eisenhower Drive. Ten minutes and they would reach their destination.

As soon as they checked in, Skelter crashed out on the bed nearest the door, having not slept the night before. Lucy laid her pyjamas on the other.

Lucy went out for a walk to try to clear her mind wandering aimlessly in and out of souvenir shops along

Duval Street until she ran out of island. At the Southernmost Point, the tourists stood in line for photographs beside the giant concrete bollard with its slogan '90 miles to Cuba'. As she gazed towards the horizon, she wondered if maybe she had reached the end of the road with Mark? Despite desperately wanting it not to be the case, the image of him – gun still smoking in his hand and Wolf's body on the bloody floor – would not go away.

Far from a relaxing escape, the visit to Key West turned out to be more like a prison sentence for two incompatible cellmates. Sparse conversation, meaningful communication non-existent, they drifted further apart. By the morning of the last full day, Skelter did not emerge for breakfast until Lucy had finished hers and gone out.

He took out his mentor and placed the little, green God on the table in the garden, alongside a plate of mixed fruit and lifted a coffee cup to his lips. *It's all turning to rat shit, Buddha, and I don't think I can stop it. I screwed up. Should have checked the body. That was sloppy. I'm over the hill, and the irony is, I know it. I have to stop, now, just when she wants me to. With the inheritance, our future's secure, but she doesn't trust me. Shouldn't have lied to her. Not going to forgive me, is she? What a bloody mess.* The coffee he drank, the fruit he left untouched.

55
Reality Check

Florida
Sunday, November 7th 2004.

Skelter swung his legs off the mattress, lowered the volume on the radio alarm and headed for the shower. Lucy groaned, turned over and buried her head in the pillow.

Don't go back to sleep now, she heard him shout above the cascade. Taxi will be here for seven thirty.

God, wont he ever let up. she said to herself. *Why did we open that third bottle last night?*

'Shower's all yours,' he said breezing in, bollocks swaying in the slipstream.

Does he have to be so bloody chirpy? By the time she had

struggled out of bed, he had his case beside the door – packed, strapped and tagged.

'Come on, love.'

Lucy ignored him and plugged in the hair dryer. 'Go fuck yourself,' she muttered under her breath as she sat on the edge of the bed and rooted around in her bag for paracetamol.

Skelter stowed his flight bag under the seat, buckled the belt and settled in next to the window with his nose buried in a book.

Beside him, Lucy sighed, and took out her phone. A quick scroll showed no new messages. She switched the device off and settled in her seat. No point in saying anything, the mood he was in. All that fuss, God knows, they made it, didn't they? And with time to spare. So anal with his obsession for being early. Why would anyone want to hang around an airport for two hours when they could sleep in? She closed her eyes and snoozed only to be woken by the voice of the pilot.

'Good morning ladies and gentlemen and welcome aboard this Delta Eagle flight to Miami. Flying time will be approximately 45 minutes. The weather is sunny and clear, so we expect a smooth trip. Sit back, relax and enjoy your flight.'

The 'Fasten Seat Belts' sign came on with a ping and Lucy buckled up and thumbed through the in flight magazine. The flight attendant performed her animated safety drill as the plane taxied in preparation for take-off. By the time they had reached the end of the runway,

Lucy had dozed off again, but as the little CRJ 700 rolled forward, she opened her eyes.

He looked away, out of the window. Engine noise increased as the aircraft gathered pace towards the point where the pressure beneath the wing exceeded that of the air flowing over it, generating the lift required to achieve flight. A steep climb followed through the low cloud belt and up into the sunshine.

The whine of the landing gear retracting ended with a thump as the undercarriage doors closed. *How could she be so relaxed?* He tried to get into his book as they levelled off and turned onto the flight-path heading. Bright morning sun streamed in, illuminating the page of his thriller, its golden rays warm and comforting. The seat belt sign went out, but he remained buckled, while she released with an exaggerated flourish.

After only twenty minutes in the air, Skelter noticed a shadow fall across the text, and he looked out at a bright blue cloudless sky. It seemed strange, but he carried on reading. A few minutes later he looked up again, surprised to see the sun shining through the windows on the opposite side of the aircraft. The seat belt warning light came on again. A flight attendant walked along the aisle checking seat belts, the forced smile upon her lips betrayed by the anxiety in her eyes. Skelter winked at her. She looked away. His pulse quickened, he checked his belt buckle and looked at Lucy.

'We've changed course. One hundred and eighty degrees. Sun's moved across. Something's up, we're heading back.' Not wanting to give her any hint of his anxiety, he kept his voice even, unsurprised at the apprehension on her face. Something familiar there, something he saw in the hallway at Mitch's – fear.

Brow creased, a look of concern as she nodded towards the grim-faced cabin crew strapped in tight at their landing stations.

In the calm, measured tones that all officers learn at training school, the pilot announced they would return to Key West but that there was no cause for concern. Something about a warning light in the cockpit, routine precaution, FAA regulations. Skelter wasn't buying the 'routine precaution' crap. One look at the cabin crews' faces blew that one out of the water. He glanced out of the window. They were losing altitude, entering the cloudbank. He looked at Lucy, she at him, her white knuckles above the armrest. He placed his hand upon hers and smiled. She entwined her fingers with his. The descent went on too long. He was sure they must be close to the deck but still nothing but dense cloud. He gripped her hand tighter. The passengers nearby looked worried, tense. Still no break in the cloud. Suddenly, the aircraft shuddered and the engine pitch changed. Adrenaline rushed through his veins. They said goodbye to each other with their eyes.

'Landing gear,' he said. 'Normal'

She nodded and forced a smile.

It was a lie, and she knew it. Skelter had heard the sound of undercarriage hundreds of times in his career and this did not fit any profile in his memory banks. The aircraft started to vibrate.

They broke through the clouds at around six hundred feet. He sucked in a sharp breath. There was the airport ahead. They were going fast – too fast – he was sure. The hydraulics whined as the flaps lowered cutting the speed. Four hundred feet now. Flared for impact. Fire tenders, four of them, racing hell for leather alongside the runway, strobe lights flashing blood red. She gripped his hand so hard his circulation had stopped, her head crushed against his shoulder. One hundred feet now, bracing; bracing. Wheels slammed into the concrete, the wing dipping dangerously before correcting. The plane hammered along the runway as the fire tenders raced to keep pace. His ears filled with the roar of the engines, as the pilot applied reverse thrust, blue smoke visible through the window as the wheels shed rubber. Inside the cabin which, until then, had been quiet, the sound of people praying broke the silence. It was then that the nose-wheels burst a tyre. The aircraft slewed across the runway towards the leading fire tender. The vehicle swerved to avoid the plane, which gouged a furrow in the grass as it careered out of control at breakneck speed. The airframe screamed as it twisted under the strain, popping rivets.

Baggage rained down from the overhead lockers as the front oleo leg buckled and the nose ploughed into the ground. They shuddered to a halt. Silence descended and hovered for several seconds.

On their feet in a heartbeat, the cabin crew wrenched the doors open and deployed the emergency chutes. Smoke poured into the cabin and, somewhere behind Skelter, a woman screamed. He unbuckled, reached down, pulled off Lucy's shoes, then kicked his off and got to his feet. The smoke stung his eyes blinding him.

'Down. Get down Cariad,' said Skelter pulling her to her knees. Below the smoke level, he could see okay but, despite the nearest exit being behind them, passengers instinctively scrambled forward. A man tried to climb over him. He elbowed him in the chest. 'Don't panic,' Skelter said in a calm voice, 'keep low and follow. We'll all get out.'

He pushed Lucy ahead of him as other passengers began to move. They were fortunate that the aircraft was only half full. People shuffled forward, stooping to keep under the smoke, some crawled on their knees. He held onto Lucy's dress and drove her forward. His eyes smarted again as they reached the chute. A stewardess, kneeling at the door, forced a smile. Skelter winked at her as he bundled Lucy out and jumped after her to slide down the escape way. At the bottom, he grabbed Lucy's hand and pulled her onto the grass. 'Come on, Cariad, we need to get away from here.'

Fire tenders pulled up and their crews went into their well-rehearsed drills.

Despite the crisis, the evacuation continued in a smooth and orderly fashion. As they walked away from the plane, Lucy gripped his hand tight. 'It feels so good,' she said.

'What does?'

'The grass under my feet, our feet, don't you think?'

'I'll tell you what feels good.'

'What?'

'This.' He stopped, held her by the shoulders and kissed her. Kissed her in a way he had not done since they were first lovers.

When they separated she tried to speak, but he closed her mouth with his. He came up for air. 'What matters is us, Cariad. We mustn't throw this away it's too important, too precious. Whatever it takes, I'll do it, I can't lose you, not now.' Lucy hugged him so hard he gasped for breath. 'I thought we –'

'I know, Mark. I know.'

A bus came out to meet them and take them to the terminal, where the airline arranged a free bar for the passengers.

'Well, Cariad,' said Skelter, raising his bourbon to her gin and tonic. 'We'll not be catching our plane in Miami.'

'So long as we get home sometime, I don't care, Mark, I'm just glad to be here. Funny how something awful puts things into perspective. I see that now. I know what is important.'

'And me, Cariad.'

56
Fifty Not Out

Herefordshire, England
Thursday, November 18th 2004

Skelter had a fair idea what to expect, he knew his birthday must involve music and that Lucy would sing. Beyond that, he would just be speculating so he played along, making no protest when she blindfolded him and sat him in the back of her father's Range Rover. The duration of the journey rather gave the game away. He had had lunch with his father-in-law at the golf club several times. It was the obvious choice.

The first faces he saw when he arrived, were Brick's and Turbo's. Hanging on Brick's arm, Caroline Warren, a few years older than when he had last seen her, but looking younger and more attractive.

'Great to see you, boys. You too Caroline, you look great. How are you?'

'Dry, H. Not touched a drop in over three years, thanks to this lovely man.' she squeezed Brick's arm.

'Well done,' he said.

Brick winked.

Turbo shook Skelter's hand. 'Happy birthday, pal.'

'Thanks, and congratulations by the way.'

'How's that?' said Turbo, turning to the petite brunette next to him.

The heavily pregnant woman looked him in the eye. 'He doesn't mean your medal or your promotion, knob head,' she said. 'Thank you, H, it's a boy. We're going to call him Mark.'

This took Skelter aback. 'Wow, I am honoured, Janice. What about that Lucy?'

'It's a lovely gesture. Mark Thompson. Nice ring to it. We're delighted for you both.'

'Good job on the Medal too, mate,' said Skelter.

Turbo shrugged. 'Cock up in the paperwork somewhere, should have gone to some other Thompson, I reckon.' He winced as Janice elbowed him in the ribs.

Lucy headed to the stage to speak to the band and check her keyboard equipment, while her father, Rollo, made a beeline for the bar.

The surprise appeared at the edge of Skelter's vision. 'Natalie, great to see you. When did you get here?'

'I flew in the day before yesterday, staying with my ex-husband, bless him. Come give your old mother-in-law a kiss, you lovely boy.'

Skelter obliged. 'How's Kenya?'

'Hot as always, which is good for business. Fully booked for six months. Tourism is booming.'

Rollo appeared with two glasses of wine and handed one to Natalie. 'Here's to the birthday boy.' They all raised their glasses and drank his health, including Caroline; gin and tonic without the gin.

'So where are you living, Brick?' Skelter asked.

'We just moved back to the U.K. Not quite sure where we'll settle yet. We fancy somewhere quiet.'

'Do you?' said Skelter, 'now that is interesting.'

'Forget it, mate, I'm retired. She would kill me.'

'You had better believe it,' said Caroline. 'We have both had enough excitement to last a dozen lifetimes, thank you.'

Skelter grinned. 'Me, too. Wife's orders, but I have a plan that doesn't involve anything dangerous or dodgy.' Skelter looked at his two comrades with his serious face. 'What it does come with is vacancies for adventurous, outdoor types. Would suit ex-military personnel. No foreign travel involved.'

Brick raised his eyebrows at Turbo, cocking his head.

'He's taking the piss.' said Turbo.

'Deadly serious, I'm a landowner now. I have to settle down and act in a responsible manner. Or, to use Lucy's language, I have to grow up.'

Janice threw her ten pence worth in the ring. 'Give the man a chance, listen to what he's got to say.'

'Go on - we'll humour you,' said Turbo. 'What's it all about?'

'Tell you later,' said Skelter, 'after the band, in the break maybe. I guess they'll be having one.' He could not help a smile; they were nibbling at his bait. *Be terrific to work with the boys again, it would, Buddha, boy, fingers crossed, eh?*

Lucy and the guys were on top form and Natalie joined in a duet with her daughter. Their rendition of Etta James's 'I Just Want to Make Love to You' left both Skelter and Rollo a little warm under the collar.

Later, when the music had finished and everyone was mellow in drink, Skelter outlined his plans for the adventure centre to Brick and Turbo.

'Sounds like a great idea to me,' said Turbo, I'll have to talk to Janice but can't see it being a problem, her being a Jock. Her mum and dad are still living in Glasgow. 'You can count me in. You should run it past Lofty.'

'On my 'to do' list. The estate has Red Deer and he would be perfect for running stalking courses.'

'None better, mate, he grew up in the highlands, stalking with his dad. He'd be perfect if he ever leaves The Regiment. He's still a kid mind, few years in him yet, I reckon.'

'Thirty-five is hardly a kid, even if I am technically old enough to be his father,' said Skelter, 'still, he might be pleased to know there's a job waiting for him when he comes out.'

'Amen to that,' said Brick, 'especially one that uses all your soldier skills. Rare as rocking-horse shit, jobs like that.'

'So, Brick, what about it? Can I tempt you?'

Brick looked at Caroline.

Skelter interjected with a sweetener. 'There's a pair of cottages on the estate, not sure what condition they are in, but we can soon bring them up to scratch. Part of the package.'

She shrugged. 'It's not like we have any

commitments, is it? The lease is up on the flat in three months, so moving is not a problem.'

'You would be happy with that?'

'I hate to say this, Brick, but I'm more content than I have ever been in my life.' She squeezed his muscular arm and looked at Skelter. 'This man saved me from myself, H, and I know he would love to work with you again.'

'That's it then, Mucker,' said Brick, 'let's seal it with a drink. Caroline?'

'Tonic and Lime, please.'

'Come on Walrus, I'll give you a hand,' said Turbo.

Rollo approached with Natalie on his arm. 'So, my boy, you have survived to the half century.'

'Looks like it. And your daughter has stuck by me too, not that I am worthy.'

'Pack it in Mark,' said Lucy. 'He's only after the sympathy vote, Daddy.'

'Well, he is wasting his breath. Tell me, what will you do with the new house, now you are going to move to Scotland?'

'We'll rent it out for the time being, until we get settled, at least,' said Lucy.

'You realise your new home in Speyside is close to Bunny's pile? Less than an hour's drive, even on those roads. Simon was tickled pink when I told him his big sister was moving near to where he spent most of his school holidays. You must look him up.'

'We plan to,' said Skelter, 'being neighbours'

'Excellent, I'll call him, bring him up to speed.'

'That would be great, thanks.'

57
Therapy Revisited

Leominster, Herefordshire, England
Tuesday, December 14th 2004

Skelter drove Lucy to the old house on the outskirts of Leominster, with some misgivings, but considered on balance that the sooner she spoke to her therapist the better. So far, she had experienced no problems related to the episode with Wolf, but he knew from experience it was just a matter of time. The sun hung low in the grey morning, hazy and vague. Lucy turned up the collar of her coat against the chilly dry as they stepped out of the car. Judith greeted them at the door with a warm and welcoming smile.

'Come in out of the cold, I've just chucked another log on the fire. Coffee?'

'That would be lovely,' said Lucy.

'When have I ever refused your excellent blend?' said Skelter.

Judith led the way through to the lounge and settled them into separate chairs beside the crackling fire.

After a few minutes, the psychotherapist entered with a tray and set it on the table. 'So, how are you both? This is a first, you both together.'

'Just to be clear, Judith, anything and everything we say here is confidential. Nothing can be revealed outside?' said Skelter.

'Correct, unless you're going to tell me you've murdered someone.

The colour drained from Lucy's face.

'Can we do this without recording the session?' asked Skelter.

'If that is your wish.' She turned her attention to Skelter's wife. 'Lucy?'

'I would feel better if we didn't.'

'Of course.'

'This was my idea,' said Skelter, 'We're here for Lucy, she needs to talk to you, a bad experience, an incident, shooting...'

'Perhaps it might be more productive if you tell me, Lucy,' said Judith.

'Sorry,' said Skelter, 'I would like to stay, if it's all right.'

'That is up to Lucy.'

Lucy nodded. 'I'd like Mark to stay.'

Judith turned to Skelter. 'Did you witness the shooting?'

Skelter shook his head. He had no wish to incriminate himself. Lucy had agreed to keep his name out of the story.

'You may observe but please do not speak unless asked.'

He nodded again, coughed as if words were stuck in his throat, but said nothing

Judith's face showed no emotion at this and pushed the coffee across the table and picked up her own cup. She took a sip.

Skelter could not help but be impressed. *You would not want to sit at the poker table with her, Buddha, buddy.*

'Take your time, Lucy,' said Judith in a soft tone. 'When you are ready.'

Lucy glanced at her husband and placed the cup on the coffee table. With a deep breath she began.

Judith listened, Lucy unloaded, but mentioned only that an armed intruder had been shot. She did not name her husband as the shooter. Skelter behaved, keeping his lip firmly zipped. When Lucy had finished, Judith offered her opinion. 'It may well be beneficial for you to come and talk through your concerns. 'You are moving into a new house in Hereford, I understand?'

'Well,' said Lucy, 'we are moving, but there has been a change of plan. A little further afield than Hereford. Scotland, Speyside. I was wondering if it would be practical to talk over the phone.'

'Oh,' said Judith, wrong-footed for once. 'It is not ideal but it can work. Tell me, have you heard of Skype?'

Lucy looked at Skelter.

'It is a form of VoIP, voice over internet protocol. It's

new, allows you to talk one to one through live link on your computer. I'll send you the details,' said Judith.

'Sounds exciting, thank you,' said Lucy.

'Well done, H.'

'What for?'

'You know what for,' said Judith with a laugh.

'Keeping my mouth shut, you mean?'

58

Memorial

Mitchell Estate, Speyside, Scotland.
Sunday, May 15th 2005.

Skelter looked up at the big sign spanning the gateway; Mitchell Adventure Centre. The early morning spring sunshine baptised it with warm a golden glow. He had a sense of achievement not experienced before, not even when he passed selection for The Regiment. It had been a steep learning curve.

'You have done a fabulous job, Mark. Mitch would be so proud.'

'We did it together, Cariad: you, Turbo, Brick and all the team. The estate workers have been amazing.'

'Mitch was well liked and respected.'

'And he only came over twice a year,' said Skelter.

'Just shows what a good workforce he had. And they seem to like you.'

Skelter managed a smile. 'So far, so good, eh? They're real grafters, I'll say that – and they know their stuff. The foresters made a cracking job of the assault course.'

'And the cabins, don't forget the cabins,' said Lucy. 'The kids will love sleeping in them, when you aren't making them sleep out under canvas, eating berries and earthworms that is.' She squeezed her husband's arm and kissed his cheek. 'I am so proud of you, Mark.'

'Put him down, lass, I know where he's been.'

'Turbo, good morning. Ready for the big day?'

'They told me 'never volunteer for anything', but I thought I'd break the rule as it is such an occasion.'

'Run that by me again,' said Skelter.

'I'd like to volunteer to run the beer tent,' said the grinning Yorkshire man.

'You've more chance of being struck by lightning, mate.'

Turbo looked crestfallen 'Worth a try. What time's kick off?'

'Memorial service in the church at nine, back here for ten thirty, grand opening at twelve and the kids are due at two thirty, all sixteen of them.'

'All under eighteen, aren't they?'

'Aye, they have two adults with them; teacher and a nurse.'

'All the bases covered then.'

Skelter breathed a sigh. 'It's been a frantic six months, but it's been worth it.'

Turbo's nostrils twitched. 'Old puffing Billy's here, unless I'm very much mistaken.'

The words had hardly left his lips when Brick stepped out from behind the gate lodge, trailing a plume of smoke. Alongside him, appearing years younger than she had any right to, Caroline Warren looked relaxed and gorgeous.

'Morning all, good day for it,' said Brick.

The others nodded in agreement.

The village church was crammed to the cloisters. So many people turned out to pay their respects at the memorial service that many had to listen to it outside, through speakers installed in anticipation of the numbers.

Skelter walked forward and stood in front of the lectern. He gazed upon the sea of faces, most of whom were strangers or recent acquaintances. Lucy smiled encouragement from the front row. Turbo winked. The lump swelled in Skelter's throat as his left hand tapped the Buddha through the pocket of his suit jacket.

'Mitch Mitchell,' he began, 'made me what I am. I have no delusions of grandeur, but I can be proud of what he helped me become, with his encouragement and guidance. Without his hand on my tiller, I would have foundered on the rocks a long time ago. He showed me the value of education. He showed me how to be the best I could be, and to believe in myself; to realise that the only limit was my imagination.' The lump in his throat felt like a golf ball. He composed himself and then, with a slight tremble in his voice, he continued. 'Today, we are here to honour his memory and to carry on his work

346

through the Mitchell Memorial Adventure Centre. We want to give young people a chance to learn about themselves, to instil in them the values he taught me and provide a unique experience that will enrich their lives. This will, we hope, make them better people for it. God bless you, Mitch.'

There was dead silence throughout the church. Skelter moved away from the lectern and walked back to his seat beside Lucy. The minister stepped forward.

'We shall now sing Hymn number forty-two, 'Abide with Me'. Please be upstanding.'

'That went well,' said Brick, as he stuffed the bowl of his pipe with tobacco.

'Yes,' said Lucy, 'that was a lovely tribute, Mark.'

'Thanks. Nearly lost it in there for a minute.'

'You did fine,' she said squeezing his hand. 'He had a brilliant send off. You've done him proud, all of you,' she said, looking at Turbo and Brick.

'I'll second that, laddie,' said a tall kilted man with a shock of flaming red hair.

'Thank you, Hamish, I appreciate that.'

'Nay bother, we could not have wished for a better man to take over the reins. Ye've proved your worth here these last six months.'

'I'm humbled by the warmth of my reception here. I can't fill Mitch's shoes. Nobody could ever do that.'

Hamish offered Skelter his hand. 'No, laddie, but you are doing a pretty fine job of walking in his footsteps.'

Skelter shook the offered hand warmly. Tight lipped, he nodded. 'Thanks again, it means a lot.'

Skelter's Final Duty

Made in the USA
Charleston, SC
29 September 2016